LEISURE BOOKS  NEW YORK CITY

A LEISURE BOOK®

December 1993

Published by

Dorchester Publishing Co., Inc.
276 Fifth Avenue
New York, NY 10001

Printed in the United States of America.

TWICE THE HARD CASES! TWICE THE HONEYS! TWO PISTOL-HOT ADULT WESTERNS IN ONE BIG VOLUME!

KANSAS CITY CHORINE

"Kick your pants off and walk backward," the gunman ordered. "And no tricks! Try anything and your guts'll be sizzling in the sunshine!"

Spur sighed. This wasn't his day. "What kind of man are you? You'd use your pretty wife to rob innocent men?"

The gunman snorted. "Elsie, go over there and do what you do best—get the man's pants off!"

The young woman smiled, walked to McCoy and bent over.

Spur flipped his left boot up into the air. He caught his gunbelt as it sailed up in front of him. McCoy simultaneously pulled the blonde to him and unholstered his Colt. A second later he had its muzzle pressed against the screaming woman's throat....

PLAINS PARAMOUR

Jack Hastings panted as he made the noose. He stared down at the groaning man. Doubt clouded his brain but he quieted it. This wasn't killing. It's never killing during a war. It's doing a job that has to be done, and this was a war.

"You killed them," Hastings said as he knelt and slipped the noose around Fields's neck. "You killed my parents! You raped my mother! You didn't think anybody was left but I saw it. I saw it all!"

He pulled the rope tight. Fields coughed and opened his eyes. "What—what—"

Hastings smiled. "You're getting what you deserve, Yankee!"

Lester Fields's voice was scratchy. "You're the one! You've been killing my friends!"

He laughed. "Yeah. And you're gonna join 'em—in hell!"

The *Spur Double* Series from *Leisure Books:*
BODIE BEAUTIES/FRISCO FOXES
DODGE CITY DOLL/LARAMIE LOVERS
DAKOTA DOXY/SAN DIEGO SIRENS
COLORADO CUTIE/TEXAS TEASE
MISSOURI MADAM/HELENA HELLION
RAWHIDER'S WOMAN/SALOON GIRL
INDIAN MAID/MONTANA MINX
ROCKY MOUNTAIN VAMP/CATHOUSE KITTEN
SAVAGE SISTERS/HANG SPUR McCOY!

SPUR
KANSAS CITY
CHORINE

1

Don't want to blow myself up, Jack T. Galde thought as he walked through the town. Gingerly gripping the denim-wrapped bundle, he peered around the corner of Maple Street. No one in sight.

Galde quickly cleared the last forty yards and approached the hulking brick building from behind. The Forestville Bank had been built to withstand anything but dynamite, he mused, as he crouched near his predetermined spot.

A few faint peeps from the tree beside him startled the man. Just a bird waking up, he thought. Don't get all riled up, Galde! Everything will go fine. Nothing could go wrong now. You've planned too carefully.

Galde placed the bundle on the ground and unwrapped it. Five sticks. Should be enough, he mused.

The man worked quickly, sweating in the darkness. He stuck a blasting cap into one of the long, red tubes and attached five feet of fuse to it. That was just enough to reach behind the tree.

Satisfied by his handiwork, Galde nestled the bomb against the bank's left wall and trailed the fuse into the clump of small saplings, checking with his fingers through the darkness that nothing would impede the fuse's slow burn.

That finished, Galde returned to his hotel room. Excitement ripped through him as he silently climbed the stairs. He was doing it again. Another bank. Another load of money and gold. Another fast escape and another search for a new target.

It invigorated him, this game of hide and seek, these aliases and phony names, the way he'd work his way into some small town and then, when he was trusted, rob the bank, kill anyone who got in his way, and ride out of town.

Galde went into his room, closed the door and swallowed a mouthful of whiskey. In the dim light spilling from the kerosene wall lamp he smiled and raised the bottle to his lips again. No, he told himself. You don't want to get drunk. He returned it to the rickety table. Time enough for drinking later.

Galde checked the sky through the cracked window. Blue light tinged the eastern horizon beyond the livery stable. Sunrise wasn't far off and he was right on time.

Twenty minutes, the stocky man mused. He had twenty more minutes to wait.

Then he'd never have to face the simple-minded fools of Jacksonville again.

Smirking, he gave himself a whore's bath in the

cracked basin and used the hard lye soap. He then changed into his riding clothes and packed his old carpetbag. Dress for the occasion, he reminded himself.

At 5:20 Galde left his hotel room, lugging his saddlebags. He untied his horse from the hitching post in front of the hotel and rode her out of town 200 yards, then turned back and halted his mount behind the bank. No one should be going back there this time of morning. He tied the sleepy mare to an oak tree and grabbed his saddlcbags.

Three minutes later he heard boots kicking through the dirt and keys jingling. Bud Ormond was arriving right on time. Pulling a red kerchief up around his face, Galde slipped down the far side of the bank and peered around the wall. The tall, blonde haired, hatless man struggled with the lock in the bank's front door.

"Damn!" he muttered.

Galde sidled up to him, silently drawing his six-gun. He pushed its muzzle against Ormond's back.

"What th—"

"Shut up!" Galde hissed. "Just open the door and walk in like nothing unusual's happening, unless you want me to blast your worthless guts all over the street, Ormond!"

"No. No!" The young man finally turned the cylinders and pushed open the door.

Galde shoved him inside the cool building, removed the key from the lock and quietly locked the door from the inside.

Ormond still stood facing away from him, his knees shaking.

"Turn around!" Galde growled.

The banker did, presenting a shadowy face.

"Listen up, Ormond. I want you to open the safe. Now!"

The man glanced around him. "But—but Mr. Drithers isn't here and I—"

"Look, Ormond, I ain't trying to make a deposit, just a withdrawal!" He motioned with his six-gun. "Move your ass before I blow you to bits!"

"Sure! Sure!" The thin man hustled to the rear of the bank, stumbled between the two oak desks and crouched next to the waist-high, iron safe.

"Hurry!" Galde growled as he followed him.

Ormond flipped the lock twice to clear it and began working out the combination. His fingers faltered.

"I'm—I'm sorry, I—" Ormond began.

"Just do it!"

He successfully entered all three numbers and pulled the handle. The heavy door swung open.

"Stand up and back towards me. And don't try nothing!"

"I—I won't." He moved toward Galde.

When he was four feet away, the bank robber grunted. "Far enough. Lay down with your head facing the left wall."

The man looked at him quizzically. "You—you ain't gonna kill me?" His face in the growing light was confused.

Galde smirked. "Not unless you try anything."

As the man got into the prescribed position, Galde bolted for the safe. He reached into it and pulled out three small bags. Testing their weight he knew they had to be filled with gold coins. He stuffed them into the saddlebags he'd carried with him. Two more searches with his hand revealed neatly stacked piles of ones, tens and twenties, along with two hundred-dollar bills.

Galde snarled as he emptied the safe into his saddlebags. Not much, but enough for a while. He closed the bag and stood upright.

"You—you finished now, mister?" Ormond asked.

"Yeah. Almost. Why?"

"Cause—cause I'm gonna piss my pants."

Galde laughed.

"Hey, I know who you are!" the banker said, looking over his shoulder. "You're Emil Jackson!"

"Get your ugly face back on the floor!" Galde yelled.

The young man did so.

"I ain't Emil Jackson. My name's Galde. Jack T. Galde."

"But—"

"Shut up!" Galde retrieved a Bowie knife from its sheath on his belt and walked up to the downed man.

"Whatcha doing now?"

"I'm gonna tie you up, boy, so you don't go hollering around that the bank's been robbed." He knelt behind him. The early morning light, shining in through the bank's front windows, glinted on the six-inch blade.

Galde rammed it down. Hard. Ormond convulsed as the steel sliced through his spine. The knife came down again and again, ripping up the man's back, shattering his nervous system.

Ormond's head lurched back. He twisted and flopped on the floor. Galde flipped him onto his back and drove the knive into the man's pulsating chest.

Stab. Hurt. Kill. Blood spread slowly over the polished marble floor.

Galde sheathed his knife in the living flesh again and again. The smell of blood rose up from the body as Bud Ormond kicked two last times and lay still.

Sweating, grinning, Galde rose, plunged the knife into the dead man's throat and stood back. Lugging his heavy saddlebags he slipped out the front door and walked around to the back of the bank.

Dawn broke fully in the east as he approached his horse. No one had seen him. He'd timed everything perfectly, down to the last detail. Galde chuckled and hefted the saddlebags onto his horse.

The yellow light illuminated dark red stains on his right hand and sleeve. Cursing, Galde threw down the bag, wiped off the blood with fresh oak leaves, ripped off his shirt and dressed in a fresh button-down.

Voices. One, high-pitched, was Betty Jane. He didn't know who the man was and didn't care. Betty Jane must be going into work early that day. He smiled, bent and lit the fuse with a sulphur match.

That done, Galde mounted his horse and rode up to Hawkin's Hotel.

Two men greeted him as he arrived there. The town was waking up, just in time to watch the show. He should have two more minutes. He walked inside, saw that the dining room wasn't open yet—as he knew it wouldn't be—and then walked out.

One minute.

A female scream pierced the dawn. Galde smiled. No more time. He looked at the bank.

The slow burning fuse met its end.

The explosion was intense, ear-shattering, as the five sticks of dynamite detonated. The building lurched on its foundations, rattled and slumped. Thousands of bricks noisily toppled as dust rose in a huge cloud. As it cleared, the Forestville Bank lay in ruins. Its ceiling had collapsed and all but one of the walls now lay scattered on the dirt.

"You there!" a male voice said. "Emil Jackson!"

Galde spun around. George Ryman, the barber, waved his shaving brush at him as he ran up. "What happened?"

"Hell if I know, Ryman. I was just trying to get some flapjacks when all of a sudden the whole place went up." He shook his head in mock anger and sorrow.

Ryman peered at the ruined bank. "Was anyone inside? Did anyone get killed?"

"I don't know. Didn't see anything."

Men and women ran out of hotels and their homes in every state of dress. The agitated people filled the street with their cries and shouts.

The barber shook his head. "Can't imagine something like this happening here." He cocked his head toward Galde. "Can you, Jackson?"

"Nope. Never came to mind."

Ryman threw up his hands and trailed off to join the crowd approaching the bank.

Galde joined them, mingled, expressed his shock and dismay, spoke of how he had fifty dollars in the safe. After twenty minutes of this—and well after the sheriff had found three bodies inside—he slipped away and mounted his horse.

Riding out of town, Galde finally allowed himself to smile. He guffawed, startling his mare, as he left Forestville behind him forever and rode out to find his next opportunity.

2

The passenger car rattled on its iron trail, jolting Spur McCoy from a drowse. He blinked twice, shook his head, sat up straight and pulled the telegram from his pocket.

His job didn't seem any easier upon re-reading the message. All that General Halleck had been able to give him were the bald facts: a string of small towns in Missouri and Kansas have been hit with bold bank robberies and murders. Five banks have been cleaned out. No witnesses attest to seeing anything of importance. Twelve men and three women—one pregnant—have been murdered in direct connection with the robberies.

Maybe that's why no witnesses are talking, he thought. They're dead. McCoy stuffed the telegram back into his pocket.

Staring at the length of ankle the fancily dressed woman seated across from him was daringly showing, he sighed. Not a hell of a lot to go on.

The thirtyish, red-haired woman smiled as she saw Spur eyeing her ankle. She smoothed down her skirt, cutting off his view, and straightened her back.

McCoy slumped in the seat and pushed his brown hat over his face. It was a long way to Kansas City, Missouri.

A far cry from most ex-soldiers, but Spur McCoy was now a member of the United States Secret Service, a branch of the federal government originally created by an act of Congress in the year 1865 to protect U.S. currency against counterfeiting, as well as to ensure its safety at all times.

Later, the Secret Service's duties were expanded to include those crimes which crossed state or territorial lines. Soon it became involved with other federal business, since it was the only federal agency with law enforcement personnel.

Fresh from a distinguished career in the Union Army, during which time he rose to the rank of captain, McCoy went to Washington, D.C. to serve as an aide to Senator Arthur B. Walton of New York, an old family friend.

He joined the Secret Service soon after it had been formed and served for six months in the Washington office. When his superiors realized that McCoy was not only a crack shot but the Service's best horseback rider, he was transferred to the St. Louis branch and was assigned to handle all cases west of the Mississippi River.

These two factors had been of the utmost importance in giving McCoy the dangerous assignments, for the law had only recently settled into most of the western United States and in some places hadn't quite done even that. Yet.

The work was tough. It commanded his absolute attention. Spur had no roots—no sweethearts, no established friends, no hometown affections. He was a loner. Though he'd had his share of pretty ladies his only constant companions were a Colt .45 at his hip, the Mexican coins ringing his hat, and a hankering to do justice.

Spur McCoy was the kind of man who was made for the untamed, turbulent American west: fearless and vigilant. He was making it into what he could.

The city withered under the burning summer sun. McCoy slapped his new mount's rump, strapped on his sparkling, serviceable saddle and walked the beast to the Kansas City General Mercantile. Broad Street was dusty and filled with countless horse droppings. After stocking up on coffee, beans, hard tack, canned peaches, pears and beef jerkey, Spur loaded up the saddlebags, checked his carpetbag one last time, and headed for the local marshal's office.

Frank Porter was a big, ungainly man. His rough clothing hung on his frame and he extended a hand to McCoy.

Spur quickly explained his job. The marshal had heard of the robberies and spat into the dented spittoon when Spur mentioned them.

"Cowardly thieves!" he said. "They should thank their lucky stars they didn't hit my town. Hell, I'd have them all hanging by their necks if they'd come into Kansas City!"

Spur smiled. "That's why they didn't trouble you, Porter. Seems like these thieves avoid larger towns, preferring to do their dirty work in small, isolated ones. Less chance of being caught, more chance of being successful."

"Can't understand why there've been no witnesses," Porter said, chewing his lower lip. "It just don't seem right that nobody saw anything."

"Maybe those fresh bodies lying in the ground all over the state could tell us something," Spur grunted.

Porter glanced up at him. "Is that all you know?"

"So far."

"Not much to go on." The big man swatted a fly that buzzed around his sweating forehead.

"Nope. The robberies have all occurred on a fairly straight line heading west from here. I'm assuming they'll continue in that direction. Got a map?"

The man grunted, flipped open a creaky drawer in his desk and slapped a much-folded piece of paper onto it. "It's the best I have. Shows all the settlements and towns—and most of the large farms and ranches—from here to Colorado Territory. Some of it's even to scale."

Spur flopped into a chair and studied the map. Though crudely drawn it did indeed detail at least five more towns west of Jacksonville, the site of the last brutal, puzzling bank robbery.

"Can you get me a copy of this, Porter?" Spur asked.

The man smiled. "If you can wait a minute or so I can probably do one up."

The man soon covered a three-inch square piece of paper—the back of a whiskey bottle label he'd soaked off—with squiggly lines and uncertain block letters. Finished, he shoved the map over to Spur.

The Secret Service man nodded. "Guess that's the next place," McCoy said, stabbing his index finger on a tiny circle marked Holmes.

"Not much there," Porter said.

"Didn't think so. Is it big enough to make it worth a bank robber's time?"

The marshall mulled it over. "Sure, I guess. It's grown since I was out there last."

He folded up the map. "Thanks, Porter. Maybe I'll stop by on my way out once I've got this thing taken care of."

The lanky man grinned. "Ain't you cocksure. Why you so certain you can find those bastards? You don't know enough to piss at it."

Spur shrugged as he stuffed the map into his pocket. "It's my job."

Vanessa Thompson glanced out one of the paned windows that led from her parlor. A squat, dark figure walking down the street riveted her eyes. Vanessa gasped. Could it be? Yes, it was. It surely was. Her prayers had been answered. There, right there, walking down the street of Holmes, was a preacher man. Newly arrived, judging from the carpetbags he was carrying. A new preacher had come to Holmes!

She threw off her apron, gussied up her hair, and rushed out of her simple home.

"Excuse me, sir!" she called at the now departing figure. "Hello!"

Apparently oblivious to her, he kept up his steady, slow pace. Vanessa quickly overtook him and stopped before the man.

"Excuse me." She smiled broadly at the man who wore a simple dark suit and a clerical collar. "I was wondering if—if—"

"Yes?" The man's voice was soft, melodic. Above the white collar his face was fleshy, cleanly shaven, with small jowls, piercing black eyes and short-cropped hair.

Vanessa was pleased. "Well, it just has to be a sign from God that you've come to our town," she said quickly. "Here I've been praying for a new preacher for three weeks now and—and here you are!"

His smile broadened. "Are there souls to be saved here? Is there drinking? Fornicating? Dancing and gambling?"

Vanessa smirked. "You can't imagine—begging your pardon. Preacher, ever since my husband departed from this world of fleshly pleasures, leaving the church without a guiding light, the sin in this town has gone on unchecked." She shook her head. "I can barely buy a bolt of cloth or visit Aggie the milliner without running into one of those—well, *those* kind of women on the street!" Her cheeks paled. "I don't know who you are, why you're here or how long you can stay, but I'm ever so glad to see you!"

The preacher dropped his bags and spread out his arms. "With a welcome such as this, and with such a vivid portrait of this town's involvement with the Fiend, I believe the Lord has guided my footsteps." He looked into the sky above him. "This is where I was meant to go. This is my new home." He looked down at her. "If I can rely upon your help, dear sister of Christ, perhaps we can drive out the evil that thrives here."

Tears quelled up in Vanessa's eyes. "Yes. Yes! I—I—" She was speechless at this occurrence.

"Let us pray!"

And Jack T. Galde prayed.

The flat, featureless land had never known a mountain. One hour outside of Kansas City, endless acres of farmland stretched around Spur McCoy. Riding down the wide, dusty trail he passed fields of chin-high corn, green wheat and stubbly alfalfa. Spur hoped the towns Marshal Porter had mapped out were near the trail, as he'd indicated. Otherwise, they'd be swallowed up in the vast croplands.

Dozens of small farms and several fenced ranches dotted the area, as too did empty plots awaiting future human efforts. The land was dry, cracked and covered with scrawny weeds where streams and spring water hadn't yet been diverted to give it nourishing moisture.

Spur glanced his boots at his mount's flanks, urging her to pick up the speed. He was eager to begin his job.

Up ahead on the trail a figure lay sprawled on the ground. Spur rode quickly up to it. It was a woman. He halted his horse and rushed to her.

The blonde beauty lay face-up, one arm behind her back, eyes closed and fluttering. The rips in her red dress revealed much more than a woman should reveal in public. The woman's lips parted and locked together.

He didn't see powder burns or wounds. Spur touched her cheek. The woman opened her eyes and looked up at him. "Help me," she said in a pain racked voice.

Spur nodded. "Don't you worry, ma'am. I'll take care of you. What happened?"

This was puzzling. He didn't see anything physically wrong with her. Maybe she'd been raped . . .

"They came at me. I—I was walking to my sweetheart's ranch and they—they—" She squeezed her eyes shut and turned her head away from McCoy.

"I see."

"Water." She coughed. "I need water. And food."

He walked to his horse. As Spur reached for his canteen he heard rapid movement behind him.

"Hold it right there, mister!" a female voice said.

He turned, of course. The *injured* woman was on her feet, grinning and pointing the business end of a six-gun at his heart. She ran her left hand through her wild, dirty-blonde locks.

"Ma'am?" he asked.

"Don't you *ma'am* me, buzzard dick!" she spat. The blonde's eyes flashed at him. "I don't need your help. I don't need any man's help! I just need your money. Give it to me. Now! Empty your pockets!"

"Look, lady." Spur began. What the hell had he gotten himself involved in?

She racously laughed, maintaining her aim with a steady, sure hand. This was no injured woman. "Don't those big ears of yours work?" she asked in a gruff, unfeminine voice. "Cut the talk and hand over your money. Unless you wanna die out here in the dirt!"

Spur straightened his shoulders. This game had gone far enough. "You really don't wanna use that, woman! You think you can outshoot me?"

Jubilant chuckles emerged from her generous bosom. "You really want to find out?" She looked at him slyly. "Pa always said I was the best shot in the county. Heck, you don't know nothing about me. I've got the advantage. I caught you by surprise. You're just a dumb man." Her eyes were wild. "You and all men. You're pigs. Pigs! Buzzard dicks! And you're gonna throw your money down on the trail!"

"What're you gonna do after that?"

Spur relaxed. The woman was crazy, out of her mind. He'd talk her out of it.

She lifted her unplucked eyebrows. "Why, what I always do. I'll cut your balls off and make 'em into a purse!" The blonde hardened her visage. "Now give me your money?"

Spur smirked at her. "Just put down the gun and get on home, woman. I'd hate to have to kill you."

She hesitated, her cheeks flushing. The blonde's right hand trembled. "Oh—oh *hell!*" She threw down the gun.

Upon impact it discharged, sending a slug into the dirt and an explosion rippling through the hot summer air.

"Jesus!" Spur said. "You mean that thing was loaded?"

The woman looked at him. She arched her back, pressing her full breasts against the tattered bodice of her bright red dress. The material strained, threatened to unravel.

Spur allowed his gaze to travel below her chin. A pert, hard nipple peeked through the cloth.

"I didn't really wanna kill you," the woman said. She slid a hand between her legs. "I don't wanna kill any men. There's too much they can do for a lonely woman." She rubbed.

Spur shrugged and bent to retrieve her weapon. "Sorry, but I've got business to attend to."

Her right hand became more urgent, violently stroking her groin, pressing the thin material to her body. "Come on, mister! I *need* you! Right now!"

Spur was only human. The sight of the woman pleasuring herself in front of him, in broad daylight, set his body in motion. But he killed off the desire before it had a chance to build. "Sorry. I said no."

The blonde woman pouted. She gripped her bodice with her left hand and pulled hard. The material ripped apart and her dress fell to her ankles. Not a shread of cloth remained on her.

Wasn't she full surprises, Spur thought.

The harsh sunlight revealed every curve, every swell, every forbidden part of the woman's body. He stood, stunned, drinking her in. At least he could enjoy the show for a minute before he rode off to Holmes.

"Now, mister. Now!" the blonde said, her hand

moving up and down, pressing, rubbing, furrowing her yellow pubic hairs. Legs parted, knees bent, she rocked up and down as erotic sensations pulsed through her body. "I can't wait any longer. I can't! Git that thing out and use it on me! Come on!"

Her eyes locked onto his. She parted her lips, panting, writhing before him in unashamed ecstasy, giving him an open invitation to ravish her.

Spur felt himself responding again. He tried to fight it off but the woman's unexpected, outrageously sexual performance dug into his loins and wouldn't let go. She raised her left arm to him, her fingers parted, pleading.

Spur grunted as the pressure in his crotch rose to a painful, aching degree. He took a step toward her, mesmerized by the fire in her eyes, drinking in her passion, consumed by the lust she transmitted to him.

The blonde smiled as she rubbed herself. So near. So close. So willing. Spur walked to her. He dropped her now forgotten six-gun to the dirt, unbuckled his pants, ripped open the buttons and shoved them and his gunbelt to his feet.

"Yes! Now! Right now! I'm ready and wet!"

The words—their power—overwhelmed him. He stood before her in his long underwear. Her left arm closed around his waist, gripping him to her nude body.

No time for rational thought. No time for headwork. She was warm, soft. She crushed her full breasts against his shirt front. Spur looked down at the top of her yellow hair. No, he thought. No.

Yes!

"What the fuck're you doing with my wife?" a gruff voice barked behind him.

Spur threw the woman from him. He spun around, panting, to face the man who'd yelled at him.

3

"I said, what the hell're you doin' with my wife?"

The beefy, armed man glared at Spur, coughed and spat on the ground.

McCoy automatically reached for his Colt .45. Damn! It wasn't there!

"How the hell're you gonna grab your hogleg? You're standing in your underwear, asshole!"

"Your wife's plumb crazy," Spur said. He felt the tension in the air. "First she tried to kill me, then she offered herself up to me in such a way that no man could refuse."

The man smiled. "That's my Elsie." He glanced over McCoy's shoulder. "Come on over here, honey!"

The naked blonde strolled up to the gunman, stood beside him and smiled sweetly. "I done right?" she asked.

"Yeah, honey, you done right. Just like I told you

to do. Sure got him all fired up, thinking you'd let him stick it in. You did a good job, Elsie; didn't leave nothin' out."

"What the hell's goin' on here?" Spur asked.

The big man snarled. "Don't go usin' filthy language like that in front of my Elsie!" he thundered. "I've killed a man for less than that!"

"You're as crazy as she is," Spur said.

It had been a trap, of course. A well-planned, well-executed trap. They'd gotten him right where they wanted him.

The thick man grunted. "Hell no! Neither of us are. Just a little trick I dreamed up one night while I was packing it to her." He fingered her hair with his left hand. "Back to business. Kick yer pants off yer boots and walk backwards. And no tricks! Try anything and your guts'll be sizzling in the sunshine!"

Spur sighed. This wasn't his day. "What kind of a man are you? You'd use your pretty wife to rob innocent men?"

He snorted. "Hell, I'd have my mama spread 'em to get a few extra dollars—if I didn't think she'd scare 'em away. Now do it! Don't bend over, just kick 'em off."

Spur worked his pants lower, twisting his legs, pulling, tugging at them, alternating boots. He finally freed all but the waistband. He looked down. From the man's viewpoint they should look like they were still tangled up.

"That's as much as I can do. They must've caught on the heels."

The gunman snarled. "You think I'm that stupid? Try harder, asshole!"

"Check them yourself."

"Elsie, go over there and do what you do best—get that man's pants off!"

The bare assed young woman smiled, walked to McCoy and bent over.

Spur slipped his left boot up into the air. He caught his gunbelt as it sailed up in front of him. McCoy simultaneously pulled the blonde to him and unholstered his Colt. A second later he had its muzzle pressed against the screaming woman's throat.

"Sonofabitch!" the big man said as he dropped his aim. His eyes grew wide. "You move faster than a rattler!"

"You're gonna lose Elsie faster than that if you don't drop your weapon and ride outa here!" Spur warned him.

He laughed. "Hell, kill her. I can always get another cunt. Plenty more like that out there!"

"You bastard!" the woman screamed.

"I don't believe you," McCoy said. "She's too valuable to you. What other woman would live with an ugly, fat coward like you? A man who has to hide behind a woman to separate innocent men from their money?"

The man blubbered. "*Coward?*—you—I'll—"

"I'm calling your bluff! You won't do nothing except what I tell you to do. Understood?"

The big man's face reddened as he nodded. "Damn! I had it all planned. Everything. Elsie and me practiced for two weeks. This was our first time!"

"Ah, you're making my heart bleed for you! Now throw that gun onto the dirt and get your fat butt outa my sight!"

"What—what about Elsie?"

Spur paused. "Hell, I'll worry about that when I don't have to see your ugly face! She's a looker."

"Now wait a minute—"

"Drop it!"

He sighed, cursed, snorted and threw the gun into the dust.

"Move!" Spur commanded.

The big man turned and walked down the trail toward Kansas City, kicking the dirt, hollering and moaning.

When he was out of sight Spur released the woman. Elsie turned to him, trembling, her eyes bright with fear.

"Are you gonna—I mean—"

Spur smiled as he retrieved his pants and dressed. "No. Just don't try that again, little lady. Is he really your husband?"

She nodded. "He forced me into it. I don't mind saying I enjoyed teasing you—you're a handsome man. But I hate him!" The bitterness in her voice was convincing.

"Best thing I can think of for you to do is to leave your husband as fast as you can and settle down somewhere else. Get him out of your life."

She nodded. "I suppose you're right."

McCoy gathered up the two weapons, stuffed them into his saddlebags and mounted. Before he rode off he looked back at the fetching, naked woman. "And get some clothes on, you hear?"

"Yeah, might as well."

Spur rode off for Holmes.

* * *

Joshua Golden, Jack T. Galde thought as he scrubbed his face in his hotel room. That was his name. A new name, a new profession, a new town ripe for the picking. He'd installed himself in a matter of hours.

With the support of Vanessa Thompson, the concerned, church-going citizens had flocked to him. The late hours he'd spent boning up on the Bible, recalling the lessons his mother had given him on her knee when he was a screaming brat, had paid off. He'd fooled them all with his talk of God and Satan and Heaven.

Hal Phillips, Holmes' unoffical lawman, attended church every Sunday morning. So did the mayor, half the citizenry and the largest depositor in the Western Bank. He'd worked his way into the puny power circles of the town, gained the people's confidence, worked hard to establish a reputation as an honest man of God.

It had been difficult—excruciatingly difficult. He'd had to lay off liquor and never got to watch the dancing girls at the Glittering Garter Saloon. He hadn't had a woman for over a month. Late at night that tore him up inside. But he knew that in the long run it was well worth it. He'd live a life of luxury as soon as he'd stripped this town of its wealth.

Galde wiped the chilling water from his face. He'd done it. He'd made his moves and carefully planned. Now he'd wait until the time was right.

Holmes, Kansas, was a small town west of Kansas City. Named after its colorful founder, Quentin Holmes, it was a gathering place for local farmers and ranchers to buy, sell, exchange goods and to do some drinking.

Quentin Holmes, now deseased, was a man who appreciated the finer things in life—especially *art*. At least, that's what he told the first residents. After building the bank, church and general store, he'd established the lavish Glittering Garter Saloon. Every night, 'ladies', imported from various shady parts of various shady eastern cities, put on a show that made the local men drink more and think less.

Though the founder had died years ago, the saloon was still the center of the life for most of the men who lived there.

Spur rode into the town that had been carved out of a centuries old, dried river bed. He checked into a hotel, discarded his carpetbag, rubbed cold water on his face and set about to business.

He stood on the boardwalk that fronted the Calvin Hotel, hands on his hips, thinking, looking around.

"Excuse me, but you look lost," a pleasantly feminine voice said behind him.

McCoy was pleased at the voice's owner. A well-formed, primly-dressed woman in her late thirties smiled at him in a wholesome manner. Twirling a white parasol over her left shoulder, she chuckled, "You look *very* lost. Can I be of any help?"

Spur tipped his hat. "Thanks, ma'am; just got into town." He was somewhat irritated by the interruption but figured she might be some value to him.

"Well, there's not much here—not really." The

woman proffered her right hand. "I'm Vanessa Thompson, widow of Charles Thompson."

Spur took it gently. "Spur McCoy."

Withdrawing her hand, she lowered her parasol. "It is powerfully hot out here today. Would you like to come to my parlor? I'm afraid I've never been much of a woman who could stand heat."

"Gladly, Mrs. Thompson."

They'd soon installed themselves in the widow's front room in the small, plain house beside the church.

"Well, what's your business here in Holmes,if you don't mind my asking?"

"Not at all." He took the cup of cool tea that she offered him and began spinning a cover story. "I've just left St. Louis looking for a place to settle down. I'm a printer and was thinking to start a newspaper."

"A *newspaper?* In Holmes?" She laughed. "Mr. McCoy, I assume you've already decided that this isn't the place. Why, most of the folks around here don't read. I know that because they haven't read the Bible, the only book *worth* reading. And furthermore, nothing ever happens worth reporting! It's a lazy town with lazy people."

"That may be," Spur said, and sipped the cool liquid, "but I've heard Holmes is growing. How many people live here now?"

"Oh, let's see—I'd say about two hundred or so—but mind you, most of them have farms and ranches nearby. Maybe about fifty in Holmes itself."

Spur nodded. "Many new folks moving in here?"

Vanessa shook her head. "Not many. Let's see—there's been three in the last month. That's quite a few. A young girl by name oh—oh, I can't remember, flounced into town yesterday in a scarlet dress with even brighter lips." She sniffed. "The young lady—if I can dare to call her that—is working in the Glittering Garter Saloon." She smiled broadly. "And two weeks ago the Reverend Joshua Golden answered my prayers. He's been preaching every Sunday. A fine enough man, though perhaps his style's a little soft for my sake. Reverend Golden's doesn't drum up nearly the thunder that my late husband used to call down in the pulpit." She allowed herself a fond memory—it flickered across her face like a summer breeze. "And then some drifter showed up here a few days ago." She curled up her nose. "Someone should inform him of the values of regular bathing."

"And that's a lot?" Spur shook his head. "Guess this might not be the place for a newspaper. Still, I'll be around for a few days, thinking about where to check next." He placed his cup on the small table beside his chair and rose. "Thanks for your hospitality, ma'am."

She nodded pleasantly at him. "I hope to see you in church Sunday morning if you're still in town. Preacher Golden told me he's planning a soul-searching sermon and I don't think you should miss it!"

"No promises, Mrs. Thompson, but I'll do my best." He walked to the door.

"And if you see that brazen hussy on the street, tell her I'm expecting here there, too!"

Spur walked out into the relentless sunlight. The

drifter Vanessa had mentioned was a possibility—not a strong one, but a possibility. Of course, a gang could ride into town at any moment and rob the bank.

But that didn't fit the picture. These thieves did things quietly. They were smart.

He began to wonder if Holmes was the thieves' next target. It seemed too small, even for a western town, even with the riches of the surrounding farmers and ranchers that had presumably been deposited in the small bank that he was passing.

Still, it was something to go on.

Reaching the front of the Sullivan Hotel, Spur stared at his new mount as it quietly lapped at the trough. The drifter might be one of the thieves, but it wasn't likely. He'd check him out just in case. And after that?

He stroked the horse's smooth, shimmering flank. Maybe he should leave Holmes, move on to the next town. Even now the thieves might be killing more innocent people. Even as he stood here another safe might be suffering from the blast of dynamite. Even then—

"Becky!" a dusty man in riding clothes yelled as he bustled up to Spur.

"Sorry to disappoint you but I'm not your Becky." Spur's voice was sarcastic as the hulking man stormed up to him across the dusty street. "She sure must be an ugly gal for you to mistake me for her!"

"Not you, asshole!" the man said. "The horse!" He curled is upper lip before looking down. His sunburned face blossomed into a boyish grin, exuding joy as he gazed at Spur's new horse.

''Becky, where ya been? Huh? I never thought I'd see you again, you old girl!'' He reached out for the mare's neck.

Spur blocked his hand. ''Begging your pardon, sir, but that's my horse you're ogling. Kindly keep your hands off.''

The narrow-eyed rancher grabbed McCoy's arm and wrestled it away. ''The hell I will! I'll touch my own horse whenever I want! This here's my Becky. I'd know her in a minute!''

''You're wrong,'' Spur said.

''Bullshit!'' His face reddened. ''Someone stole her off my ranch three days ago. I've been up day and night since then lookin' for her.'' He drew his gun, his face showing the strain of unaccustomed thought. ''You must've stole her! You must've been the one! Now give her back right now!''

''Come on, mister! You made a mistake!''

''No. You're the one who's made the mistake, horse thief!''

He cocked his revolver.

4

"Try to stop me!" the big man yelled. "I don't mind shooting a horse thief! Hell, that's legal around these parts. That's my Becky. You stole her from me and boy, we don't cotton to your kind around here!"

Spur waved off the armed man. "Hey, look, I don't know what you've been drinking, mister, but that's my horse. I bought her fair and square in Kansas City just this morning. Paid fifty genuine U.S. dollars for her. So if I were you, mister, I'd holster my weapon and try to think things out before you go and accuse me of being a horse thief!"

The rancher spat. "Hah! I know my Becky when I see her! Can't imagine why you'd be so stupid to bring her here right after you stole her, but I figure that's what you is—stupid!" He waved his six-gun menacingly. "You just back off, boy, and let me take Becky home with me!"

Spur controlled his anger. "This isn't your horse. I bought her. She's mine."

The man guffawed. "An' I suppose you got a bill of sale, right?"

"Damn straight I do!" Spur pushed his right hand into his pocket and retrieved the small paper. He thrust it out toward the man. "All legal and everything. I don't think your horse thief stole her, rode her out to Kansas City and sold her all in the space of three days!" he said as the big man peered at the paper.

"It's possible." He squinted, staring at the receipt as if it were written in Chinese.

"Try to think straight, pal. This isn't your Becky. This isn't your horse. She's mine." Spur grabbed her reins protectively. "It's all there. Read it!"

The rancher's shoulder slumped as he stared at the bill of sale. "Hell, I—I don't know. Never was much for letters." He glanced up. "Hey Hal, git your butt over here and read this here thing for me!" He waved it in the air.

A thin man with thick glasses sauntered up. "What seems to be the trouble, Burt?" he asked.

"Just read it!"

"Okay, okay."

"This man seems to think I stole his horse," Spur threw in. "I can't convince him otherwise."

"Well, you've convinced me," the man said, after scanning the paper. "This horse is your rightful property. If you did steal his Becky, this isn't her. Sorry, Burt; it's all here. This horse was purchased this morning in Kansas City."

Burt stomped on the ground. "Damn. Hell! I was sure this was my Becky!" He looked wildly at the thin man. "How we know he didn't just get someone to write that up all fancy like? Couldn't he've done that?"

"It looks good to me. Besides, he wouldn't bring her here to town."

Spur patted the mare's head. "Anyone can make a mistake, Burt." He snatched the bill of sale from Hal's hand. "Hope you find your horse—wherever she is."

"Sorry for the trouble, stranger. I'm Hal Phillips, the unofficial law in these parts. Well come on, Burt; let's have a drink. Think you need a cooling down."

"Well. . . . well . . ." he stammered. "I still think that's my Becky!"

Spur shook his head as the two men walked off. He patted his horse once again and rambled down the street, taking in what few sights the small town had to offer. He tipped his hat at two elderly women who, upon seeing him, nodded politely but scurried away. He saw a young man walking hand in hand with a freckle-faced girl, the two of them oblivious to anything but each other.

A block down the street a pudgy, sweating, hatless man dressed in black—with a backwards white collar—approached him. As soon as he saw Spur the man hurried forward.

"Hello. New in town?" the man asked, mopping his slick forehead with a stained handkerchief.

"Sure am. Just arrived today."

"Well, on the behalf of Holmes, let me welcome you to our town. My name's Golden. Joshua

Golden." He grabbed his jacket lapels.

"You must be the new preacher Vanessa Thompson told me about."

"You've met Mrs. Thompson? Fine woman, she is. A fine sister of Christ." He shook his head. "Well, I've got some sick folk to attend to. Hope to see you in church on Sunday. I've got a powerful sermon cookin' in my brain!"

"Don't know if I'll be around that long, but if so I'll try to make it," Spur said, somewhat half-heartedly.

Reverend Golden didn't seem to notice. "You do that. Good afternoon!"

With that the man was gone, hurrying down the street.

Spur returned to his hotel room, cleaned his Colt .45 and took a short nap. He didn't know why he was staying in Holmes. The place seemed quiet enough, and the only reason he'd gone there was the assumption that the thieves would rob the local bank. He had no evidence to support this except a stubborn idea in the back of his head.

McCoy flopped down on the hard, small bed and thought it all out.

Later, after dark, Spur once again roamed the streets of Holmes. By the light of the nearly full moon he saw a dirty man, dressed in tattered clothing, walking aimlessly, dragging his left foot.

The drifter?

Spur sank back into a heavy shadow and watched the man for a few minutes. He looked into windows, stood outside a hotel for a while and stared inside before wandering off.

McCoy sighed. He didn't seem the kind of man who'd murder innocent people and rob banks. If he had he certainly wouldn't be so poor, and Spur guessed that the man wasn't in some sort of disguise. Anyone who went to those lengths to rob a bank would probably enjoy the fruits of his dirty work.

The drifter seemed harmless. Spur shrugged and headed into the nearest bar. He might as well have a drink.

Jack T. Galde pulled at the hot, constricting collar around his neck as he strolled. He hated the damn thing, hated the town he was in, hated pretending to be a preacher. Most of all he hated that fuckin' Vanessa Thompson, the widow lady who watched his every move as if she was testing him. Hell, he'd like to throw down a bottle of whiskey and show her how much a man of the cloth he really was.

Of course, he couldn't do that. Too much was riding on this. Through discreet inquiries he'd discovered that the local bank had deposits in excess of $20,000—a huge sum, compared to what he's been getting lately. Some of it was held in trust for one of the founding father's nephews who lived on an outlying ranch with his adopted parents.

For that much money he could force himself to wait a few more weeks until he got back to enjoying the finer things of life.

Speaking of, Galde thought, as he spied a blond-haired, beautiful girl waltzing down the boardwalk toward him. She was a magnificent creature, all hair and lips and breasts and thighs, wrapped up in a tight green dress.

She was the kind of woman that any man would want. The kind of woman he wanted right then. Damn! What in hell gave him the idea to dress up in that old preacher's outfit he'd stolen a while back? Why couldn't he just be an ordinary man here? If he was he'd take that delicious package, rip off her clothing and pound it into her until she screamed for mercy.

He felt lust seize his veins. He didn't stop looking at the girl as she approached him. Seeing his outfit, the young woman slowed her steps.

Galde's face twisted up into hatred—not at the girl, but at the way he'd tricked himself into denying the good things of life. "Young woman, are you a Christian girl?"

She looked down as she walked up to him. "That's not for me to say, reverend."

Inwardly, he hoped not. Maybe he'd have time for one quick—no. Not now. "Find out. Come to church this Sunday. It'll do you good."

Hell, it'd do *him* good, seeing her there while he sweated his way through another one of those damn, demanding, exhausting sermons. He could glance at her tits every time he said the word "God."

"Sorry, preacher; I always sleep late on Sundays." With a dazzling, white-toothed smile, she skipped away and disappeared into the Glittering Garter Saloon.

Damn her! Galde pulled at the collar again and trudged off to visit the sick old woman who'd just willed her entire fortune to the church. At least he could pick up a hundred or so before he hit the bank—if the old broad managed to kick off soon. Very soon.

He sighed. The problems of being a preacher in a Kansas city town. Galde didn't know if it was worth it.

The man turned around and looked back at the Glittering Garter Saloon. Maybe he could meet one of the girls who worked there, somehow, someway, pay her enough money to keep her mouth shut and have a little fun with her.

Sure. He could hire a carriage for her and they could meet out of town some afternoon. He'd tell her to bring a bottle of whiskey and pay her fifty bucks for the little adventure.

He felt excitement course through him as he planned it out. That could take care of his worst cravings for a week or so until he was figuring on leaving anyway.

Then he sighed. It was too risky. He couldn't do anything that might ruin the image he'd built up for himself in Holmes. Not with that damned Vanessa Thompson breathing down his neck every second.

If she found out about it—and she had her ways and spies—he'd be kicked out by the townsfolk. Once he'd lost their trust he'd have to move on to the next town.

No. He'd worked too hard, suffered through too much bullshit to ruin it now.

He'd just have to play the upstanding, clean-living preacherman for a week more. Just a week.

Well, maybe less. Five days. He thought of the blonde girl.

Four.

Spur stood at the bar, nursing a whiskey, staring at the assorted townfolk there. The stage was bare, empty, but a large sign next to it promised the wonders of real female flesh every night. *Dancing girls,* it said. Chorines with class!

He snorted, thinking he'd have to come back there later. Hell, he didn't mind a good show.

McCoy nearly dropped his glass as he saw Vanessa Thompson, dressed in a demure black dress and matching bonnet, storm into the place.

He rushed over to greet her at the door. "Mrs. Thompson. What brings you to this place?"

She eyed the glass in his hand and shook her head. "What do you think? I'm here to warn these men of the dangers of alcoholic beverages," Vanessa said smugly. "I can see you need my words as well. I also have to warn the good men of this town of the threat of loose women; to try to open these men's eyes to the lascivious, licentious behavior that goes on in this kind of establishment!"

"Now hold on, Mrs. Thompson," Spur said. "I'm pretty sure they're aware of these facts. And just as sure that they'd heard all this from you before. Am I right?"

"Well—well—that doesn't matter!" Her voice was filled with righteous wrath. "It's my duty to carry on the work of my late Charles—God rest his soul—in cleaning up this town of the evils of drink and filthy women!"

"What about the Reverend Golden?" Spur asked kindly. "Isn't that his job?"

The woman harrumphed. "I'm not so sure about the man. He preaches well enough, but he doesn't seem real. He doesn't smoke. He doesn't drink. He doesn't go with the ladies."

Spur tucked his chin against his chest. "Isn't that the way a preacher's supposed to act?"

"Yes, but they don't. Not out here, anyway. And it's just not right for a man of the cloth not to be a man of women, too. What I mean is, he should be married. Men like him make me suspicious of all kinds of things." She arched her left eyebrow.

"Mrs. Thompson, I don't want to dissuade you of your noble goal, but do you really think you'll accompolish anything in here?"

"If you try to stop me I'll be certain that you're a true instrument of the Devil rather than just a sinner," she warned him.

Spur set down his drink and tipped his hat to her. "In that case, I'll be leaving now. Good evening, Mrs. Thompson."

She ignored him.

"Hey Vanessa!" a man called out as Spur was headed out the batwing doors. "You gonna put on a show fer us?"

"Yeah. Show us your ankles! Hoo-whee!"

"Jesus will forgive you for your sins!" she hollered, "if you confess your—"

Spur left, shaking his head. As he emerged from the saloon, the drifter passed by him and headed down the block. Curious, Spur followed.

The man seemed to be going toward a specific location. Within moments he'd halted before the darkened general store. The drifter didn't look around. He simply tried the door knob.

After struggling with it for a few moments, he cursed lightly and kicked in the front window, sending it to the floor inside in a tinkling crash.

Spur ran toward him. "Hey! What the hell do you think you're doing?"

The drifter pushed out splinters of glass and jumped inside.

5

Spur bolted to the general store. Reaching it, he peered through the shattered window. All was dark inside, and the drifter wasn't in sight.

He carefully stepped through the yawning frame and drew his .45. Broken glass crunched beneath his boots. The drifter might not be a bank robber, but he was certainly a thief.

"Where are you?" he called into the darkness. "Show yourself, drifter!"

Nothing. Spur surveyed the large store. It was packed to the ceiling with every conceivable kind of dry good. One whole wall was filled with dozens of bolts of cloth. Nearby were hand tools, wire, nail kegs, rope, whips, bags that probably held seed and lime. To the rear of the store were cracker barrels, stacks of dusty canned goods, shadowy mirrors and dozens of other items.

"I said, show yourself!" he hollered again.

A glint. A whine. A glistening blade shot through the air a foot from McCoy's head and plunged into the door behind him.

"Son of a bitch!" Spur said.

Another knife flashed by him.

Spur ducked behind a solid oak counter covered with cast-iron pots and cauldrons. A clang told him of a third knife's passage.

"What the hell do you want?" Spur asked.

"Food. I'm hungry. Starvin'! And the people around here don't give a shit about that, about me. So I figured I'd just rustle up my own vittles."

"By breaking into this store? Not smart, drifter."

The voice was issuing from the far corner. Spur glanced above the counter. Straining his eyes through the murky store he made out a large wooden plaque filled with countless knifes of every size and kind nailed to the far wall.

A hand reached up and snatched one.

McCoy ducked. "Put the knife down, drifter! Give yourself up. At least they'll feed you in jail."

"Never!" he shouted. "I ain't going back there! That's what got me in this mess in the first place!"

So words wouldn't help, Spur thought, as the sound of steel against iron rang through the darkened store again. He darted across the open floor to the end of the long counter that stretched across the back. Crouching behind it, Spur waited. He knew the drifter was at its far end, below the knife display.

"Leave me alone! All I want's something to eat!"

Spur moved past the counter and pressed up against the rear wall. There he was—a down-cast, shrunken-shouldered man leaning against the corner. Spur saw a line of canvas bags on a shelf above his head. Might come in handy, he thought.

"I'll get you!" the man grabbed another knife and tossed it at the pots and pans again, then saw Spur.

"No!" he said, reaching up. His hand met empty wood.

Spur easily peeled off a shot six feet above the drifter's head. The bullet pierced a sack. A stream of white flour poured down directly on the drifter.

He coughed, gagged, wiping at his eyes as the bag unloaded its contents.

McCoy laughed as he strode over to the man. He grabbed one of his flailing arms and hauled him to his feet. Yanking him out of the flour shower, Spur shook his head. "I think you need to visit—what's his name? Hal Phillips?"

With that he pulled the man out of the store, through the opened window, down the street and into the saloon. McCoy was pleased to see Vanessa Thompson had left.

"Where's Hal Phillips live?" he yelled. "Got a ghost for him."

The lanky man with bottle-thick glasses emerged from the smoky air. "I'm Phillips. What the hell's going on now?" he asked.

"Here." Spur thrust the flour-covered man at him. "Caught the drifter trying to rob the general store. He broke a window and scattered some knives around."

"Olsen Hunter?" Hal seemed a bit dazed by the news, but fairly pleased by Spur's accomplishment. "Well, thanks—I think," he said, surveying the coughing man. "Guess I'll lock him up in my house. What'd you say your name was?" the unoffocial lawman asked.

Spur shrugged and walked to the bar. "Didn't."

Phillips shrugged. "Well, come on, Hunter." He dragged the sneezing man from the saloon.

Spur ordered a whiskey, got it and tried to pay the hefty barkeep.

"Nothin' doing," the apron said, smiling. "We need more law-abiding citizens like you around here. This one's on the house. Why not get a table and enjoy the show? It's just about to start."

Grinning, Spur thanked the man and sat at the back of the saloon. Within minutes every table was filled as the men of the surrounding area poured in for their nightly visual orgy.

A mustached, white-suited man slammed his hands down on the keyboard of a small piano next to the stage. "Gentlemen! Prepare your eyes for the vision of the one, the only, Glitter Garter Revue!"

The 30 men hollered, stomped their feet and otherwise greeted the news with enthusiasm. The piano player started in on some nameless tune. Four young women—attired in petticoat-stuffed dresses with plunging necklines—spilled out from a small door and onto the tiny stage.

They launched into a dance number. What it lacked in artistic merit, Spur thought, was compensated for by the amount of female flesh it exposed. The four girls shook, romped, highkicked and bounced around, showing as much or more than their counterparts anywhere in the country.

One young lass particularly intrigued Spur. Mounds of blonde hair lay piled on her head. She wore a dress of the brightest scarlet silk and her face shone as she moved through the routine, struggling with the simple dance steps. When the other three girls kicked, she bounced; when they bounced, she kicked.

Spur sat back in his chair and enjoyed the sight of the increasingly exasperated blonde. He didn't mind if she didn't know what she was doing, and from the whoops around him he was certain no one else did either.

The girls performed four songs, bowed low to show off their ample cleavage and, giggling, disappeared in the little room next to the stage.

The piano player quickly positioned himself in front of the door. "The girls will be out shortly, men, so try to hold yourselves back."

Spur smiled. He wanted to talk with the blonde. He wanted to buy her a drink. McCoy walked to the bar, borrowed a pencil from the apron, wrote a short note and handed it to the piano player with a silver dollar.

"Would you give this to the blonde?" he asked.

He studied it. "Sure. But you might have to wait your turn. Patrice is new here. None of the men know her." He smirked and pocketed the note.

Soon after, the girls emerged. Spur sat upright as the piano player handed the blonde his note. She looked over to where he pointed, beamed and walked to his table as McCoy rose.

"Glad you decided to accept my invitation. Can I buy you a drink, Miss. . . ."

"Carlon. Patrice Carlon. And I'd love one! A

sarsaparilla is fine."

Spur quickly got her one and returned to his table.

"I was so surprised when Jack pointed you out to me. I never had a man write me a note." The girl had a dazzling smile, perfect white teeth, a short nose and wide-open, staring blue eyes.

"I heard you were new here."

"I'm new anywhere. This is my first night. Well," she said, making a face. "My first night of *this* kind of dancing. I guess I'm not very good at it."

"I thought you were fine. A little rusty, but fine. And the men sure did like you."

She blushed. "I'm not used to all this attention—or all these men." She shivered. "Look, mister—"

"My name's McCoy. Spur McCoy."

She nodded. "Mr. McCoy, I'm not comfortable here. I hate to think what else these men want me to do for them. Or with them. Would you mind walking me back to my hotel?" Patrice fluttered her eyelashes.

He stood. "It would be an honor, Miss Carlon."

She giggled. "My, aren't you one with the fancy manners!"

Patrice took his arm and they strolled to her hotel.

Once at her door, she turned to him. "Won't you come inside?"

Spur accepted at once. She turned up the lamps as Spur locked the door.

"I hope you don't think I'm too forward," Patrice said, standing nervously in the center of her room.

He leaned against the door. "I don't think you're too *anything*, Miss Carlon."

She laughed nervously. "It's just that I figure, well, I mean, if I'm supposed to dance for all those men, and—and—, well you know, I figure I better know how." She looked up at him and squished her cheeks to her nose. "Know what I mean?"

"You've never been with a man?"

She threw her head back and laughed throatily. "Oh, heck, I've been with them. Not as many as the other girls. Just a few when I could get away from my parents." Patrice stared into his eyes. "But St. Louis doesn't grow many like you, Mr. McCoy. I think you could teach me a thing or two." Despite her bold words the young woman's cheeks colored.

"Call me Spur." He walked to her and touched her arm. "You sure about this?"

"Sure I'm sure." She pulled his arm to her waist and touched his chest. "Take off your hat, mister."

He flung it to the ground.

"Now your shirt. Take that off too!" Her voice was breathy.

Grinning, Spur unbuttoned it and let it fall to the ground. "You sure you haven't done this much, Miss Carlon? You sound pretty experienced to me."

"Not experienced," she said. "Just desperate. Kick off your boots and take off your pants." She sat on the bed, leaned back against the pillows and watched him. "I just gave you a show; now give me one!"

The boots were off in seconds. Spur unbuckled his belt and dropped his dusty trousers. He stood in his long underwear.

Patrice raised her eyebrows. "My, my, Spur, what a large bulge you have there. Could I be the cause of that pulsing growth?"

He grinned. "You know damn well you are, woman! Come on over here and take these off for me!"

"No. I wanna see you stripped naked. All the men I've been with always doused the lights before they did me. Or we were outside at night. I wanna see what a real man looks like!" She leaned back, waiting.

Grunting, Spur bent and ripped off the cotton underwear. He stood up, fully erect and gazed down at the blonde woman. "Well?" he asked. "You're seeing me now. You're seeing what you're doing to me with that pretty little mouth of yours!"

She giggled, gazing at his crotch. "I'm seeing you. I'm seeing more of you than I ever thought any man had!" She gulped. "Now show me what you can do with that thing! Rip my dress off and ride me, Spur!"

He jumped onto the bed beside Patrice and rolled her on top of him. McCoy fumbled with the buttons that ran down the back of Patrice's dress, cursed and ripped it, splaying the red material. He rustled it off the laughing woman and tore her petticoats into shreds, flinging them all over the bed as he lustily denuded her.

Patrice Carlon was on fire. She ground her crotch to his and kissed his chin and cheeks.

"You taste good," she said, running her tongue along the line of his stubbly jaw.

McCoy grunted and turned her onto her back. He

forced her legs apart and knelt between them. "Don't be so shy, Patrice," he said.

"I will if you will," she teased.

"Okay." He bent his head and took the woman's left nipple into his mouth. It hardened under his tongue, stiffened as he sucked her firm breast.

She groaned, gripped his head and forced his mouth lower, pushing deeper until he'd taken half her breast.

"Oh. Ohhh!"

Spur relished the sweet, warm flesh, the way her nipple responded, the groans that escaped from her lips. He lifted his head and enmouthed its twin, sucking, gnawing on its hard tip as she shook his head.

He rose and proudly stroked his erection, staring down at the overheated woman.

"You want this?" he asked, smirking.

She stared down at his huge organ. "Yes. Of course I do! Haven't I made myself clear?" She spread her legs and raised her crotch to him. "Put it in me. Go ahead, Spur. Stick it into my pussy."

"I don't know. I thought I'd suck on your tits for an hour or so first to really get you worked up. Thought we could take our time."

"I *am* worked up!" she said, impatient.

Spur moved his body down to hers. Gripping his hard penis, he pushed it against her wet opening and shoved. Patrice arched her back as he slid into her, filling her, stretching her like she'd never been stretched before, slowly driving her out of her mind.

"Oh, Oh god, Spur!" the woman wailed.

Their pubic hairs entwined as he sank full-length

into her. Spur gripped her head and slammed his lips onto hers. He pushed his tongue against Patrice's lips and into her liquid mouth, darting it toward her throat.

She moaned as their mouths thrashed together. The urgency at McCoy's loins drove him to withdraw and push back in, slowly, lovingly. The young woman dug her fingers into his muscled back as he began riding her, pumping, pounding between her parted legs.

Spur lifted his mouth. "This is what you wanted," he said, ramming into her. "You wanted to be fucked hard and fast. You wanted my cock in your tight little pussy."

"Yes. Yes!" Her eyes were half-closed as she writhed beneath him, lifting her hips to meet his with every powerful thrust. Patrice tossed her head, flinging blonde hair all over the pillow as he rammed into her.

Spur's scrotum banged repeatedly against her buttocks as he drove his penis deeper, deeper. They locked together, their slick bodies molding into one as Patrice gripped him with animalistic passion.

"God. Jesus! You're so tight and hot!" he moaned as he filled and emptied her vagina.

Patrice stared at him. "Give it to me. Slam it in! Set my pussy on fire!" Her eyes were alive with erotic heat as they burned into his. "Deeper. Harder! Come on, Spur; fuck me!"

He pumped faster, his hips blurring as he slammed into her velvety orifice. The familiar yet ever-new sensations made his testicles boil and heated him until droplets of hot sweat rained down onto the woman's body.

Below him, Patrice closed her eyes. Harsh, short breaths blasted out between her slick lips. She screwed up her face and strangled out a cry as he sent her over the edge, into the dark, shuddering place that sent bolts of electricity ripping through her, reducing her to a trembling, spasming woman that clutched him in her ecstasy.

Her climax was too much for Spur to take. She tightened around him, wringing his stiff penis. He felt his control fade as their bodies slammed together.

"Fill me up!" the gasping woman said, her face bright red. "Give it to me! Shoot your ball-juice!"

That did it. Waves of intense, bone-jarring excitement coursed through him. Grunting, jerking his hips spastically, he ejaculated deep into her, squirting, spewing hot male seed as he plowed.

Pleasure thundered through him. The room tilted, swerved before his lust-blinded eyes as he emptied himself with each savage thrust. His climax went on and on, extended to an incredible length as Patrice slapped her arms around his sticky torso and pushed her breasts against him.

After an unmeasurable time Spur felt drained. He gasped, puffing his breath against her hair. They relaxed. Muscles loosened. Their bodies slapped down onto the dripping bed, their hearts racing in time with each other as Patrice continued to grip his penis in orgasm-induced contractions.

They lay there, joined, panting, for five minutes. Spur finally lifted his head and looked down at her.

Patrice Carlon's face glowed. Her eyes twinkling, she stuck out her tongue and pantomimed extreme exhaustion, sucking in her breath in a comic style.

Spur laughed. "Hell, Patrice, I gotta remember to stay away from you."

She squeezed harder around his softening penis. "What makes you say that?"

"You could be hazardous to my health." He kissed the top of her head. "I don't think you need any more practice, Patrice. You sure know how to get a guy all hot and bothered."

Patrice smiled. "You complaining? You didn't seem to mind a few minutes ago. You got so wild, so furious, that I didn't know what you'd do."

Spur cupped her left breast. "No, I'm not complaining. Hell no! You drove me out of my mind, woman. Besides, you knew exactly what I'd do." He smirked and started to pull away from her.

"No. Don't! Not yet!" she said, frowning.

"Sorry. Have to give it a rest."

Patrice groaned as Spur disconnected their bodies and sat on his heels between her legs. He ran a hand over his forehead, slicking up sweat. The woman sighed and closed her eyes. "You okay, little lady?"

"I don't think so." Patrice shook her head. "You sure are one hell of a man, Spur! And I do mean man!" She feigned exasperation. "They should hang a sign around your neck warning innocent women to stay away from you."

"Now why would you say a thing like that?" He crossed his arms. "I'm decent and honest and help little old biddies across the street."

"It's your thing! It's so big—bigger than any man

should have the right to have! Spur, I didn't know if I was dying or getting off!"

"If I did have that sign would you have stayed away?" he asked, gazing down at her nude body.

"Heck, Spur, I said *innocent* women."

"Sure am glad you aren't innocent."

She smiled, smug, assured. "Good. Then you won't mind if we do it again?"

He groaned and fell onto her, sending her into a fit of laughter.

6

Jack T. Galde paced in his motel room. The small, sparsely furnished room irritated him, infuriated him. He could be living in a big house instead of being cramped up in this godforsaken dump.

Fury pulsed through him until he finally sighed and sat on the hard wooden chair he'd bought after arriving in town. It couldn't be helped. He couldn't live anywhere else. Vanessa Thompson was firmly ensconced in the parsonage and his subtle hints that he'd like to move in there hadn't made her suddenly offer the place to him.

There he was, in a backwater Kansas town, five thousand dollars richer than he'd been two months ago and yet living in a dingy hotel.

But that was the least of the problems of this job, Galde thought bitterly. Anywhere else he'd gone he could walk into a saloon like any normal man and suck down a bottle of whiskey. He could fool around with the fancy ladies and play some faro without raising an eyebrow.

Here, however, trapped in that damned preacher's outfit, he couldn't move, couldn't eat, couldn't even take a shit without risking offending someone or threatening to expose his disguise for what it was.

He needed a drink. God, he needed a drink. Something to kill his brain for a while, to numb his anger and his unfulfilled lust. Something to make him *human* again.

Sighing, his throat parched and scratchy, Galde leaned back on the hard chair and thought about his position. The people of Holmes had immediately taken to him. Their need for a preacher—a lucky break—had allowed him to assume that role without any problems.

But he suspected that damn widow, Vanessa Thompson, thought something wasn't quite right about him. She watched him everywhere, studied him intently while he preached, even checked his biblical references in church to make sure they were right. A thought gnawed away in his mind. She didn't quite believe him, the little cunt. That could make her dangerous, or at least a problem.

Hell, he'd have to speed up his plan. In just a few days he'd rob the bank and leave town. Flush with all that new wealth, where would he go? He scorned the idea of setting up another job like this one. He needed a break.

Maybe he'd take the train to San Francisco. He'd get a room in the most expensive hotel in town and fill it up with fancy ladies. He'd guzzle whiskey and women until he couldn't see or piss straight.

The thought brought a smile to the pudgy man's lips. Well, hell, maybe it was worth waiting for. Just a few more days. But first . . . he'd better call on Vanessa, assure her of his devotion to God, assuage any doubts that lingered in her holier-than-thou mind.

Jack T. Galde was a simple man. Born of a God-fearing mother and a crabber in a tiny town in Maine, he'd been reared with Bible readings and steaming meals of cracked crab, fish and clam chowder. At first he'd been taken in with the idea of God—a powerful, all-seeing deity who'd strike you down with lightning if you so much as *thought* about a girl in the way you weren't supposed to think.

Soon, however, he started having those thoughts about Mindy, a girl who lived nearby. He thought about what was under her dress and it had made his crotch pound. He thought about what she looked like under all that dark wool.

The more he dwelled on such subjects, the more his mother's Christian teachings slipped away into some deep part of his brain. He'd played with Mindy one cold winter night, sticking his hand between her legs and fingering her. No flash of divine power struck his body, only normal boyish lust. Proving to himself that his mother had been wrong about sex, he'd decided to see what else she'd lied about.

He stole money from the collection plate at church. He lifted pouches of tobacco from old Mr. Dorman's store and rolled his own smokes with newspaper. He finally picked a fight with the town bully who'd terrorized him for years, beating him with his fists until the bloody boy bawled his head off and ran screaming for his mommy.

As he stretched his horizons and grew into young manhood Jack Galde realized that the world was his. He could have anything he wanted. *Anything*. If people wouldn't give it to him, he'd steal it. If they tried to stop him, he'd hurt them.

Nothing was sacred—not women, property or life itself. Galde quickly realized that the small-town surroundings weren't big enough for him, so he left home at fifteen on his father's horse and rode to New York.

Three years in the bowels of that dirty, noisy city turned him into a hardened youth. He had his first woman, tasted his first whiskey, played his first game of poker. He ripped diamond bracelets off fat women's wrists and grabbed purses. Hiding out in abandoned buildings with other thieves and thugs he managed to build a small fortune. Galde outfitted himself in the most expensive clothing (which, uncharacteristically, he bought) and became a full-time thief, earning a tremendous living at the expense of other people. When they gave him trouble he'd flash his gun and they'd relent.

Not long after, he shot his first man. A policeman, responding to a woman's cries for help, ran after him. He dropped her purse and, cursing, turned and fired without even thinking about it. The slug pierced the cop's heart and sent him to the ground, dead.

Excited at the power over life and death in his hands, he gave up simple thievery and let it be known that he'd kill anyone, anywhere, for a price. He had many takers among the up and coming politicians and suited businessmen.

Finally, 15 years of life in New York left him cold. He headed west and began his new career. At first he pulled some simple bank robberies with a few hired guns but he soon bored of that. Three months spent hitting trains was just as tiring, so he holed up in St. Louis and invented a new way of separating people from their money.

At first he'd enjoyed the game he played. He'd settle down in a new town, earning the people's trust, drinking and eating with them, becoming a friendly local.

Then, when the time was right, he'd rob the bank, kill anyone who tried to stop him and silently ride out of town. He'd done it five times so far, pulling off each job without a hitch.

He hadn't been caught. No one suspected him of his crimes. No sheriffs were staring at wanted posters that showed his ugly face, no witnesses still enjoyed the breath they'd need to accuse him.

Galde enjoyed making his mark across the west. He relished the wide-open spaces after the deadening darkness of New York City. Moreoever, the money was easy and there were few lawmen around to try to stop him. Those few that did exist didn't have the brains or guts to find him.

Spur slumped onto Patrice, exhausted.

"Come on, honey, again!"

"Hey, I'm not a machine!" He rolled off her. He stared at the ceiling and squeezed her firm breasts.

"Patrice, you're a hell of a woman. But I gotta rest."

She sighed. "Okay. But promise me this won't be the last time."

"I promise you. Now let me take a nap."

"You're—you're not really here to start a newspaper like you said, are you?" Her voice was hesitant, unsure.

He looked over at her. "What makes you say that?"

She flung yellow hair from her eyes. "I don't know. Just a hunch. My mother, the actress, always used to say that these thoughts came into her head from nowhere. Sometimes it happens to me. And I don't think that's why you're here."

Spur shrugged. "So?"

Patrice sighed. "Okay. So don't tell me. I don't care—really I don't! Just as long as you don't ride out of town tomorrow morning."

"I may be sticking around for a day or two," Spur said, realizing that the young woman's charms had temporarily blotted out all thoughts of his current job.

"You better not leave before I have the chance to give you a going-away present." Patrice wickedly grinned at him.

He moaned. "I've got a hunch what that might be."

She smiled. "See? My mother the *actress* was right!"

Vanessa Thompason walked hurriedly to the door. Who could be knocking at this late hour? She turned up the kerosene lamps on either side of the door and opened it.

"Preacher Golden!" she exclaimed. "Praise the Lord it's you! I was a little worried, being this late and all. I was just about to retire for the evening."

Galde smiled. "Then I'm glad I'm not unduly disturbing you, Mrs. Thompson. Can I come in?"

She nodded curiously and stepped back. "What brings you here at this hour?"

"God, Mrs. Thompson." He settled into one of the needlepoint covered chairs in the parlor.

"What about Him?"

The preacher was acting more peculiar than ever, Vanessa thought, as she sat opposite the man.

He looked down in supposed anguish. "I believe I'm having a crisis of faith."

"Preacher Golden, if that's the case I don't see why you're talking to me—though I appreciate your honesty."

"Who else can I turn to but you or God?" He looked up at her wearily. "Every citizen of Holmes knows you're the most God-fearing woman around. But the Lord hasn't answered my prayers."

She was interested. "What—what *kind* of crisis are you experiencing?"

"The Fiend in the Bottle calls to me. The Devil makes me thirst for alcohol."

Relief shot through Vanessa. So he was human after all. "Preacher Golden, that's not a crisis of faith; just a hankering after sin. No man's perfect. Even men of the cloth may drink a bit now and then. Even Charles—"

"Not I, Mrs. Thompson. I fear the Devil is taking hold of me. But that's not all that I crave. That's not the lowest of the abominations that burn to control my sinful body." He peered into the woman's eyes, gazing at her.

Vanessa grew uncomfortable under his stare. She hadn't seen a man look at her like that since—since her late husband had one of his bouts of fleshy lust.

Lust! She was shocked beyond all words.

"Preacher Golden, I think you'd better go back to your room, get down on your knees and pray to be washed by the blood of Jesus. Confess your sins and you shall be redeemed!"

Galde rose. "How can I confess to evil without trying them out first?"

She sat open-mouthed as he rose and walked over to her, lowering his gaze to her chest.

"Your fine looking titties jutting out like that are driving me crazy! You're a hell of a good looking woman, Vanessa!"

Her face colored. "Get out. Get out! You're no man of God! I knew it the minute I saw you!"

Galde laughed. "Was that the minute I 'answered your prayers?' " He roared with laughter and reached for her breasts with both hands.

She slapped him away, stood and backed against the wooden chair.

"You're in league with the Devil!" Vanessa said, tight-lipped. "Stay away from me!"

"Vanessa! Let me show you the ways of sin! Let us share in the wicked delight of *lust*, my dear!"

"Abomination! Devil! I rebuke you, Satan!" Vanessa stepped backward into the chair, knocking it to the ground and crashing down after it.

She slammed onto the floor. Hurt, stunned, she saw Galde lunge down toward her. Vanessa scrambled to her feet, trying to free herself of the stocky man's grabbing hands as pain shot through her body.

"Come on, Vanessa, you know you want to!"

"No! You speak with the Devil's tongue! Abadon!"

"You're gonna dry up without some good loving in your hole!" Galde slapped her face, leered and ripped the front of her simple black dress, tearing it off at her waist.

Shocked, nude to the waist, Vanessa slapped back. Galde chuckled until she broke free and hurried to the front door. Then he was there, holding the knob firmly, trapping the woman between his arms. She looked up at him, helpless, drained of energy. Her fight had left her.

"If it's God's will. . . ." she said slowly, looking at the floor.

He laughed. "Sorry, honey, I gotta disappoint you. I don't wanna rape you."

"You don't!" Vanessa glanced at his face. "Then why are you doing this?"

"I couldn't control myself. All I want is your money. Frankly, my dear, I don't have the time." He picked the woman up, stumbled once under her weight and carried her into the bedroom. He threw her onto the quilt-covered feathered mattress, stripped off his belt and tied her hands together behind her back.

Vanessa lay in a daze, unable to cope with the

reality of the situation, watching emotionless as Galde stormed through her dresser drawers.

"Nothing. Nothing! Come woman, you must have something worth stealin'!"

Why was this happening to her? Why, Lord why?

"Ah hah! What have we here?"

She stifled a sob as he brought out a small, carved wooden jewelry case. Vanessa's cheeks burned as he opened it. Not that, she thought. Not that!

"All kinds of expensive shit," he mumbled.

Galde removed the strand of pearls her father had given her as a girl; the diamond earrings and emerald brooch, gifts of former suitors; the gold chains and all the other shameful fripperies that she'd stored away after she'd become a preacher's wife because she hadn't had the heart to part with these vestiges of her former life.

The exposure of her long-hidden secrets enraged Vanessa but she was powerless to resist. As much as she bucked on the bed she couldn't release her hands.

"Well well well. Vanessa, you can't be half bad if you've got goodies like these. And I thought you were a woman of God." He stuffed them into his pockets.

"I *am* a woman of God," she said in a low voice. "Just not a perfect one."

He looked around further but, finding nothing else of value, smiled at the bound woman on the bed. "Good day to you, Vanessa. You won't be seeing me again."

"The Lord will punish you for your sins!" she screamed. "He will find you and kill you and cast you into eternal hell-fire, Joshua Golden!"

"I don't think so, but pray to your God that someone finds you soon. Frankly, I don't give a shit." He blew her a kiss and hurried out of the room.

Vanessa pushed her face into the quilts and cried.

Patrice Carlon tip-toed out of her room. She didn't want to wake up the handsome naked man who slept there. Glancing back at Spur, she pulled her shawl tighter around her and closed the door.

After leaving her hotel she walked along in the fresh, chilled air, enjoying it, feeling it clear her mind of the sex-mists that still boiled within it.

She strolled down the short lengths of boardwalk that fronted the town's buildings—the general store, the combination post office and notary public, clothing shop, the milliner's. As she approached the bank Patrice was puzzled by the fact that its front door stood wide-open.

That's strange, she thought, even for a small town like this. Patrice walked up to the bank.

A short man ran out the door, colliding with her, nearly knocking her over and spilling the bag from his hand.

"You! Who are you?" the man asked.

Patrice reeled back. "I—I—"

"Never mind."

Two men approached a block away. The pudgy man glanced at them, then at the girl. "You're coming with me!" He slapped an arm around her head, covered her mouth with his hand and painfully yanked her along with him.

Patrice struggled against his powerful grip as he

dragged her to the horse that waited behind the bank. What in the world was happening?

When they got to the mount the man slapped her cheek hard enough to send her head spinning. She felt herself being lifted onto the saddle, then the man's body pressing against hers.

In seconds they were off and moving across the darkened landscape. The buildings sped past until they had left Holmes and were out into the countryside.

"Where are you taking me?" she asked, afraid.

"Shut up or I'll throw you off!"

Patrice looked down at the dimly-lit ground that raced beneath them, sighed and shook her head. Her mind reeling from fright and pain, Patrice held onto his pudgy sides as the horse whinnied and bolted into the unknown.

7

Spur stirred. A sensuous lethargy filled his long body as he stretched and greeted the dawn. Somewhere outside a bird chirped erratically.

He yawned, coughed, scratched his stubble and reached over to the bed beside him. His hand hit cool sheets. Surprised, he shifted to full consciousness, opened his eyes and blinked. Patrice wasn't there.

Mystified, he glanced around the room. The blonde girl was nowhere in sight. McCoy wiped his eyes, shook his head, stood and dressed a little faster than he normally might have. Not that he had anything to worry about—Patrice had probably gone to breakfast, or out for one of those strolls she said she enjoyed so much.

He stuffed his feet into his boots, slapped on his hat and walked out of the room. Still yawning, Spur did find it a little strange that the woman who'd begged him to do it again and again last night wasn't around the next morning for a repeat performance. He expected her to wake him up with her mouth—below his waist.

Then again, he never really understood women. At least not all women.

He walked out into the blazing Kansan sunshine. The street seemed unusually busy. Perhaps two dozen men crowded around a tall, lean figure. Hal Phillips, Spur thought, the unofficial lawman. Women and children ambled about, two babies screamed, dust filled the air from iron-wrapped wheels and horseshoes.

Dazed by the confusion, Spur stumbled around, looking, listening. What the hell was going on? Shouts echoed through the street but he couldn't make out any of the words.

McCoy grabbed a passing man's shirtsleeve. "Hey! What's all the excitement about?" he asked.

The calico-shirted farmer, clearly irritated at the interruption, wrestled his sleeve from Spur's grip. "Ain't you heard?" he asked testily. "Reverend Joshua Golden tried to rape Vanessa Thompson last night!"

McCoy was stunned. "I don't believe it."

He remembered the Bible-thumping, fat, black-haired, greasy-faced man.

"And that ain't all," he said, wide-eyed. "He tied her up and robbed her."

Spur said, "And that's what kicked up all this commotion?"

"No, asshole!" the wrinkle-faced farmer said, his eyes narrowing. "Then that fine new preacherman of ours robbed the bank and kidnapped that new girl who works down to the Glittering Garter—" He shook his head. "What's her name?"

Spur's pulse quickened. "Patrice Carlon?"

"Yep. Then that damned man rode out of town with the two things dearest to my heart—my money and a fine piece of woman-flesh!"

"How you know all this?" McCoy asked. "Anyone see him do it?"

The farmer glanced behind him. "Well, Mrs. Thompson tole us all about what happened to her herself. She managed to git her hands untied and walked outside. She wuz goin' to Hal to tell him about it when she seed a man barge outa the bank with a big sack, grab a blonde girl and disappear out back!"

"And Golden's missing this morning?"

"Yeah, damn straight he's missin'!" The farmer bolted toward the man who'd earlier accused Spur of stealing his horse.

"Which way did he ride?" Spur called after the departing figure.

"Everyone says east. That's what they think!"

Spur shook his head. No way. Joshua Golden—or whatever his real name was—wouldn't backtrack. It was too dangerous for a man in his profession.

Now, too late, it was so clear to him. Golden was the man who'd pulled the string of bank robberies. He'd been right under his nose but Spur had barely noticed him. And now he had Patrice Carlon!

Patrice recoiled from the stench rising from Golden's armpits but realized she had no choice. She gripped his waist and hung on. The horse wasn't galloping and hadn't for several hours, but she was unused to its movements and thought she was in danger of falling to the dirt at any second.

It had been a living nightmare, clutching to the man's broad back for hour after hour, listening to his cheery, foul-mouthed talk, contemplating her possible futures. None of them looked bright.

Why the heck did I have to go on that moonlight walk? The question pounded in her brain until long after the first streaks of dawn had spilled over onto the western horizon ahead of them. She could be snuggled up to the man of her dreams—well, the man of her current dreams—instead of getting her fanny bruised by the uncomfortable, cramped seat she'd been forced to take on a saddle.

"Yeah," Galde said, breaking into her thoughts again. "You just hold tight, blondie. Much as I hate to say it, I'm kinda glad you came along for the ride. You'll be my first woman in—hell, two, three weeks."

The loud smacking noises which issued from Galde's lips turned her stomach. She just didn't know how much more of this she could take. If she couldn't escape—which didn't seem too likely—maybe she could talk him into releasing her.

"You oughta be ashamed of yourself, hiding your thieving ways behind the Bible! I still can't believe you fooled all those people into thinking you were a preacher."

"Hell, I fooled you. Filled you with fire and brimstone until you couldn't stand to be near me. I'm a good actor." Galde chuckled at the statement.

"No you're not!" Patrice hissed, batting swirling

dust from before her eyes. "My mother's a great actress in St. Louis. She'd probably kick you out of any show you were in. You're just a thief, a common thief."

He reigned in the horse to a stop. Jack T. Galde looked over his shoulder at her. "There ain't nothing common about me, blondie. 'Cept maybe my lustings." He grinned evilly at her, showing broken, yellowed teeth. "I got a pow'rful lusting that's just itching to be satisfied."

Patrice shivered and looked away from his eyes. "It's time you let me go."

He laughed and kicked the horse to a fast walk, ignoring the woman's words.

Goldwater—named after the muddy river that ran straight through the town—was right where Marshal Porter had indicated it would be on his map. It was a rude, growing settlement of about fifty people and half as many buildings. Spur knew it was too small a place for Golden to stop in for more than resupplying.

He rubbed down his foaming horse and let it drink from a slightly green trough as he asked around about a stocky man and a young, blonde-haired woman. The townsfolk he met were uncommunicative but few seemed alarmed or interested in his words.

One old man, sitting in a rocking chair in the shade of the barber shop, summed it up: "Hell, ain't been no excitement around here for years. Sorry, feller! Your two little love-birds didn't fly into here last night or this morning."

Frustrated, Spur questioned several more people

and then tried his luck at two of the outlying farms. The first one, slightly off the trail from Holmes, was unproductive. The second one was abandoned —the windmill flying six broken vanes, bales of hay rotting in the sun, a dead horse lying in the middle of the yard.

Unwilling to waste more time, Spur trusted to his instincts. It wasn't a coincidence. Golden was the man who'd robbed the other banks and he was headed onto the next—with the girl who'd shared her bed with him last night.

He rode west, pushing his horse.

"I keep telling you, blondie; you're too dangerous. So shut your pretty little mouth and let me do some thinking!"

"Don't strain yourself." Patrice laughed, staring at the back of his narrow-brimmed black hat. "Honestly, the way you talk you'd think I was an armed criminal or something. I'm just a young girl in a very strange part of the country. How could I possibly be dangerous to you?"

He grunted. "You won't talk me into letting you go. Now or ever."

Patrice hung onto her hope. She figured he'd only take her part of the way out of town and leave her somewhere to fend for herself. "But you've got a headstart! And no one'll ever find you!"

"You're right about that. No one *ever* finds me. But that's still not a good enough reason to let you go. You're too pretty to leave here out in the middle of nowhere." He reached behind him, grabbed her hand and dragged it forward.

Patrice squirmed as he pressed it into his fat

crotch. She slapped his back and jerked her hand free. "You animal!" she said, her cheeks coloring. Then she calmed down. As much as it made her ill to think of it, she did have another bargaining tool. It was the most expensive commodity a woman owned.

"Mr. Golden—"

"The name's Galde. Jack T. Galde."

"Whatever! Mr. Galde, if—if I let you have me, you know—in *that* way—"

"You mean *fuck* you?" He grunted.

"Yes."

"Stick it in your pussy and slam it in and out?"

"Yes!"

"Bank your tight little hole until I shoot my—"

"Yes! Yes!" She sighed at his colorful description. "If I let you do that to me, then you'd let me go. Right? I mean, then you'd have everything you want and I wouldn't be any more use to you. Why don't you just stop this smelly old horse? Let's get together for a while."

His laugh was short, harsh. "Hell, I was planning on fucking you anyway. If you're even half-good I'm not fool enough to let you out of my sight. I'll fuck you for five or six days at least."

Her throat tightened. "And then?"

He laughed. "Probably won't kill you. You're too pretty to kill, with all that blonde hair."

She shut her eyes. At least that's one thing she didn't have to worry about. Patrice picked a grain of dirt from her lips. "Then how about money? I could pay you any amount you want."

Galde was silent for a moment. "How much?"

"I—I don't know. A hundred dollars?"

He guffawed. "Hell, woman I ain't counted it yet but I must've taken ten thousand dollars from that piss-poor Holmes bank! Just sit tight, blondie. We'll stop soon enough and rustle up some grub."

"Stop calling me that!" she said with sudden violence. "My name's Patrice!"

"Sure, blondie. Sure." He guffawed as they rode through the bleak, flat landscape.

The trail between Goldwater and Fagan showed many deep ruts caused by the passage of carriages and stagecoaches, as well as countless horseshoe impressions formed in earlier, wetter months. Spur stopped and studied them at regular intervals, allowing his mare to rest, but couldn't make out any regular tracks that would positively tell him that he was going the right way.

As he rode, exasperated, McCoy kept telling himself that the man may have bypassed Goldwater but probably wouldn't ride through Fagan. The town was much larger. He was sure that if he didn't find him on the trail, he'd find Golden in Fagan.

A thief like him didn't suddenly alter his plan. That was the only thing he had going for him. That, and a hunch. Spur smiled as he remembered Patrice using that word, remembering her warmth, her scent, her lust.

The thoughts quickly dissolved into a sense of urgency. If he wasn't careful all he'd have of her were memories.

"Come on, girl, faster!" Spur yelled, gently stroking the mare's flanks with his boots, urging her toward the man and woman whom he knew were ahead of him.

Patrice sat on the sand, legs crossed beneath her, her arms bound behind her back with a short piece of stiff rope. It bit into her wrists every time she tried to move them into a comfortable position but the young woman soon decided that she wouldn't notice the pain, wouldn't occupy her thoughts with anything but her biggest problem—how she was going to get away from Jack Galde.

She thought vainly of Spur McCoy, the man she'd left behind. When he woke up and noticed that she was gone, would he look for her? Would he hear about her kidnapping? Did anyone know about it? Would Spur ride out and try to save her from this smelly man? Or would he simply carve another notch on his belt and get on with his life?

She didn't know him well enough to decide.

Across from her in the primitive campsite he'd carved out in the midst of a copse of cottonwoods, Jack T. Galde threw more kindling on the fire he'd built. The dry wood caught quickly, flashing into a brilliant, temporary blaze that died down as he stuffed larger branches into it.

He went through his saddlebags and produced a coffee pot, some coffee and a bit of hardtack. Galde glanced over at the woman and smiled.

"Gourmet eats."

She sniffed at him. "I'm not gonna eat a thing," Patrice said, and turned her head from the man. "You'd probably try to poison me."

"No way. Too much of a waste." He settled down before the fire.

"And anyway, I thought you were gonna rape me. How come you're suddenly more hungry than horny?" Not that she wanted him to, of course; it was just something to irritate him with. Maybe if he got mad enough at her, he'd leave her behind.

Galde laughed. "So you *do* want it! I thought so the minute I saw you walking in town. Had the hots for me as a preacher and still have 'em for me as a thief! You want me bad, don't you, blondie?"

"Not on your life!" Patrice shook her head. "But, I mean, after all those weeks without a woman, I just figured—well, heck, I don't think you can."

He grunted. "Can what?"

"You know! Maybe you like horses."

"Hell, you're jealous of that beast? You're a strange little woman, blondie."

"Patrice!" she said hotly. "My name's Patrice!"

"Sure. Sure, blondie."

She blew out her breath. At least he hadn't hurt her or tried to rape her—yet. But Patrice had this sinking feeling that despite the man's words, despite his reassurances, he'd either use her and kill her, or simply kill her.

The thought wasn't comforting, so Patrice blocked it out by intently watching Galde filling the coffeepot with water from the dented canteen.

It could be lots worse, she thought. He could be filling *her*.

8

Spur rode for most of the day, following the invisible tracks that he was sure were there on the trail. Well after noon the steel rails of the railroad sidled up beside him, stretching out like giant, dark-scaled snakes.

The endless acres of rich cropland and their attendant farm houses and barns, as well as a few scattered ranches, gave way to open land. Not long after riding through cultivated areas, the burgeoning town of Fagan, Kansas, rose before him.

Moving into it, Spur was impressed with the place. Two-story brick buildings as well as wooden structures lined the eight main streets. As he passed three hotels, the bank, the city hall and five saloons--as well as a variety of dry-goods stores—he was startled at the town's appearance. Everything looked fresh, new, well-kept.

Hundreds of people crowded the streets, vying for space with carriages and horses of every description. The train had apparently just stopped at the Fagan station, leaving in its wake a new load of confused, belongings-loaded men, women and children standing in Fagan with their hopes and dreams.

It had grown in a few short years from an isolated crossroads to a full-fledged town. The coming of the railroad had brought with it a steady influx of city dwellers ready to eke their livings from the verdant topsoil in the surrounding countryside.

Once there they bought precious lumber, nails, barrels, wagons, cloth, horses, pots and pans, food, kerosene and all manner of life necessities before striking out to find their own piece of land.

The noise surrounding him was almost deafening. From the blacksmith came the clanging of ironwork. A group of pigs squealed as they were led by an eldery, humpbacked man. Dozens of children screamed and cried to their parents. Carriages clattered by and horses whinnied. From within the saloons a cacaphony of off-key piano music mixed with the sound of drunkards demanding more whiskey.

Saddle-weary, caked with dust and thirsty, Spur rode into Fagan. The size of the town and the activity that seethed in it made it seem rather unlikely for Golden's purposes—too large, too many people, too many possible witnesses for him to pull off the kinds of bank robberies he was used to.

However, Spur knew—*knew*—that the man had

come here and, he hoped, had brought Patrice with him. The dear girl, Spur thought. Why had she gone out that night? Would she still be back in Holmes, fending off groping cowboys and kicking her beautiful legs into the air in the Glitter Garter Saloon, if he'd just done it a third time with her?

He shook off the thought. Too late for that now. And besides, like he'd told her, he was only human. He had his limitations.

Spur tied his horse up before the National Hotel—the best looking of the ones he'd seen after riding through half the town—and registered. The price was slightly higher than he was used to but money wasn't of any importance. In his room he threw his carpetbag onto the sturdy bed and was surprised that it actually bounced. Maybe he'd get a good night's sleep.

By the time he'd finished scraping off several layers of trail dirt and donned a fresh change of clothing, the sun had set. He grabbed dinner and went upstairs. McCoy stopped by at the unmanned front desk and flipped through the register. No familiar names—such as Golden—had been recorded in the last day.

He went outside to find Golden, Patrice—or, preferably, both of them.

Even after dark, Buttonwood Street was alive with people. Young as well as old lovers walked hand-in-hand. Men streamed in and out of the ever-busy saloons. Fancy ladies daringly walked the boardwalk alone, wrapped in tight dresses that picked up the light of exterior kerosene lamps that lined the street in all the right places.

It would be fruitless to search every male face in the hopes of finding Joshua Golden—or whatever his name was. But there were always the saloons. If any of them had dancing girls, and if Patrice had made it this far—

He checked all five. Two offered shows—the Horseshoe and the Red Ace. He watched the women go through their contortions in the first saloon but Patrice certainly wasn't among them. The 'girls' were well into their thirties and beyond, and their talent lay on their chests and between their legs—certainly not in them.

He walked into the Red Ace just as the show was ending to a rip-roaring ovation from the appreciative, liquor-laced male audience. From the back of the saloon McCoy thought he saw Patrice just before the blonde-haired girl turned and ran backstage with the other five women.

If he wasn't mistaken, she was in Fagan. His mind raced. Had she been kidnapped? Of course. She wouldn't have left her clothing behind had she simply decided to leave Holmes. And if she was there, was Joshua Golden there as well?

Remembering a stage door in the alley beside the building, Spur went outside and waited there. Several other young women, in pairs or accompanied by men he assumed were Red Ace employees, left through the door. Finally, Patrice walked out, her face flushed. She'd changed into a simple green dress.

"Patrice!" Spur said.

The woman stared at him in fright, rigid for five seconds before melting and running to him. She hugged him, pressing her face into his neck. "Spur McCoy! I thought I'd never see you again!" she said.

"Likewise." He gripped her waist as hard as he dared. "You seem healthy enough, Patrice. What the hell are you doing in Fagan?"

She broke from him. "It's a long story." The blonde looked up at him with sad eyes. "Jack Galde—that's Joshua Golden's real name—kidnapped me the other night after we'd—well, you know. I just happened to be going by the bank on my stroll while he was robbing it.

"I tried to get him to let me go but he wouldn't. Nothing I did or said would convince him otherwise. And he kept threatening to rape me." She made a face.

"Did he?"

"No. That's the funny thing about it. He had every opportunity to but he never did. Maybe I was right, maybe he only likes horses."

Spur smirked at her.

Patrice sighed. "So, yesterday afternoon, he finally stopped his horse and let me off. He said I was filling his mind with all sorts of crazy thoughts and he needed to think straight right then. I think he just couldn't stand to have me around any more. I'm afraid I talked him half out of his mind." She smiled, curling up her lips in a delicious grin. "Jack told me to go back to Holmes but it seemed too far. I'd heard him talking about Fagan, and even saw a map of his one time showing where it was, and so I headed here. My feet are still hurting."

"And got a job dancing?"

She nodded. "Mr. Weatherby had an opening

and so I was on stage less than an hour after I straggled in. I was dancing before I'd even gotten a hotel room—bruised feet and everything. After all, I didn't have a dime on me. No money, no clothes, nothing. And besides—Mr. Weatherby pays twice as much as I was making in Holmes. And here we're just dancers—nothing else." She raised her eyebrows suggestively.

"I see. Have you see this Jack Galde since?"

Patrice frowned. "I didn't until just tonight. He came in during our first number. I was mortified when he noticed me, wondering what he'd do. Though he'd let me go, I'm sure he didn't expect to see me here. I waited around backstage until I finally had to leave." She looked at him fondly. "You have no idea how happy I was to see you out here—instead of that man."

Spur nodded. "So he's here. Somewhere in this mass of people." He paused. "Did Galde say what he was doing next? Was he planning on robbing the bank here too?"

"I—I don't think so. He said something about 'laying low' for a while. Seems he's got plenty of money to spend."

"Makes sense. I didn't think he'd try anything here. It's not his style."

Patrice glanced around. "Look, Spur, I'd love to talk to you some more, but not here. I—I can feel him out there. Just knowing that he's in the same town is enough to give me the creeps." She shivered.

Spur gave her his arm. "Your room or mine?" he asked.

"It doesn't matter to me," she said, taking it.

They walked off.

Jack T. Galde stared at the Red Ace Saloon from his hotel room window. The show should be over any minute now, he thought, fingering the pearl buttons that ran down the front of his red shirt.

Soon, Patrice and some man he vaguely recognized from Holmes emerged from the alley beside the saloon and strolled off, arm in arm.

He scowled. Never should have let her go, he thought. Never leave any loose ends that can come back and trip you up just when you thought everything was going fine. He should've killed her the minute he stumbled into her as he was leaving the bank. Hell, he'd killed lots of women before. One more wouldn't have made much difference one way or the other.

But when he recognized her face, saw the shimmering blonde hair, he made a snap decision and dragged her along with him. He was aching for female companionship and all the charms that were at their disposal and thought that, if nothing else, she could give it to him. And besides, those men were walking up.

After a few hours, though, he realized that what had attracted him to her in the first place soon repelled him. The golden mane, the high, youthful voice all reminded him of one lady, the woman who had haunted him for all of his adult life.

His mother.

He slammed his fist onto the windowsill, making a long red mark across his knuckles. The pain was good, Galde thought, and he repeated the motion.

Agony set his mind in motion, got his head clear of stupid feelings.

He remembered his early adoration of his mother, that woman who'd had her nose stuck in the Good Book for so long that she'd never thought to take it out and look at the real world. He remembered how he'd idolized her until he'd realized that while God was fine for those interested in storing up for the life after death—if it did exist—life itself was the most important thing. He'd decided to wring as much out of it as he could.

However, the image of his mother—with her serene, almost simple face, high cheekbones and ringlets of hair the exact shade of daffodils—had stayed with him. Sometimes, as he lay panting beside a nameless whore while bad whiskey lubricated his brain, he thought of her, remembering the pretty woman she'd been. The thoughts bothered him, angered him.

Patrice soon did the same to him. However, he just couldn't kill her, not the way she looked. As much as he despised her smart, ever-running mouth, she was too beautiful a woman to waste. So he'd dumped her in the countryside between the two small towns, hoping she'd either die out there by herself or head back to Holmes. Either way, he assumed he'd never see the blonde bitch again.

Now, her sudden appearance in Fagan presented a problem to him. Patrice was dangerous, very dangerous. She knew far too much about him, enough to get him either lynched or legally kicking in the wind. All she had to do was go and spill the details to the local law.

Galde rubbed his head. It was too early to move on. He had plenty of money to spend and Fagan was a comfortable enough town. It was also big enough that he could blend in without being noticed—as long as no loose ends were dangling around.

He felt fury boil in his gut. He should've killed her then and there and been done with it. Never too late to settle unfinished business. This time he wouldn't let his feelings get in the way.

He slammed his knuckles onto the windowsill again.

He'd kill her. Kill the little bitch with the big mouth. Kill her before she killed him.

"Good evening, Miss Carlon," the craggy-faced man in an expensive New York suit said from the front register in the Crouching Lion Hotel.

"Good even, Peter." She walked into the fairly elegant lobby with Spur by her side.

"I enjoyed the show last night. You're very good." The beady-eyed man stared at her with admiration well mixed with hunger.

"Thank you, Peter." Patrice smiled at Spur as they walked to the stairs.

"It's a pleasure to have you staying here."

She giggled as they rose and burst into laughter on the landing.

"What's wrong with you?" McCoy asked.

"See why I like staying here? Back in Holmes I was a whore. Vanessa Thompson said it to my face. Here I'm a *star*, just like my mother always said I'd be."

She extracted a shining skeleton key from the small beaded purse that hung on her left shoulder and quickly opened her room.

Spur was impressed by its size and furnishings. This was no cheap hotel, judging from the cut-crystal lamps, the lace doilies that topped two cherrywood tables and the huge bed covered with thick woolen blankets.

Patrice threw her purse onto the bed and lit the small table-top lamp that stood before the window. She reached in through the curtains and opened it. A light breeze blew the filmy material into the air. Patrice turned to McCoy and smiled. "So, you can see I'm doing well enough here in Fagan."

"Yes," he said, looking around. "Pretty impressive. There's just one problem."

"What's that?" Patrice asked.

"Galde's in town."

The young woman's happiness melted into a frown. "Heck. I'd almost forgotten about him. You're right, of course. I should have expected to see him. But when I looked out into the saloon and saw him sitting there, staring at him, I was petrified. Nearly fell off the stage."

"You had every right to be. Who knows what's going on in his mind? Maybe he's thinking that letting you go wasn't such a good idea."

She shivered. "Don't even talk like that. With any luck, he'll be gone from here by tomorrow and I'll never have to see him again."

"I don't think so," he said, walking to her. "Galde said he'd be laying low. That sounds like sticking around in town for a week or so."

She looked at him curiously as he approached

her. "You seem awfully interested in him. Was—was he why you were in Holmes?" she suddenly asked.

He shrugged. "Could be."

"Damn you, Spur McCoy!" She moved laterally away from him and stood before the bed, shaking her head. "You're such a mysterious man. I can't get you to tell me anything." She huffed, then purposefully looked at him. Her blue eyes picked up the light reflecting from the prismed kerosene lamp. "So let's stop talking, okay? After all, you still owe me that third one."

He grinned. "Well, if you insist."

"I insist all right."

"Well, then. . . ."

"And I promise not to run off in the middle of the night. I'm through with my moonlight strolls. Besides, it'll get that darn man out of my mind for awhile and do us both a lot of good."

As he went to her again, loud male voices issued up from the street below. The conversation was heated, angry. Spur ignored it and touched her shoulder. Her skin was as soft as a duck's back, he thought, as a gunshot thundered up into her room.

"What was that?" Patrice asked, freezing up under his stroking hand.

"Just a fight outside." Spur nuzzled her warm neck, drinking in the expensive perfume that lingered there. He nibbled gently on her ear.

"But they might be killing each other! Maybe—maybe it's not just a fight." Patrice moaned.

"Forget about it."

Nibble. Lick.

"Maybe it's Jack Galde robbing the bank!"

Another shot.

"Don't worry about that. We've got other things to think about."

She shook her head. "If nothing else, I'm closing the window. I can't stand hearing that noise!" Patrice broke from him and went to it.

A third gunshot rocked the night. The window shattered, sending deadly shards of glass against the curtains. At the same instant the kerosene lamp exploded. The burst was short but long fingers of liquid fire spread across the table and fell onto the carpeted floor.

"Christ!" McCoy yelled as the flames rose higher in front of the window and Patrice's scream was nearly drowned out by the screech of broken glass crashing to the floor.

9

Thick smoke curled up to the ceiling. The room brightened as flames licked along the floor and gnawed at the cherrywood table. Patrice stood frozen amid the fire as it howled and snapped around her.

Spur grabbed the woman and threw her onto the bed. Stepping around the blaze, he ripped down the curtains and slapped them at the flames, quenching small portions of them but fanning others.

The fire continued to spread. Cursing, coughing and ignoring the itching in his eyes, McCoy knocked over the table, grabbed up the yet untouched end of the oval rug and roughly folded it in half. As that portion of the fire died out, the curtains combusted. Fire licked the wallpaper.

Spur glanced around, bolted for the pitcher and

dumped its liquid contents onto the flames. They sizzled and sputtered out.

Sighing, he turned around. Patrice sat up on the bed, back straight, her face calm. She folded her hands in her lap but didn't look at him as she spoke. Tears ran down her eyes in the now darkened room. Fresh air blew in from the broken window and swirled out the noxious fumes.

"That was Jack Galde," she said, ghostly in the smoke. "You were right. He's trying to kill me."

Spur went to her. "You don't know that. It could have been a stray shot from the fight in the street." He paused. "But even if it wasn't, you can't stay here. You better spend the night in my room."

Patrice glanced at him and nodded. "Okay." She was still pale.

"Just in case that bullet was meant for you, I don't think it would be a good idea for you to be seen outside right now. Any ideas?"

The question seemed to bring her back to life. Patrice rose and strode to a large trunk near the basin. "Something in here might help. It's a bunch of costumes that Mr. Weatherby lent me to use in the show. Everything just about fits me." She rummaged through it for a few minutes and soon held up a plain black dress, shawl and bonnet. "Will this do?"

McCoy nodded.

Five minutes later Spur left her hotel room and casually walked half a block down from the Crouching Lion. Not long afterward he saw a woman leave the hotel. She was dressed in black, a shawl pulled tightly around her face, her hair invisible beneath the bonnet. The figure hobbled along toward the National Hotel, looking for all the world to be an old, lame woman.

He followed her from a suitable distance, inconspicuously glancing around to be sure no one else was showing any interest in Patrice.

She soon disappeared inside the National. He hurried after her and joined her in front of his room. Once inside, Patrice threw off the bonnet and laughed at McCoy as he turned up the lamps.

"How exciting!" she said as she unwrapped the shawl and ran her fingers through her hair. "Did I give a convincing performance?"

He nodded. "You didn't attract any attention. You were perfect." Spur kissed her nose.

She murmured and touched his shoulders. "Care to help an old lady out of her clothes?"

He feigned disinterest. "Hell, I don't know, ma'am. Why, you're old enough to be my—my—"

She playfully punched his chin. "I'm old enough, all right! Just help me out of these crinolines. I'll show you how old I am!"

He unbuttoned and unsnapped. The tired, stiff dress fell to the floor. Though he'd seen her in the same condition only minutes before, Spur admired Patrice in a new light as she stood before him dressed only in petticoats and a thin chemise. Her skin was as white as her undergarments.

"Anything else I can help you with?"

She smiled and lifted her hands above her head.

Spur gripped the bottom hem of the chemise and raised it slowly. It revealed a flat stomach and pouting belly button. Patrice giggled as he bent and slapped a kiss on it. Raising his head once again he lifted the chemise higher, exposing her delicious breasts.

"You got a helluva nice pair there, grandma." He acknowledged each nipple with a slick, fast suck. Patrice moaned and writhed as he pulled the chemise past her head and off her arms.

Spur knelt before her, gazing up at her breasts before lowering her petticoat. She kicked it off. Underneath it, another layer of soft cloth still hid what he wanted to see so he removed that too, revealing yet another petticoat. The hunger built within him. He ripped the flimsy material in his haste, finally sending it to the floor.

Her thighs were silken marble—perfect, unblemished, curved in all the right places. Between them, a hand's width below her navel, a patch of blonde hair beckoned him.

Patrice stood naked before him—unashamed, unabashed—an alive and sensual woman. Looking down at him, she held out her arms. Spur rose and locked her in a tight embrace. Her breasts crushed against his powerful chest and their mouths sought out each other, lips parting, tongues clashing. She slipped off his hat.

Without breaking their oral contact, Spur unbuttoned his shirt, wriggled out of it, and then kicked off his boots. Her hands beat his to his fly. Twenty fingers pulled, prodded, pressed and finally managed to free the cloth flap from its prison. Plunging his tongue in and out of Patrice's warm mouth Spur lowered his pants and underdrawers.

He moaned as her hand touched his stiffening penis. Her cool fingers slid around it, gripping him in an erotic embrace. His groin boiled as the woman's touch stroked him, encouraged him and soon worked its magic.

Patrice slid her mouth from his and dropped to her knees. She gazed at the erection that jutted out from his hairy crotch precisely before her eyes. She licked her lips.

"Patrice, you don't have to—" His voice was husky.

"Have to? I *want* to. I've wanted to ever since I saw it!" Her head moved forward. Her lips parted.

Spur felt his knees threaten to give out as liquid heat engulfed him. He steadied himself by placing a hand on her shoulder. The sensations were overwhelming, overpowering, as they flooded through his body.

Hot. Tight. Soft. Demanding. The warmth moved down, farther and farther, her lips sliding along his shaft. Spur stared down at the woman in disbelief, shaking his head as lust shot out from his crotch and spread through his body.

Her head moved up, then down; up, down. Soon blonde hair flew in the air as Patrice hungrily worked him over with her mouth, drawing it deeper into her, embracing it with her tongue, welcoming it.

She pulled off and stared up at him, her eyes glazed, her lips shining. "Grab my head and make me do it!" the panting woman said.

He covered her pink ears with his hands and gently slid back into her. She moaned as she took him. McCoy pushed slowly into her yielding mouth, luxuriating in the silky feeling.

The tension in his groin mounted. He increased

the speed, slipping faster into her, moving her eager head to meet his thrusts.

Deep. Deeper. He felt Patrice's throat relaxing, opening, accepting him until his scrotum slapped against her chin.

It was too much for him to handle. He quickly pulled out of her and stepped back, gasping, his penis trembling, shining in the golden kerosene light.

"What's wrong?" Patrice asked, looking up at him."Don't you like it?"

"No. I mean, nothing's wrong. It's just, ah, a little too soon for that."

She smiled and jumped to her feet, sending her breasts bouncing. "Then let's move on to the second course. Whaddya say, lover boy?"

He grabbed her and lifted her from the floor. Three steps took them to the bed. After laying the woman on the light pink blankets, Spur stepped between her legs and knelt. He touched her knees and spread them.

"You *have* to," Patrice said with a wry smile.

He glanced up at her and pushed his face into her mystery. The young woman sighed as his red moustache meshed with her soft pubic hair and his tongue licked, tasted, probed.

Her musk set him on fire. He spread her lips and tongued her tight button, flicking back and forth, up and down. Patrice squirmed on the bed and moaned as he pleasured her. Sucking, nibbling, licking, he sent her on a ride into ecstasy that tortured her to a shuddering, shrieking orgasm.

"Spur!" she cried.

Merciless, he did it again, tonguing her to a second climax seconds after the first had subsided. Patrice locked her thighs around his head as she trembled and bucked and rode out the exquisite moment of pleasure.

"Not again!" she said, gasping, puffing. "Please, Spur, mercy!"

She relaxed her legs. McCoy straighened up and gripped the base of his penis. He moved forward as the woman stared into his eyes. She shivered. He plunged, all at once, driving into her, filling her up with his lust.

Their bodies joined in a primal dance. He withdrew and slammed back in, groaning, gripping her shoulders. Patrice undulated beneath him as she accepted his thrusts. Each withdrawal seemed to make her hungrier for the next.

Their heated bodies rocked together in a steady, slow rhythm. Spur sucked in her left breast, forcing it into his mouth as he continued to pound into her. The soft flesh was delicious, warm. He moved up on it and teethed the nipple, gently digging into it. Patrice grabbed his head and forced it down, directing him to chew harder.

He switched to her other mound and worshipped it. Patrice groaned as McCoy stimulated her all over again. He never let up on his steady pumping, sliding in and out of her with primal urgency.

He popped his mouth off her breast and lifted himself onto his hands.

"Oh god, Spur," Patrice said. "Just fuck me."

He grunted and pounded into her, quickening his thrusts, driving into her yielding body with ever-demanding urgency. Unsatisfied unless he fulfilled her needs, Spur moved his body higher until his penis rubbed against her clitoris. Patrice grabbed his pumping buttocks and forced him deeper, faster, harder until their crotches banged together and the bed creaked beneath them.

"Jesus, Patrice!" Spur said as sweat flowed off his body.

Her face took on a new glow. Her mouth opened in a soundless cry, breasts flushing, body trembling, muscles tightening around his shaft.

The increased pressure inside her sent Spur into a frenzy. He bucked and pumped and rammed until the bed banged against the wall, the world went black, his body exploded, and he felt his seed shooting, squirting, rushing into her opening in mindless ecstasy.

Drained, spent, emptied, Spur slid down onto the panting woman, burying his face into her slick breasts, gripping her shoulders, hugging her until his body shook off the powerful release. Patrice patted his hair, stroking it, murmuring soothing words as he slowly regained his senses.

Soon afterward he lifted his head. Haggard, dazed, he looked up at Patrice. The woman's face wavered until his glazed eyes adjusted and sharpened the image. When he saw her clearly, Patrice was smiling at him, radiating joy and fulfillment.

He grinned momentarily and flopped back down onto her breasts.

Stupid! Stupid! Galde stormed around in his room. It had been a stupid idea, stupidly planned, stupidly executed. His face burned as he thought of what his old friends back in New York would say if they knew how he'd bungled the simple job.

Now it was clear. He should have waited until the right moment, not gone tearing off into the night with his rifle, blasting into the empty-headed bitch's room, hoping he'd blow off her face.

Galde remembered how he'd waited, crouched on the roof of the building opposite the Crouching Lion Hotel, watching, waiting until the right moment. Then the fight broke out and he saw his opportunity, but had missed his shot. He was sure that all he'd done was start a fire and clue the blonde woman—and the man he'd seen through the shattered window—to his plans. A stupid mistake.

He tipped up a bottle of whiskey and swallowed down the burning, smoke-flavored liquid. Three gulps later he set the bottle on the table and snarled. The alcohol flowed through him, cobwebbed those parts of his being that he didn't want to face.

You're losing it, Galde, he thought. You're losing your touch. Maybe it's time you quit the business and opened up a whorehouse.

Hell, getting soft on the yellow-haired girl and then letting his anger rule his actions wasn't like him at all. Was it the pressure of his last job, all that Bible-spouting that had mixed him up?

Galde smiled. Yeah. That must've been it. He was okay, stronger than ever, and had enough money to ride out a few weeks more in Fagan.

So he'd kill the girl right, once and for all, and

wait until he saw where the wind took him.

As long as it wasn't hanging from the end of a rope he'd be happy.

10

"You ain't going nowhere, boy!"

The crowd of Fagan newcomers parted down the middle of the street, allowing the passage of a speeding, red-faced youth closely followed by a burly man, Winchester in hand, eyes snarling. Thick, curly black hair stuck out from the bull-necked gunman. His clothes were tattered and caked with dirt.

Looks like trouble, McCoy thought, seconds before the young, pimple-faced buck slammed into him, stared into his face with surprise, stiffened and sighed as he heard the approaching man.

"Johnson! I warned you time and again. Keep your dirty paws off my daughter!"

"But Mr. Salt, I—we—"

"Shut up! But did you listen? No. You let your hot blood get the best of you! Now she's good for nothing, shamed, used like a goddamned whore!

You made her unfit for any upstanding man in this great country of ours! I'll have to put Missy out to pasture with the cows!"

Spur pushed the boy from him. If it got too dangerous he'd step in and try to straighten things out.

Johnson turned around, trembling, eyes lowered to the ground as he faced his enemy.

"Gee. Mr.Salt, I—I didn't mean nothing' by it. Just havin' a little fun."

Enoch Salt lined up his rifle with the face that pitched before him. "What the hell you mean by that? You sure as shit meant something by it!" He puffed in rage.

"But we—"

"You got two choices, Johnson!" he barked, cutting off the youth's words. "Marry my Missy—right now. Take her to the preacher and get it done up all legal like. Or give me three bucks."

The boy was startled. "Three bucks? What in heck for?" he asked.

"So I can get you *buried* after I blow your guts into the street! Don't want you stinking up the place!"

"Hey, Enoch, Myers charges five for a box and a plantin'. Price just went up," a man called from the crowd that had gathered around to enjoy the confrontation.

"I didn't say *properly* buried!" he thundered.

"Daddy!" a thin, high voice said, followed by the appearance of a plain-faced girl. She frowned as she pushed through the people and walked up to Salt. "Really, daddy! You're shaming me in front of all these people! How dare you? Why don't you just get on back to the ranch!"

"*I'm* shaming *you*?" He grunted. "Looks like Johnson here already took care of that."

"You don't understand," she began.

"The hell I don't!"

"It isn't what you think. Nothing happened!" Missy said, grabbing her father's thick arm, trying to lower his aim. "I already told you nothing happened!"

Enoch glanced at his daughter. "Don't try to protect your lover now. Too late for that, Missy."

The girl violently shook her head. "I'm not protecting him and he's not my lover. Use your head for a change, daddy!"

"My head, huh?" he said, still glaring at the young man. "Girl, you waltzed into the house a half hour ago with a smile on your face and a rip in your dress. You'd been out walking with Johnson in the woods. I don't see how there's any other explanation."

"You would if you'd only stopped and listened," the horse-faced girl said. "Tommy and I were out walking. I tripped and fell. My dress caught on a stick and that's what tore it up." She turned to Johnson. "Tommy was nice enough to help me up. So I gave him a kiss on the cheek. That's all that happened. I swear it! You're just making things up in your mind. You don't trust me. Just because mom ran off with that—"

"It's true!" Tom Johnson said. He took a step forward. "Look, Salt; I've put up with your bellowing and your thundering and your bullshit for far too long. I'm tired of being accused of things I ain't even done, tired of having to get Missy back home before it gets dark, tired of you and your big mouth!"

Salt puffed, blinked his eyes, stared at the boy and slowly lowered his rifle. "Well—" he stammered.

Missy went to the youth. "You tell him, Tommy!" Her eyes shined.

"And—and as much as it would hurt my pride to have you as my father-in-law, if you weren't such a foul-minded man I'd ask your daughter to marry me!"

Missy gasped and kissed his cheek.

Enoch Salt pondered for a minute, chewing on his lower lip, then laid his rifle against his shoulder. He shrugged. "Well, hell, boy; if you're man enough to stand up to me, I guess you're man enough to marry my Missy." He grunted again and turned to head for home. "And Johnson!"

"Yes sir?" the boy instantly responded.

"You have my daughter back by—by—" The big man faltered. "By ten. Ten o'clock!"

Tom smiled. "Okay—*dad*."

Spur shook his head and walked away from the little scene, leaving the two young people to carve out their life together.

He continued on his rounds, checking the local hotel registries for recent arrivals. The first three had none that sounded familiar, but the fourth—The Jason Lomax Inn (Fine European Appointments, the sign said)—had one "Jake Gould" registered in room 305. That could be Galde, Spur thought. Same initials.

He memorized the room number and walked back outside into the hot sun. Spur moved down to

Patrice's ex-hotel. He studied the buildings that sat opposite from it. Murphy's General Store was directly across. The building's gabled roof seemed tall enough. Galde could have climbed to the roof and easily shot into Patrice's window. Hmmmmmm.

Still unsure if it had been a stray bullet that started the fire, as he'd told the girl to reassure her, or if Galde was indeed bent on killing Patrice, Spur went to the sheriff's office.

A shirtless man in black pants stood busily scrubbing his face.

"You the local law?" McCoy asked.

The man dried, flung the towel onto the table near the basin and nodded. "Yep. Can't you see the silver star pinned on my chest?"

Spur nodded.

The man slipped on a gray muslin shirt. "Name's Frank. Tex Frank. And before you ask me what I'm doing with a name like Tex in the middle of Kansas, it's short for my real name, Tezcatlipoca." Frank tucked in the tails. "And before you ask me what in hell that means, my father was interested in Mexican shit and he slapped that moniker on me. So you don't have to ask me why I like to be called Tex." Done dressing, the man smoothed down the shirt and smiled. "So what can I do for you?"

Blinking at the man's unusual verbal style, McCoy stuck out his hand. "I'm Spur McCoy."

"Don't ask me to shake your hand," Tex said. But he laughed and quickly pumped it.

"Right. I'm here in town looking for someone."

Frank sighed. "If you can't find her in one of our saloons, you just ain't looking."

"No, a man. He went by the name of Joshua Golden in Holmes but his real name seems to be Jack T. Galde."

Tex sat behind his chair and started shuffling a deck of cards. "Hmmm. Nope. Doesn't sound familiar." He rippled the deck. "You a sheriff, too?"

"Sure. See the star on my chest?"

Frank guffawed. "Point taken."

"No, I'm with the government. Secret Service."

A whistle. "Well, I sure as shit've heard about you folks but never expected to meet one of you."

Shuffle. Shuffle.

He peered at Spur with a cocked head. "How do I know you just ain't farting out hot air about this?"

"I've got papers proving my identity back in my hotel room and can bring them to you."

Cards slapped against each other, interlacing, merging into a single stack, only to be divided once again by bony fingers. "No, no. I pride myself on being a good judge of character. You seem to be who you say you are. So why're you looking for this—who the hell was it?"

The man's manner and his constant card-play were annoying but this was his only possible source of information in the town. "Galde. Jack T. Galde. I'm convinced that he's the man who's been robbing small towns all over this part of Kansas, in a line stretching west from Kansas City. He's hit five banks so far and killed at least twelve men and women."

The shuffling halted momentarily, then continued. "Sounds like a real bastard." Tex's face went dark. "You think he's here in Fagan?"

Spur nodded. "Friend of mine saw him just yesterday in the Red Ace Saloon. And he may be registered at the Jason Lomax Inn under the name of Jake Gould."

He sighed. "Trying to find him in this crowd'd be harder than finding a virgin in the Four Jacks." He rippled the cards again, shuffling, shuffling.

"I don't know for sure, but I think he tried to kill my friend—a lady—last night in her room in the Crouching Lion Hotel."

"Ah. Patrice Carlon. I heard about that. Seems she set fire to her room, burned up a rug, a table and some curtains, then disappeared."

Spur grinned. "I was there when it happened. Someone shot through her window and knocked over a lamp. That's what started the fire. And as for her disappearing she spent the night in my room."

The sheriff nodded. "Well, I don't know what to tell you. If this Galde is in town to rob my bank I sure as hell'd like to get him. And even if he ain't thinking to do any thievery, a man like that—a woman killer—don't deserve to enjoy his breath." He slapped the cards down onto the table and rose. "Anything I can do to help you, you just let me know."

"I sure will, Sheriff Frank. I don't know that you can help me; just wanted to warn you of possible future troubles in this little town of yours."

"Yeah. Never hurts." Tex's face was a mask of boredom but tinged with intrigue.

"You—you got something about those cards?"

Tex smiled. "Keeps me from drinking."

McCoy shook the man's hand and walked out of the office. Before he closed the door behind him he once again heard the shuffle, shuffle, shuffle of the devil's picture book.

11

After grabbing lunch with Patrice, who said she was still sleepy from last night's exertion and wanted to take a nap, McCoy left her in his room and walked the streets of Fagan, searching for Jack T. Galde. As he assumed, however, there were far too many people in the town, far too many faces to watch.

Taking a new approach, Spur went to the small, white church that sat a hundred yards out of town. Inside the air was still, dusty and heated by the relentless sun. At first he figured that it was empty but a grunt from between the first two rows of pews told him he was wrong. Spur walked up the middle aisle to find a man dressed in black, crouched down on his knees and reaching under the front pew.

''Preacher?'' he said.

Startled by the voice, the man banged his head

on the wood seat, said something low and unintelligible and slowly rose to his feet. As soon as his face was visible McCoy relaxed. It wasn't Galde.

"Hello!" the wrinkled preacher said, rubbing the red circle of bare flesh that surmounted his skull. "I'm afraid you took me by surprise. That wasn't the most dignified position for you to catch me in. Sorry about that," the round-eyed, sweet-faced old man said.

"No problem. I didn't think you were here."

The wizened man waved around with both hands. "I'm always here. Morning, noon and night. I even sleep in a little room off from the altar, just to be sure that whenever one of my flock needs help I'm there. What can I do for you?"

"Well, it's kind of hard to explain. Have any preachers come here recently from out of town, looking for work, or to start up a new church?"

The man shook his head. "No. Thankfully, no. Some of my flock seem to think I'm too old to keep on doing this. If any new man had shown up I'd suppose I'd be sitting somewhere doing nothing, reading the Bible and rotting." He dusted off his large hands.

Spur nodded. "I didn't think so. Actually, the man I'm looking for isn't really a preacher but a bankrobbing murderer by name of Jack T. Galde, or Joshua Golden."

"May God forgive him of his sins," the elderly man automatically said. "You believe this—ah, gentleman has recently arrived here in Fagan?" He scratched his left leg.

"I know he has. He was seen a few days ago.

Since Galde used a preacher's disguise in the last town he was in, I thought that he might have—"

The old man smiled. "I see. Well, I hope you don't think I'm this Galde. That is, unless he was sixty years old, bald and truly devoted to our Lord."

Spur held up his hands. "No, sir. I don't believe you're him. But if any new preachers come in to see you, let me know, okay? I'm staying at the National Hotel. Name's Spur McCoy."

"Fine. I'll do that. Well, I've got to retrieve that hymn book. It's somewhere down there under that pew." He hesitated and stared meaningfully at it.

Spur grunted, bent down and picked up the book. "Here you go, preacher. And thanks."

The man beamed. "Thank you, Mr. McCoy. Good day."

Galde sat in a corner of Smith's Saloon, nursing the bottle he'd bought two hours earlier. He set the half-empty whiskey on the table, burped, shoved the unruly black hair from his eyes and frowned.

He had to kill her, he knew. Had to silence the little bitch. But how? He couldn't rush into the Red Ace Saloon and blast her head off while she was dancing. Too risky and he'd just get himself killed.

Though he'd always worked alone, Galde found himself considering hiring on some extra guns. Always prideful of the excellent work he'd done up to this point the thought of using other men didn't appeal to him. But this was a crisis situation, one that he had to take care of immediately if he wanted to save his ass from the gallows.

He slumped lower in his chair and took another swallow from the bottle. As always the alcohol soothed him even as it burned up his guts.

Okay. Tonight. That'd be as late as he could move. He'd get the girl tonight, take her out of town and kill her. The old feelings stirred in him: the excitement of the chase, the thrill of seeing bright blood spattered onto the ground, the ecstasy of determining who lived and who died.

Two young men walked by, sucking whiskey, packing six-guns. They looked like the type of men he needed—old enough to have experience but young enough not to give a damn about what they did.

"Hey, come over here!" Galde said.

The taller, slimmer of the two glanced at him and snarled. "Leave us the fuck alone, fat man!" he said, and guzzled another mouthful.

"Yeah! We're gonna go screw some women!" His shorter friend grabbed his crotch and lewdly squeezed it.

Galde controlled his temper. "Fine. Then you *boys* go find your girls. Guess I was wrong. Guess you wouldn't be interested in earning fifty-dollars tonight." He looked away from them.

Four feet scrambled over to his table. The flushed, drunken youths stared at him.

"What'd you say? Fifty-dollars?" The older one said, quickly losing his snarl.

Galde smirked. Always gets them by the balls—money that is. "No, go on and get your women if you don't have time to talk to me."

The two sat at his table. "Hey, mister, anything you want done we can do. Ain't that right, Kurt?"

he said, slamming down his bottle.

"Yeah, Matt. Whadya want us to do?"

Galde smoothed on a smile. "You boys old enough to work for me?"

"Shit, I'm twenty, and Matt here's nineteen," Kurt said, his bloodshot eyes focusing on the pudgy man. "That's old enough for anything you could have in mind." He burped. Twice.

Galde had already decided to try them out. He had a gut feeling about the pair, a talent he'd honed on the rough streets of New York.

He let them sweat it out for a few minutes, glancing at one, the other, then away, drumming his fingers on the slick, ash-covered table.

"Come on, mister, what do we gotta do to get that money?" Matt asked.

"Can you boys keep your big mouths shut? Can you do what I tell you to do, take the money and get the hell out of town for a few days?"

"Shore!" Kurt said.

"Shit; with money like that I'd kiss this town's ass goodbye and ride outa here faster than you could spit!"

Galde snorted. "If you're still interested tonight, show up behind the livery stable at dusk. Don't bring anyone with you and don't tell anyone you're going there. I'll let you in on everything you need to know then. Now get your butts off those chairs and leave me alone."

The two youths stood, nodded, flushed, swallowed more whiskey and wandered away.

Galde watched them go. They'd be there, eager. They'd do anything he wanted to get their hands on that kind of money. And after they'd helped him get the big-mouthed bitch he might even pay them. He patted the revolver in his holster.

Might.

"Nervous?" Spur asked Patrice as they entered the Red Ace Saloon.

She looked at him and pulled a lock of blonde hair from her forehead. "About dancing? No. I'm used to it by now. But I'm sure not too happy thinking that that man might come in here again tonight." She blew out her breath and shook her head. "Why don't we leave? Tonight? Let's go back to Holmes. You can ride me there and I'll get the next train back home. I'm tired of this place, tired of the men and—"

Spur smiled. "It'd be more dangerous for you to ride at night than it would be to dance up there in those lights." He stroked her arm. "Relax, Patrice. If you still feel that way tomorrow morning I'd be glad to accompany you back to Holmes. Or, at least see you off at the train if it comes through here. Try to put it out of your mind."

Patrice's pretty face fell. "That's easy for you to say. You don't have a crazy fake preacher trying to kill you."

"Now don't think about it. Just dance up a storm out there. If you are going back home tomorrow you might as well do it with a little extra money."

"You're right, of course." She clasped his hand, blew him a kiss and disappeared backstage.

Spur got a drink and settled in at a small table at the rear of the saloon. It quickly filled with noisy, armed men eager for a little diversion from their daily lives. Spur took it all in, checking every face, looking for harsh features and black hair attached to a fat, short body.

Galde didn't show up.

He smiled curtly as two youths settled in at his table.

"Sorry, mister," the younger said as he sat down, "last table in the place."

He waved his lack of concern and nursed on his whiskey. After seeing Patrice safely through the show and then into his bed he'd check room 305 of the Jason Lomax Inn. Maybe this Jake Gould was Jack Galde, maybe not. But it was high time he found out.

The six dancers came on stage in tight silk dresses, all red, all designed to show off every curve of their bodies. The men watching them hooted and hollered, slamming their boots onto the wooden floor and nudging each other as they shouted what they'd do to the girls.

Patrice shined as she moved through the first dance, an uncomplicated romp across the stage. The two men seated on either side of Spur stared at the women unblinkingly, drinking whiskey, panting.

"Hell, Kurt, have you *ever* seen such fine female flesh?" one slurred.

"Fuck, no. Not out there on the ranch. Sure puts me in mind of doing something but just lookin' at them." He stumbled to his feet.

Kurt grabbed the back of his pants and yanked his friend down onto his chair. "Just sit there, Matt. Don't forget we gotta work tonight."

"Aw hell! Fuck the money!"

Kurt leaned across Spur. "Now you listen here,

boy! We're gonna do our work and collect our pay. We're a team. If you run off, leaving me alone, I won't get a goddamned dime! Just watch the fuckin' show!"

Spur leaned away from the streams of sodden breath that the youth shot across his face. Boys will be boys, he thought.

"Oh—oh, hell. Okay, Kurt. I guess'll it be worth it." He grumbled into his drink.

"Damn straight it'll be worth it! Now shut up and let me enjoy those pussies!"

McCoy sighed and watched as Patrice went through the dazzling moves. The piano player was far better than the one who'd provided the music at her former place of employment, but his efforts were nearly drowned out by the hoots and thundering, full-throated yells that the overexcited men blasted out at the women.

The number ended and the women bowed, then quickly began the second. As they leapt and kicked, showing off their finely-shaped legs and petticoats, a beefy, red-faced man stood and walked toward the stage.

Spur was instantly behind him. From the back the man could be Galde, though he hadn't seen the thief enter the saloon. He tapped him on his back.

"Leave me the fuck alone!"

Spur grabbed his shoulders and spun him around. It was Enoch Salt, the father who'd threatened to kill that boy for taking his daughter on a walk.

The whiskey-lubricated man glared at McCoy, rocking back and forth on unsteady feet. "Hell, I'm first!" he yelled. "You can have 'em later." He struggled against Spur's powerful grip. "Let me go, dammit!"

"Sit down, Salt! Those are dancing girls, not whores! No one's having them—any of them."

"The hell I ain't!" he said. "Just try to stop me! I'm gonna fuck 'em right on the goddamned stage!"

Spur released the man and slammed his doubled-up fist into Salt's jaw. The blow didn't faze the man.

He grinned. "You tryin' to pick a fight with me?" His hand flew down to his holster.

Spur blocked Salt's grab and jerked the arm backward into an unnatural position. Enoch howled as McCoy punched him in the gut, driving his fists into the fleshy belly, forcing him backward with the force of his blows.

Salt banged against a table, upsetting it and spilling him to the ground. A whiskey bottle smashed beside him as cards and poker chips rained down on the big man. He groaned, lifted his head, then slumped, unconscious.

The music halted. Patrice and the other girls on stage stood looking at the downed man.

"Er, go ahead with the show, ladies," McCoy said, and tipped his hat at Patrice.

She smiled. As the dancers started kicking away Spur dragged the big man over to his table, huffed and sat in his chair. The man was heavy.

"Mighty fancy fist work," Matt said, grinning.

"Thanks." Crossing his legs, he rested his heels on Enoch Salt's stomach and watched the rest of the show.

By the time it was over Salt still hadn't moved.

Spur bent toward him and felt the man's wrist. He was alive but still unconscious. He poured his drink onto the man's face.

"Come on, wake up!" he said.

Salt spluttered, blubbered, and wiped the stinging liquid from his eyes. "What—wh—"

"On your feet, man. You've got a date with the sheriff."

With tremendous effort he lifted the huge man, draped his left arm around his shoulder and dragged him from the saloon. Patrice emerged from backstage as McCoy neared thc door.

"Hey! Where you going, Spur?" she called.

"Sheriff's. I'll be right back." He turned and threw her his room key. "Go there and stay inside. Don't open the door for anyone but me, Patrice. I'll be back soon as I havc this lover locked up for the night."

Groaning, he dragged him off to the sheriff's office four blocks away.

Patrice fanned her face. She was tired, as always, after her energetic performance. All through the hour-long show the blonde had looked forward to its conclusion and to once again sharing Spur's room. The hungry-eyed men in the saloon disturbed her, but the pleasing absence of Galde made it tolerable. She refused a dozen offers of drinks from a variety of men and sat sipping her ginger ale at the table closest to the bar, where she felt safe.

Tired, scared, she tried to rouse enough energy and courage within her to walk to Spur's hotel. It wasn't far but, it was far enough to make her hesitate. Why the heck did he have to go and leave her alone like that?

Two young men approached her. Patrice sighed, readying her response of "No, thank you; I'm drinking sarsaparilla."

"Ma'am," one of the youths said, and pulled his hat from his head. "Me and Matt here was wonderin' if you'd allow us the honor of escorting you to your hotel."

Well, at least the boys were trying a new approach. "I'm sorry, but I'm waiting for my friend—the one that beat up the big, strong man a few minutes ago?" She fluttered her eyelashes and turned away from them.

"But—but—"

"No thank you." Her words were even, level, tinged with the slightest bit of anger.

"Look, ma'am, we just want to—"

"These two boys bothering you, Patrice?"

She turned. Elias Weatherby walked up to her table, glaring at them behind thick, round glasses.

"They were just leaving, boss."

"Fine. Get the hell outa my saloon! If I catch you bothering one of my girls again I'll do more than kick you out!"

"You don't scare us!"

"Come on, Matt, let's go! We have to talk!" He slurred his words.

Kurt dragged his friend out of the bar.

Patrice sighed. "Thanks, Mr. Weatherby."

The middle-aged man smiled paternally at her. "No problem. Always like to look after my girls. You have someone to walk you home?"

"No," she said. "He had to take that man to the

sheriff's office."

"Allow me."

Pleased, Patrice rose and the two left the saloon. Outside the air was cool, refreshing. She felt safe with him, safer than she would have walking alone or even with one of the questionable men from the saloon. They walked along, arm in arm, through alternating patches of light and darkness as they passed the kerosene street lamps that dotted the broad avenue.

Patrice was wrapped up in her thoughts. Should she tell Mr. Weatherby that she was leaving in the morning? It wouldn't be right not to. But why mess up things before she absolutely had to? But then again. . . .

They passed another light. A dark alley yawned near them. Patrice turned to him. "Mr. Weatherby, I have to talk to you about something."

He gestured with his right hand. "Talk away. I already think of you as my daughter, Patrice."

"Well, it's about my job."

"You don't like working for me?"

"No. Not that at all. It's just that I don't know how much longer I can stay here in Fagan. There's this man—"

Powerful hands gripped her waist, twisting her from the man's arm. Patrice screamed as a shadowy figure slammed the butt end of a revolver onto her employer's head. He slumped to the ground.

A hand quickly covered her mouth, muffling her shrieks. She kicked, flailed her arms and bit at the grasping fingers as the two men pulled her into the bowels of the alley.

12

The man's weight around his arm felt like it was about to snap his knees. Groaning, Spur yanked, pulled and shoved a blubbering Enoch Salt toward Sheriff Tex Frank's office.

Salt drowsed along the way, his big body slumping down, further hindering their progress. Each time the man's chin hit his chest McCoy backhanded him, rousing Salt for another half-block or so.

It took him nearly ten minutes to clear the distance between the Red Ace Saloon and the sheriff's office. He finally halted before the closed door, yanked the knob and kicked it open.

He shoved Enoch Salt forward. The big man stumbled, blinked at the bright light and melted into a heap of pulsing flesh at Tex Frank's feet.

"Brought you some company," Spur said.

"I can see that. What's old Salt done now? Tried

to kill Tommy again? Or maybe looked up old Gussie Graysom's dress?" The sheriff chuckled.

"He tried to rape six ladies in full view of thirty or so men."

Tex whistled. "Red Eye Saloon, right? That's the first time he's tried that—at least in that saloon."

"He's drunker than a skunk. I tried to stop him but he wouldn't quit so I punched him." Spur rubbed his knuckles. "When that didn't make a dent I pounded his gut for a couple minutes. He finally crashed into a table and went out like a lamp on a windy day."

"I'll look after him. You—you brought him here all by yourself?"

"Sure. Why?"

"Oh, nothing. It's just that Salt must weight three-hundred pounds."

McCoy shrugged. "Need me for anything else? I have a lady waiting for me."

"Nope. Thanks." The sheriff walked to his desk and reached for the well-thumbed paying cards.

They slapped against the polished wood as Spur left to go find Patrice—safely locked in his room, he hoped.

Suffocating, she bit. Salty blood flooded into her mouth as Patrice sunk her teeth into the tender fingers, ripping them, tearing flesh from bone.

"Shit!" the shadowed man whispered as he hustled her down the dark alley. He slapped her cheek. "Fuckin' bitch like to tore off my finger!"

She coughed, spat blood, gagged against the relentless, pressure.

"Grab her throat but keep her quiet!" Kurt said

as they neared the alley's rear.

Hands tightened beneath her chin. Patrice gasped, gagged as her air was cut off. Frightened and enraged, she drove her knee into her captor's groin. He screamed and dropped to the ground, freeing her head.

"What the fuck—"

Patrice elbowed the second man, taking him by surprise. Butting his chest with her blonde head the woman succeeded in shoving him back against the wall.

"Hell!" he said.

She jabbed her foot between the man's legs as he went for her. For one terrifying second he gripped her foot, threatened to tear off her leg, then sank to the ground with a groan.

"Don't let her get away!"

Jubilant, Patrice shot down the alley, her skirt rustling and dragging in the dirt. She wiped the slimy vein juice from her lips and forced her legs as fast as they'd go.

Sooner than she'd hoped, she heard the men following behind her. Where to go? Her mind raced as she exited the alley, not stopping to glance down at her prone employer. Without thinking she turned to the right and ran for the saloon.

If only it was still open—Light spilled from below its doors half a block down.

"Fuck Galde. I'm gonna kill her myself! She smashed my balls something fierce!"

Fast. Faster. Patrice felt her legs ache, her heart protesting at the unprecedented strain that she was forcing it into.

"Get her! *Kill her*!"

Panting, sickened from the taste of blood, Patrice raced into the Red Ace Saloon.

"Jule! Your gun!" she gasped, her legs faltering as she tried to clear the floor between the door and the man. "They're—tried to kill—coming now!"

The piano player whipped out a Colt .45 and trained it on the door. "Hang tight, Patrice!" he shouted.

Matt and Kurt stormed in, weapons drawn. Jules fired twice, shattering the ceiling over their heads. The startled men bolted from the saloon as fast as they'd entered it.

Patrice looked away long before the explosions had stopped echoing in the saloon. She squeezed her eyes shut as her ears rang from the gunshots. Revulsion rose in her throat. "Are—are they dead?"

"Nope," Jule said. "But they're gone."

She sighed.

"I don't think they're coming back, but I better get you into Mr. Weatherby's office. It's safer there." The piano player paused. "Hey, you all right, Patrice?"

"No."

She was sick all over the floor.

Spur ran back to his hotel and up the stairs. He banged on the door. "Patrice!" he yelled. "Patrice, you in there?"

No answer. The short hairs on the back of his neck itched. Either she wasn't in there or she couldn't answer.

He slammed his shoulder against the door, once, twice, hurling all his weight and strength into the move. The second impact sent it buckling on its hinges. It flew open.

His room was dark. Spur turned up the flame.

It was also empty.

Galde fidgeted in the darkness as he waited by his horse a hundred yards from the livery stable. The two boys should have been there five minutes ago as far as he could reckon. Where the hell were they?

''*This* was why he didn't use help. *This* was why he worked alone. If something went wrong he only had himself to blame, not empty-headed youths or trigger-happy gunmen.

Three minutes later the two youths ran up to him, holding their crotches. They were alone.

Rage boiled in his gut. He knew they'd fail. He knew it!

''Stop playing with your dicks and tell me where the fuck the girl is!'' he blasted.

''Jesus!'' Matt said. ''She—she—''

Kurt grimaced but stood tall in front of the man. ''We lost her, Galde. She got away. And damn near took our balls with her!'' He massaged his groin.

''I shoulda known better than to trust two *boys* like you,'' Galde said, fuming.

''But she didn't do it alone,'' Matt said. ''We knocked out her boss but this other guy showed up and shot at us.''

He sneered. ''So you shit your pants and came crawling back here.'' He shook his head. ''Damn!''

''Hey look, Galde, we tried. We did our best!'' Kurt slammed his fist into his hand.

''Right.''

He turned around, pondering. What to do? What to do? His hand slid under his coat to the sheath that hung from his belt.

Which first. Which first.

After a minute, Galde turned around. "All right, boys, I guess it couldn't be helped," he said.

"Then—then you're not mad at us anymore?" Matt asked, his voice filled with astonishment.

Galde smiled at the nineteen-year-old boy. "Mad? Hell no. Anyone could have fucked that up. She's not an easy girl anyway you look at it."

In the white light spilling down from the moon above, Kurt's face relaxed. "Gee, that's awful nice of you."

"Since you tried I might as well pay you boys something for your trouble."

"You—you don't have to do that," Matt said.

"Shut *up*, Matt!" Kurt poked him in his side.

Galde grinned and approached the two young men. They stood shoulder to shoulder, close enough for a fast, clean job. "I've got my money right here in my pocket." He pretended to fumble around in his coat. "This should pay you for all the work you've done for me."

The knife flashed up and into Kurt's chest, ripping, tearing, plunging full-length. He quickly yanked it out and stabbed Matt's heart, twisted it, withdrew and sheathed it again in Kurt's gaping wound.

The young men coughed liquidly, their eyes wide, screams gurgling in their throats. Galde sliced up their chests with powerful strokes, switching from one to the other, cutting into their bodies like they were hard butter.

Bones snapped under the knife blade. Tissue ruptured. The two young men's hearts beat slower, spasmed, pumped blood out of the slits in their chests.

Matt sunk to his knees, his arms jerking as Galde plunged his knife one last time into Kurt's body and savagely ripped it out. The twenty year old youth slumped to the ground, coughed, lay still.

Trembling wth rage and exultation, Galde turned his attention to Matt. Even when the youth slammed down on his back he continued stabbing, grunting, sweating, straining as the sickly stench of fresh human blood filled his nostrils. He hacked him to death.

Finished, Galde removed his knife, threw it into the trees behind him and stood, shaking, smiling. He glanced down at the bodies, kicked them and walked to the water barrel to wash the evidence off his hands and clothes.

They wouldn't fail him again.

"Patrice!" Spur yelled as he burst into the Red Eye Saloon.

Jule met him with a gun. McCoy quickly learned what had happened from the piano player and went into Mr. Weatherby's office. He gathered the woman up in his arms and carried her to Frank Tex's office.

"Could you keep her here for awhile?" McCoy asked the surprised young sheriff.

"Sure. Always have room for a fine looking lady." Tex tipped his hat.

"She was nearly kidnapped again. At least three

men want her dead." Spur pointed at the man. "Don't let me down, Frank!"

"I won't. Trust me."

Spur headed for the door.

"Hey, McCoy! Where you going?" Tex asked.

"To find Jack T. Galde!"

Rushing with the thrill of the murder, Galde walked his horse down the main street, brazenly daring any of the few men on the street to accuse him of anything. He'd remove all traces of blood from his clothing, hands and arms, and had left the knife in the woods. He was safe for now but knew he had to get out of town as fast as possible.

No sense in sneaking out, he told himself. He'd already checked out of his room, his horse was loaded with his money and those few possessions he'd decided to bring with him. It was time to leave.

Rain fell, light at first, then more heavily. With confidence bursting through him, Galde didn't flinch as he approached the sheriff's office. Glancing inside, however, made him falter. He saw a flash of blonde hair as the sheriff ushered a woman into the jail in the rear.

Patrice Carlon? He shrugged. Might as well clean up one last problem before he left.

After tying up his horse in front of the sheriff's office, he walked in.

"Sheriff!" he called. "Anybody in there?"

"Just a minute." The man's voice came from the doorway that connected the jail with the rest of the office.

Galde went to it, pressed his back against the wall and drew. He waited, patiently.

Tex Frank walked out. "What can I do for—"

He pushed the Colt's barrel against the man's side and fired. The bullet lodged deep inside the sheriff's body. Tex groaned and groped at his holster but Galde fired again, slamming a lead slug into Frank's chest. The man dropped.

He grabbed the keyring that stuck out of the sheriff's pocket and hustled into the jail.

There were two cells. One contained a snoring drunk. In the other—

Galde tried the first key. It opened the lock. Patrice looked up at him.

"Not you! Not again!" she wailed.

He stormed to her, back-handed her into a daze, scooped her off her feet and carried her outside into the driving rain.

Galde threw the woman onto the saddle, mounted up and rode fast out of town, gripping her unconscious body with his powerful thighs as he left Fagan behind him forever.

"Jake Gould checked out three hours ago," the bored young woman behind the registry at the Jason Lomax Inn said after he'd asked.

"You sure?"

She smirked. "That's my job, mister."

Spur hurried out and walked through the rain back to Tex Frank's office. Nothing. He didn't know where Galde was, what he was doing. What the hell was happening?

His hat's broad brim drooped, sending a shower of chilling water onto his face. Spur wiped it away and hurried as the rain suddenly stopped and the moon came out from behind the clouds.

The front door lay open. He drew and cautiously advanced on the office. Walking inside, Spur sighed. Tex Frank lay in a small pool of blood. He stepped over the man and checked the jail cells. Patrice, of course, was gone.

Moving back into the office he looked down. The dead sheriff's hand lay sprawled near a dark red smear on the floor.

Galde. It must have been Galde.

He ran outside. Fresh horse tracks led away from the sheriff's office to the west. Judging from the depth of the impressions they'd been made by a horse carrying two people.

Spur ran for his mare, his boots splashing mud over his pants.

Dammit! Dammit! Dammit!

13

Patrice dreamed.

She was back in her parent's home in St. Louis. The large brick building was comforting in its familiarity. The scent of roses from vases placed before the windows filled the air. Curled up in the library in front of the fireplace on a huge couch, was Patrice. She clutched the oversized leather bound volume of Shakespeare in her hands, eagerly devouring each Elizabethan word.

''Patrice, I want to talk with you.''

She didn't look up. ''Not now, daddy; he's just about to meet her.''

''Now!''

Something in her father's voice made her obey. She looked up. And screamed.

Galde rose behind her father. He swung the big axe, slicing, lopping. Her father's head rolled off his trunk and bounced like a rubber ball across the polished parquet floor. It stopped before her.

She dropped the book, terrified.

Her father's severed head looked up at Patrice. "You shouldn't have left home, baby! You shouldn't have left home."

Wind blasted against her cheeks. Patrice blinked, realized where she was and sighed. Rain pelted down onto her face. Cold, wet, aching, she tried to cry but the tears wouldn't come. After the terrors that she'd suffered in the last couple of days all she could do was laugh and cling to the horse's bucking neck, laugh at the absurdity of it all, laugh at what fate had dished out to her. Better to laugh than to cry.

"You finally wake up, blondie? I've been listening to your snoring for at least an hour."

Galde's voice was gruff, loud against her ear. She was immediately aware of the way his body pressed against hers, of how his arms holding the reins pinioned her sides, how his thighs molded to her legs

"I don't snore but, yeah, Jack, I'm awake. Couldn't stay away from me, could you?"

He laughed. "No, blondie. Decided I had to throw you a fuck before I killed you. That's why I didn't slit your throat back in your cozy little cell. What were you locked up for? Whoring?"

She ignored the question and the threat. "Won't you take no for an answer?"

"I'm used to getting my way," he said into her ear.

The night was dark. Wind slashed against them, throwing up the horse's mane in rippling sprays.

The rain increased in intensity until it seemed that the sky had opened up and was pouring an ocean down on them.

Their overburdened mount strained through the sucking mud below them. It couldn't manage more than a fast walk and made its displeasure known to its rider by whinneying and snorting every few feet.

"Atta girl," Galde said to the horse. "You know, blondie, your round ass sure feels good against my dick." He pushed his rain-soaked crotch against her and rubbed up and down. "I can't wait to shove it in you."

Patrice recoiled from the contact. "You had your chance, big mouth, but you decided not to. I think I was right; you like horses. Heck, I knew you were weird the first time I saw you."

She moved forward, trying to free herself from his demanding groin, but her cramped position didn't allow her much room. Patrice was horrified to feel the man's penis erecting against her bottom, hardening, stiffening.

"Horses, huh?" Galde said. "That ain't the horse getting me ready to go like that. You'll think of horses when I'm banging you, blondie."

"Talk, talk, talk. That's all you ever do, Jack Galde!"

Maybe if she could get him to stop, she could get away. Maybe.

"Just wait, little girl. You'll get it. You'll get what you want."

Patrice sighed. "And then what? I suppose you buy me a white dress, marry me and we'll settle down on a little farm somewhere. You'll raise corn and I'll—"

He laughed. "Go ahead, dream, blondie. I'm gonna fuck—" he thrust his penis against her—"fuck you to death!"

"With that little thing? Hell, you better get a couple of men to help you." Despite the brave words fear festered inside her, gnawing away at her courage.

"Bitch!" He spat the word at her.

The wind howled, the rain splattered down, and the horse took them further and further from Fagan, through dim cornfields and endless acres of farmland that appeared to Patrice to comprise a gigantic, ghostly trap.

They couldn't have more than a few minutes headstart on him. Spur kicked his mare's flanks, urging the horse faster along the muddy trail. A fresh breeze blew the clouds from the sky and revealed the full moon hanging mute above him.

In the dim light he could still see the dark impressions against the duller mud beneath him. They had gone this way.

McCoy cursed as he rode, cursed at Enoch Salt, cursed at himself, but mostly cursed at Galde. The man was incredibly singleminded about Patrice Carlon. He'd kidnapped her twice, hired two men to try a third time, shot through her window and set her room on fire.

Though he was tenacious he still hadn't gotten what he wanted from the beautiful blonde-haired girl. At least he hoped he hadn't.

The trail stretched straight ahead before him, cutting a narrow path between eye-tall cornfields that looked gray in the moonlight.

Clouds swept in overhead. The light dimmed to the point where Spur could just barely make out the trail. He squinted, following the tracks, and slammed his hand down on his head as the wind threatened to whip off his hat and carry it into the air.

"Come on, girl," he said to the horse, patting its neck as the beast struggled through the mud. "They can't be far ahead. We'll get them."

The storm seemed unsure of itself, sending down showers that lasted seconds, covering and freeing the moon of its cloud cover. Ignoring the weather he rode on and on, following the dim tracks, hoping that he wasn't too late.

"Why don't you just kill me."

The words shocked Patrice even as she said them. An hour of Galde's lewd talk and the events of the last few days had broken her, leaving her an exhausted girl who was too tired to fight anymore.

"That's no way to talk, little lady," Galde said. "You gotta fight. Besides, I don't fuck dead women. That's why I never married." He guffawed.

Patrice snapped out of her mood. "Heck, no woman would ever marry you. Not unless she was deaf, dumb and blind."

"That's the spirit!" Galde chuckled. He pumped his ever-present erection against her and thrust his tongue into her wet ear.

"God! Stop it!" She squirmed, violently flinging

her head aside to free it from his mouth. The motion sent her off balance. Her body slid to the right in the saddle, pushing against Galde's arm.

"No, you don't!" he said.

She allowed him to push her up. "Fine," she said. "Well, if you're gonna do it anyway, I might as well enjoy it." She reached behind her.

"Hey, no tricks, blondie! I mean—"

Patrice slid her hand between their bodies and gripped his groin.

"I'm warning you!"

She stroked, blanking out all thoughts of what she was doing, pretending the man behind her was Spur.

"Ahhhh!"

Hating the feeling, holding back a gag, Patrice feigned interest in him. She cooed and rubbed her back against his chest as she massaged the pulsing bulge.

"Maybe I was wrong. You're not so small after all."

Only about half as big as Spur, she thought.

"That's more like it! Yeah, blondie, play with it! Play with my rod!"

They rode on.

"What're you gonna do with this thing?" she asked.

"You know!" he said, irritated. "Can't you just grope and keep your big mouth shut?"

"But I figured you'd want to keep it open. I figured you'd want me to suck you."

"Jeezus, blondie!" Galde gasped in her ear. "The way you talk I—I don't know if I—"

"Just enjoy it."

"Oh God. Stop, little lady; stop! Not yet. Jeezus! I'm gonna—get your hands outa there!"

He halted the horse and dropped the reins. When his arms left her sides Patrice punched his fat crotch and slid off the horse.

"Shit!" Galde yelled.

Rain slammed down, blinding her as she landed in the mud, rolled over and ran into the cornfield.

"Come back here, blondie! Finish what you started! When I catch you I'll make you—"

His words were lost in the patter of raindrops on the broad leaves and wind that rustled them. Patrice ran blindly through the corn wincing as the sharp bladed leaves cut her wrists and hands. Choking with excitement and achievement, the blonde haired woman moved deeper into the field.

It was alive with motion, as if it were the back of a huge hairy animal. Patrice stumbled among the stalks, darting through them without direction, terrified that she'd hear his voice again behind her.

The storm swelled above her, dumping its load onto the parched land. Patrice kicked off her shoes and ran.

"There you are!"

Galde's voice terrified her.

"I see you, blondie! Guess what I have for you! Now stand still and let me fuck you, girl!"

Patrice hyperventilated. The leaves slashed at her soaked dress and slapped against her cheeks. She kept on running as the crashing behind her got louder.

"Bitch!"

Galde tackled her, his pudgy body slamming into

hers. Patrice shrieked as the stocky man drove her into the mud face first.

"Thought you could get away, huh? Not this time. You're gonna get what you want!"

Patrice pulled her head from the sucking mud and spluttered. Exhausted, she didn't resist as Galde turned her onto her back and knelt over her, straddling her legs. Patrice wiped mud from her eyes and blinked.

"All that dirty talk and your hand getting me all excited!"

Lightning crackled across the sky, outlining his bulky form. He fumbled at his crotch. "You're gonna get it."

"No. No! Not here! Not like this in the rain!" she said.

"Shut your mouth, blondie! I've waited too long."

Galde unbuttoned his pants. Though she couldn't see it she knew it hung there, ready, eager.

The thought revolted her. The thought of this man—

Patrice screamed as he threw up her soaked dress. His clammy hands gripped her thighs and spread them apart.

"Take it, bitch! You love this! You're a god-damned whore! A whore who'll do anything I want!"

She slapped at him as he ripped her petticoats off her, tore her dress to shreds. Lying there on the cold, muddy ground, huge raindrops slapping onto her nude body, Patrice Carlon screamed on and on.

"I like a bitch who fights," Galde said, as he

lowered himself onto her and the storm howled around them in the thrashing cornfield.

Wind transformed the rain drops into elemental weapons that blasted at Spur's face. Shivering, he rode his uneasy mount along the trail. Intermittent lightning terrified the horse but lit up the tracks that marked Galde's passage—horseshoe prints that were quickly melting in the rain.

A few miles out of Fagan Spur saw a dark figure on the trail ahead. He halted his horse, studied it, but couldn't make out any details. He rode slowly up to the figure and soon realized it wasn't a man.

A horse stood there next to the cornfield, water sheeting off its flanks, tossing its head. Its reins were tied to a bunch of stalks.

Galde's horse? Yes. They must have gone into the cornfield. He could have chased her in there. Spur quickly secured his mount. He wiped water from his eyes and surveyed the area. Broken stalks showed where they'd entered the field. He tore into the six-foot high sea of dripping, wind-tossed plants, following the path of destruction.

Though it didn't seem possible the storm grew stronger, the wind whipping the razor-sharp leaves around McCoy as he drove into the tall, stiff plants. The darkened sky offered him little light but Spur could just make out the trail of broken stalks before him.

The wind slapped the leaves against his body. Lightning ripped through the night, illuminating it. The trail he was following suddenly split into two paths. They'd separated. Frustrated, Spur headed down the left one.

The rain suddenly lightened but the gale force winds tugged at his body, threatening to pick him up off the ground. He bent and pushed forward as the blasting air all but obliterated the trail by flattening every single stalk of corn and then whipping them upright.

A female scream emanated from somewhere inside the field. Patrice! The scream repeated again and again. With the trail gone and wind in his ears, the cornstalks confused him. He lost his bearings and staggered around in circles between each howl before getting back on track.

Spur struggled across the field toward the voice, toward the scream, as jagged bolts of light flashed and darted above him.

14

"Hold still, blondie!" Galde said. "Dammit, let me in there, girl!"

"No. Leave me alone, Jack!" Patrice writhed beneath him, snapped her legs together and screamed. The hideous man jabbed against her stomach as he clumsily tried to penetrate the squirming woman.

Somewhere she'd found the will to fight off the evil smelling man. Patrice pressed her hands against his chest, trying to push him off her. But his wiry strength was too great for her. He grabbed her thighs and forced them open.

"Now, blondie, take it!"

Wind whipped their struggling bodies. Cornstalks broke and fell around them. Patrice slammed her legs shut again, straining them against Galde's powerful hands.

As he cursed, she grabbed one of the thick stalks

from his back. *Use it,* she told herself. *Use it to stop him.*

Patrice slammed its blunt end down against his back.

"What the—" he said.

She smacked it onto his head savagely, fighting with every ounce of strength left within her. Patrice screamed and kept flailing away with the thick stalk.

"Fucking bitch!" Galde wrestled the stalk from her hand and threw it above him where the wind carried it away. "Don't do that again!" he said, still leaning over her.

She gripped a second broken stalk and slammed it into his face, thrilling to the small victory she'd won.

Galde hit her, slapping his palm against Patrice's cheek. She ignored the pain and continued beating.

He yelled again but his words were lost to the violence of the wind that steadily increased above and around them

Scratched, gasping, tripping over loose, wet cornstalks, Spur ran toward the screams. She should be straight ahead, but by the way the wind shifted and moved around him like a conscious being, he knew that he could be hurrying toward the wrong spot while Galde . . . .

It had been a long time since he'd witnessed a midwestern storm and he'd forgotten how powerful they could be. Flashes of blueish white light sparkled continually in the puddles before him as he struggled to save Patrice.

There, in the distance, in a blinding flash of lightning, he saw two figures on the ground ahead of him. A man and a woman. Patrice. Patrice and Jack Galde.

McCoy drew his Colt .45 as he approached the struggling pair. He was raping her. The bastard was raping her!

"Galde!" he yelled, but the words drifted above him. A hundred feet separated them. Spur ran as the air filled with leaves and stalks and dirt clods that swirled and eddied and danced.

A mass of airborne earth splattered against his face. He cursed and wiped his face, hurrying toward the pair.

Fifty feet.

"Galde!" he howled. "Leave her the fuck alone!"

He still couldn't hear him but from the way the man and woman wrestled it was clear that he hadn't raped her yet. He'd arrived just in time.

Spur fired a shot into the air and bounded toward them. Even when he got into range he still couldn't get a clean shot that wouldn't hit Patrice as well.

"Dammit, Galde!"

He was twenty feet away.

The shadowed man whipped around to face Spur, gripping a naked Patrice to his chest.

"Go ahead and shoot, fucker! Go ahead!" Galde screamed. "Shoot, but you'll have to kill your little bitch if you want to kill me!"

More lightning. McCoy had to lean forward to prevent the slamming wind from throwing him onto his back. "Come on, Galde. It's over. Let the girl go."

The big man laughed. "Fuck you!"

"You can't escape this time. There's no way out."

"Throw down your gun! Throw it behind you and let me and blondie here go. Do that and I won't kill you!" he shouted above the wind. Still pinning Patrice to his chest, Galde drew his revolver and pressed it against the woman's head. "You got that, mister? Throw it down or she dies!" he screamed.

Spur hesitated. "If you kill her then I won't have any reason not to kill you."

"Hah! You won't take the chance. I got all the cards, mister. Drop your weapon and back off!"

McCoy started to respond, then looked above the dimly lit man. Lightning lit up a huge funnel cloud that twisted and moved across the flat land, eating it up in its elemental hunger, whirling the earth into a chaotic ruin. It moved straight toward them.

Spur stalled. "Hell, Galde," he said, glancing at the tornado. "Maybe you're right."

The fat man laughed. "Course I'm right. I'm always right. Now throw down your gun."

In less than a minute the tornado would be close if not directly overhead. He raised his arm over his head, as if to fling his Colt behind his head.

"Well! What're you waiting for?" Galde screamed.

Spur stared at him.

The wind intensified, blasting their bodies, whipping the broken cornstalks into tortured flight.

"What the hell?" Galde yelled.

"Bad storm!"

The man slowly rose, bringing Patrice with him. He stared around at the thousands of plants that flew through the air and battered into them.

The storm's voice shrieked as it thundered down onto them. Five seconds, Spur thought, staring at Patrice's dark form.

Four. Three. Two.

One!

A tremendous wind blasted into them. Spur felt the world shake as the tornado knocked him to the ground, flattening him like it had the corn, sending him crashing to his back. His revolver flew out of his hand. The storm tugged on him, trying to rip his prone body from the earth, trying to suck his 200 pounds up into its vortex of destructive fury.

The howl was unending, eerie. Spur gripped the muddy dirt, digging his fingertips into it as he struggled to save his life. The wind tugged on his skin, pulling his face with invisible fingers until Spur felt it would rip it off.

Foot-square chunks of earth rushed up around him and disappeared into the blackness above. The ground heaved as the storm passed.

He cursed into the mud as he clung to it, riding out the tornado, hoping that it would spare Patrice but take Galde into its spout.

Finally it lessened, grew weaker. McCoy searched for his revolver, patting the ground beside him with his hand even as the tornado still pressed against his chest. It wasn't there.

Damn! He heard Patrice's screams above the wind as he struggled against it, raising his torso with tremendous effort, gasping for breath.

Lightning crackled overhead. He glanced over. The two still laid side by side on the ground as Spur searched for his gun. A renewed blast of air sent him crashing onto his back, knocking the oxygen from his lungs. Moaning, he lay there, still fumbling for his weapon. Where the hell had it gone?

Finally, he scrambled onto his knees and dove into a four-foot high mound of cornstalks next to him. The gun, he told himself. Get the gun. Forget everything else and get the goddamned gun!

McCoy slid through the sharp leaves and thick stalks, pushing through them, frantically searching. He dug to the bottom of the pile. Nothing. Damn!

He poked his head out from the vegetation. Patrice lay sobbing where she'd been while Galde was on his hands and knees, throwing leaves over his shoulder.

Good. He didn't have his gun either. Spur lunged into another, larger pile and searched it. As he did so the storm suddenly dropped off. The silence was incredible.

"I'll kill you!" Galde said.

"You gotta find your gun first! Why don't you get on your horse and get the hell outa here!" Spur said.

"No way! I don't leave jobs half-done!"

Where the fuck was it? He burrowed into the pile, grasping, digging, looking, spitting shredded leaves from his lips and pushing them from his eyes.

Something hard pressed against his hand. He gripped the stock and shot to his feet only to see Galde's back disappearing into the darkness. He fired over his shoulder.

Damn!

Patrice lay curled up on the ground, naked, crying.

As the tornado's eye passed overhead the eerie calm was shattered by deadly winds. Spur fought them, walking into its force. It shut his eyes, pounded at his legs. Like a blind man, he stumbled forward toward the departing Galde. He kicked and ran even as the storm pushed the air out of his lungs and left him gasping. Get him, he told himself. Get him!

It soon lessened. Cursing, he peeled open one eye and looked down at Patrice who lay at his feet.

"You okay?" he shouted.

She shivered and clutched her arms to her bare breasts, but nodded.

"I'll be back!"

The tornado had cleared a path though the cornfield, stripping it clean. Spur ran through it toward the horse that he hoped would still be waiting for him. The wind kicked up globules of mud as he raced through it, fighting for breath.

It was impossible to see where Galde was but he ran on, hoping he'd hit the trail somewhere near his horse.

Finally he was there. His horse stood ten feet away—alone. He twisted around his head, searching the trail in both directions, but saw nothing but blackness.

Damn!

He couldn't leave Patrice there.

The cursing man ran back through the stripped cornfield and quickly squatted beside her. The wind had died to a stiff breeze.

"Patrice," Spur said. He shucked off his coat as the naked woman sat up on the ground. "Here. Wear this."

Patrice slipped it around her shoulders. "I just wanted to say—thanks." Her voice was thin.

He nodded, scooped her up in his arms and stood. He carried Patrice back to his horse.

"He got away," she said, shivering and pulling the coat tighter around her.

"For now. I'll get him. Don't you worry your pretty little head about that."

She nodded. "If you hadn't gotten here just then, he would have—he would have raped me."

"I know."

She looked up at the man who carried her. "Who are you, Spur McCoy?" The battered woman's voice was charged with wonder. "Who the hell *are* you?"

"It's a long story. We'll talk about it later. Now I have to get you back to town."

She gripped his arm. "No. I mean NO! Let's get him first. I can wait here, or ride with you." She laughed. "Heck, I'm used to that."

"Okay."

They made it to his horse. The beast stamped, flung its head back and forth as the tornado finally left the area. Rain splashed down onto them as Spur deposited Patrice on his saddle. He slipped up behind her and kicked the mare's flanks.

The excited, frightened beast bolted into action. Figuring that Galde wouldn't return to Fagan, he rode west into the steadily increasing rain.

Patrice reached down and gripped her legs.

"Why—why would that man do this to me?"

"I don't know, Patrice." He kissed the top of her head as they rode.

The sky opened up, pouring down huge drops. The ground quickly turned into a liquid mass of thick mud. The horse faltered, whickered and slowed to a walk.

Galde had a headstart. The rain was getting worse. He could feel the half naked woman shiver —uncomplainingly—in front of him.

Sighing, he turned the horse around and headed for Fagan.

"Why're you doing that?" Patrice asked.

"I just thought better of it. Plenty of time for me to catch up with him in the morning. Besides, I don't think blue skin goes so great with blonde hair."

She sighed and they rode back to town.

He cut across farmland once they approached Fagan. His newest problem: how to get her into his room in her condition without being seen. Spur finally halted his horse in a small stand of trees behind his hotel. A long stairway led up behind the building to the second floor. They should be able to make it.

But first . . . .

McCoy unbuttoned his soping wet pants and dropped them to his ankles.

"Hey, Spur," Patrice said, watching him. "We're soaking wet and I'm kinda tired."

Grunting, he pulled them over his boots and handed them to her. "Put them on. Helluva lot better for me to walk in there in my long underwear than you to be—like that." He motioned to her body.

She nodded and dressed. They dashed to the hotel, ran up the stairs and entered the hallway. A fashionably dressed, red-haired woman looked up from the key she was trying to use on her door. She blanched at the sight of the dripping, bizarely dressed people.

"Hello, Anne," Patrice said, as they shivered and hurried into his room under the woman's now amused but curious eyes.

Inside, Spur turned up the lamp, stuffed himself into dry pants and hurried out to hitch his horse in front of the hotel.

On his return Patrice was rubbing her nude body with a soft towel.

He took quickly stripped. They dried each other and jumped into bed. They struggled to get warm as they huddled under the covers. Once she'd stopped shaking from the cold Patrice turned to him, her blue eyes darting back and forth.

"Did all that really happen? I mean, I'm not dreaming, am I?"

"Afraid not. I guess you're just one unlucky woman, Patrice."

"Oh no." She shook her head. "If I was, I wouldn't have met you and I'd be—well, I don't know what I'd be now." She grabbed his hand under the quilts. "You said you'd tell me what you're doing out here. Remember?"

He nodded. "As I said, it's a long story."

She snuggled against him. "I've got all night."

As he talked Spur thought of the man who was out there, still free, riding away into another town, another disguise.

15

The storm had passed.

Exhausted, Jack T. Galde slumped in his saddle and dropped the reins. The horse nickered as she felt the man's control over her relax. Roused from his brief nap, Galde shook his head and looked around him.

Dawn broke fully, charging the eastern sky with brilliant light and stinging his eyes. Blinking, Galde yawned and surveyed his surroundings. Where the hell was he?

The land around him spread out in unvarying monotony. He'd left the farms far behind; only cresting streams, gulleys and clumps of trees broke up the landscape.

The muddy trail stretched out below him so he knew he was still headed in the right direction. During the worst of the rain he'd ridden blindly, hoping he was following the trail, hoping the tornado hadn't blown him far off course.

I feel like shit, Galde thought. Memories of last night's misadventures rocketed through his brain—the girl grabbing his crotch while they rode, running through the cornfields, trying to rape her, the tornado, the other man showing up and his hurried flight from the area.

Shame burned his cheeks. Galde punched his thigh and cursed. He *was* losing it, losing the killer instinct and the razor nerves he'd enjoyed on the dirty streets of New York. All this play acting, the waiting, the easy living, were eating him up like a worm in a corpse.

Okay, he thought. Enough of this. He was tired of the wide open spaces, tired of small town people with smaller bank accounts, tired of running, and especially tired of a certain blonde-haired bitch who was spending most of her time screwing up his life.

He added up his money in his head. Must have at least ten thousand. Hell, that's plenty. He'd head back to New York and set himself up there again. Maybe he'd open a whorehouse and charge five bucks a fuck.

Galde smiled at the idea. That'd be great. Easy living and easy robbing. Heck, it'd almost be legal stealing. It would certainly be better than what he'd been doing. Anything was better than this.

He headed back into the sunrise for Fagan. If that asshole who'd stopped him last time showed up he could take him with no problem—especially since it was daylight and there wasn't a damned tornado chewing on his butt.

Galde rode, letting the horse pick its way slowly through the four-inch deep mud, drowsing to the low sucking sounds of four hooves pushing in and out of the thick earth.

A half-hour later he saw a town in the distance. He must've passed it in the night without even seeing it. He rode on, pushing the horse harder. Maybe he could get a few hours sleep before catching the train to Kansas City.

As he approached it, however, he was quickly aware that the town was dead. Doors banged open and shut in the light breeze. Whole buildings had shifted, bent, leaned at unnatural angles. Some lay in heaps of broken wood on the ground. Weeds grew thickly through the main street. Nearby, a windmill in front of an abandoned farmhouse creaked erratically with two missing vanes.

Just my luck, Galde thought as he rode into the ghost town. The dead buildings depressed him, reminded him of how his career had been going. He snapped out of it. Sleep, I need sleep.

Galde rode among the remains of broken dreams, skirting shattered watering troughs and sun-warped barrel tines. After travelling its length he tuned back and finally stopped before the farmhouse. Should be good enough, Galde thought. Maybe he'd even find a bed.

After tying his horse up in the barn he walked on stiff legs into the house. He stepped back as the stench of rotten flesh rose up around him.

Gagging, holding his nose, Galde stared down at the decaying remains of some wild animal's lunch. Where the cow's skin hadn't been ripped from its bones it had shriveled into a dark brown mass, revealing putrifying green flesh beneath it.

The dead cow's stench was so revolting that he quickly backed out. He put his hands on his hips. This wasn't his lucky day, he thought, and settled for the barn. He remembered seeing dried hay there so at least he could make himself some kind of bed.

Galde walked into the shaded building. Shafts of light penetrated its roof, spilling onto the ground. Fatigue shot through him as he thought of sleep. Working slowly, he kicked the dried hay into a corner of the barn, near the stalls, and leaned back.

Just a little nap, Galde took himself. Just a few minutes and I'll ride back to Fagan.

Within seconds he was snoring away, lost in a nightmare filled sleep.

Spur left his hotel room before first light. The sleep had done him good. He felt strong, sharp, ready to go. Jack Galde, he thought, your time has come.

He was several miles out of town by the time the sun stained a few high clouds in front of him. Riding by the cornfield and seeing the tornado's path of destruction, Spur wondered what kind of man this Galde was. What drove him to do the things he did? What made him so bent on terrorizing a young woman who'd never done anything to anyone? What kind of man could kill innocent women, and pregnant women to boot.

He couldn't understand it, but that didn't bother him. All he had to do was stop the man, stop his rampaging path. Galde was a tornado on legs.

McCoy had left Patrice in his room, telling her to push a chair under the door and stay quiet until he returned. The sleepy girl had nodded and kissed him for luck before he left.

McCoy worried about her but realized the man who posed the greatest threat was somewhere ahead of him.

The muddy trail didn't show any fresh tracks. The rain had continued for some time after he'd turned back to Fagan.

He rode until mid-morning. By then clean horseshoe imprints dented the sun-drying mud. He had no way of knowing if they'd been made by Galde's horse or not, but it seemed likely. The distance between them indicated that the horse had been leisurely walking.

Spur raced his horse, watching the tracks blur beneath him. They continued on unbroken, clean, firm prints that stretched toward the west.

Two hours later he saw a ghost town beside the trail. Just when he was about to stop and give his mare a drink, another set of tracks from the opposite direction criss-crossed the first and trailed off toward the town.

He dismounted, squatted beside them and studied the prints. No doubt about it. They'd been made by the same horse. Galde must have changed his mind, turned around and stopped at the ruined town.

He peered at the seemingly deserted settlement. No one was in sight but the tracks led directly to it. The man was in there, somewhere. Spur rode into the town, following the prints.

Galde had ridden up and down the scrub-covered street, he learned, then headed away from it toward the ruins of a nearby farm.

He cautiously rode up to the gray farmhouse, dismounted and walked his horse closer. The mare fidgeted, fought his tugs. Spur covered its muzzle with a hand to halt its whickering. He didn't want Galde—or whoever was in there—to be warned of his approach.

The tracks led to the barn. Bootprints stretched between it and the farmhouse, then back again. Galde was in the barn.

Spur tied up his horse to a dead sapling and studied the building. It was a huge barn and looked sturdy enough. Faded red paint peeled off it like diluted, dried blood.

He walked silently, peering into the opened double-doors. All he could see were stacks of yellowed hay and patches of sunlight.

Moving with Indian silence he stopped beside the doors and listened. Above the sighing of the wind that whistled through loose timbers he heard a long, sonorous sound of snoring.

Galde was asleep.

McCoy smiled and drew his revolver. He'd reloaded it back in his hotel room. He gripped his Colt and stepped softly before the doors.

Jack Galde lay sprawled on a stack of hay. His fat belly and chest rose and fell with the rhythm of sleep. Nearby a horse stood calmly munching the dried grass.

Easy target, he thought. Almost too easy. Spur was disturbed—this wasn't like the man. Knowing something of Galde's abilities he stepped back out of the doors and moved around to the side of the barn. McCoy pressed his eye to a knothole and peered inside.

Galde continued to snore for two minutes. He suddenly sat up, fully awake, revealing the gun he'd hidden in the hay. The pudgy murderer killed off the words he'd readied on his lips and looked curiously around the barn.

Spur smiled. He'd outfoxed him. That gave him more time to decide how to approach him.

Of course it would be easy enough to simply blast the life of the man through the cracks in the wall, to be done with the man forever. But that wasn't his style or the style of the Secret Service.

Bring him alive, the directives stated. If you can't, just bring him back any way you can and have a damn good explanation of why the suspect is dead.

Galde glanced around the barn, shrugged and stood.

Spur decided it was time to move. He slipped along the wall toward the doors.

"Galde!" he yelled.

Silence.

"Galde! It's all over. Come on out!"

No answer.

Spur bent around the corner and looked inside. The horse was still there but Galde was nowhere in sight.

Where the hell had the man gone? McCoy searched the place with his eyes—none of the hay-mounds were big enough to conceal the obese man's bulk. Aside from a few broken barrels and two pitchforks the place was empty.

Even the stalls in the rear of the barn had been crushed and lay in stacks of lumber, ruling that out.

The hay loft. Spur glanced up at it. All he could see was the front of it where the wooden ladder extended down to the floor. The rest of the loft was out of his line of sight and lost in shadows.

He was up there, of course.

"Come on, Galde; I know you're up there. Give yourself up. You'll get a fair trial."

Faint snickers issued from above the barn floor.

"Don't make it hard on yourself," McCoy said.

Silence.

"What do you expect me to do, ride away and leave you here?"

"What the fuck business is it of yours?" Galde shouted. "I never did nothing to you!"

"I'm a government agent assigned to track down the man who's pulled off a string of bank robberies and murders in this state," he said evenly. "What is it—five banks so far? And thirteen murders?"

"Yeah."

"Thirteen innocent men and women. You killed women, Galde! A pregnant woman!" Spur shouted.

"Big fucking deal. She was an ugly bitch who got in my way. I do that to people who get in my way!"

"You scare me, Galde. A woman killer who breaks into banks at night when no one's around, then sneaks out of town with your tail between your legs."

He paused. No reaction. "And you couldn't even rape Patrice. You couldn't get it hard. Just what kind of a man are you, Galde?"

"Ten times what you are!" he screamed. "Get the fuck out of this barn unless you're ready to eat my lead!"

"Then come on down here and face me like a man. Stop hiding up there like a little girl. Show me your face, Galde!"

"So you can blast it off? Keep dreaming, lawman!" he snorted.

"I can wait all day." He still couldn't see a thing in the hayloft—no movement, no man.

Spur quietly moved to the ladder that led up to it and climbed. The dried wood creaked as he moved. Damn! He barged up it and fired a shot just in case the guy decided to give him a premature greeting.

"Come on up. Come on up to your death!"

Spur gripped the floor and hauled himself up. Galde stood there, weapon drawn and aimed at McCoy's chest. The fat man's face was slick with sweat but he smiled.

"You won't shoot me unless I shoot you first," he said. "Is that how you play?"

McCoy nodded. "That about sums it up." He studied the man's right shoulder, watching for movement beneath the seam-splitting gray shirt as a patch of sunlight burned into it.

"I like this kinda game."

It came. Just the faintest trembling, the tell-tale signs of muscles knotting and preparing for movement. McCoy dove as the finger squeezed. He slammed into Galde's legs, knocking him to the floor howling in rage and surprise as his bullet slammed harmlessly into the far wall.

"Jesus!" Galde yelled.

The move sent Spur's weapon skittering out of his hand. Spur grabbed the pitchfork that lay beside him and used it to flip the gun out of the man's hand. It fired as it impacted on the wooden floor ten feet away from them and skidded to the edge of the hayloft.

"Come on." He rose to his feet and towered over the thief. "Give me a good reason not to rip your guts out with this thing!" He waved the pitchfork menacingly.

The man scrambled back on his hands. "I thought you played fair," he said as his back banged against the wall.

"Not with shitheads like you!" he growled.

"W—wait! Maybe we can work something out." Galde's face crumpled with fear. "I got lots of money in my saddlebags. Take whatever you want. Just don't kill me!"

"Why shouldn't I do both?" Spur jabbed the sharp steel needles against Galde's bulging stomach.

"I got some hidden." His voice was desperate. "I'll tell you where!"

"Too late." Spur lifted the pitchfork above the cowering man, flipped it end-to-end and smashed its handle onto Galde's skull.

The man groaned and slumped over.

McCoy smiled. He should sleep for a while. The blow wasn't hard enough to have killed him, and he'd aimed for a fairly safe spot.

Just to make sure, he bent and reached for the prone man's arm with his left hand, still gripping the pitchfork.

The pulse was regular, steady.

Spur straightened up and nudged the tines against the man just to make sure he was truly unconscious. He pushed hard, harder.

Galde sprang from the wall and slid on the hay-slick floor toward his gun, a hideous scream strangling out from his throat.

He threw the pitchfork. Galde caught its business end in his hands before he slid off the hayloft and plunged, howling, ten feet down to the floor.

A scream echoed through the barn. Spur grabbed up his Colt .45 and looked over the edge, grimaced at the sight, and slowly descended the ladder.

The man and the pitchfork had changed places in the fall. It had hit the ground first, tines up. Galde had slammed into it, impaling himself on the sharp metal points.

The weight had broken off the wooden pole. Galde lay face down. Slender shafts of steel jutted out from his back.

Spur shook his head. It was over.

16

Spur lugged Galde's body onto the man's horse, tied the wrists and ankles together below its belly and led it back into Fagan. When he got there he stopped in front of the sheriff's office. He shook his head remembering that the man was dead but went in anyway.

The office was spotless. The blood stains had been scrubbed away. A young man looked up at Spur as he walked in. He looked vaguely familiar but McCoy couldn't quite place the face.

"Can I help you?" the youth asked.

"Yes. I got a dead man outside."

His eyebrows shot up. "A dead man? How—why—I mean, you killed him?"

"That's right. Jack Galde. He's the one that murdered Tex Frank last night."

The boy squirmed. "I see. I didn't know who'd done it. I'm—I'm the new deputy here. Tex deputized me yesterday, on account of how I'm gonna be a married man."

Then he remembered—the boy who'd challenged Enoch Salt when he accused him of raping his daughter.

"Is Missy Enoch's father still in his cell?" Spur asked, exhausted.

"Nope. I let him out this morning. He wasn't too happy to see me but he was sure happy to get out." The youth peered out the window. "How'd it happen?"

Spur waved off the question. "I'll be back to tell you every detail later. But I need some rest now. Hope you understand, Tommy."

"Sure. I think."

He jerked his head toward the door. "You might as well bring him in here."

"Okay."

Spur glanced once more at the pudgy man and then headed to his hotel. After hitching his tired horse, he climbed the steps and knocked on the door.

"Patrice?" he asked.

No answer.

He knocked harder. "Patrice? You in there?"

The door flew open. A storm of blonde hair rushed out and grasped him in soft, white arms. Patrice Carlon gazed up at him, relieved, her cheeks flushed.

"Spur!" she said. "I was hoping it was you."

He kissed her, right there in the hall, a long, lashing kiss that nearly sent him off his feet.

"Come on." He gently pushed the woman back into his hotel room.

She looked at him tentatively. "Did you—I mean, is he—well, did you find Jack Galde?"

Spur nodded. "Not far out of town."

"And is he . . ."

"Yes, Patrice. You won't have to worry about him anymore. He can't hurt you—or anyone—ever again."

She sighed. "Well, that's over." Patrice shook her head. "I still can't believe it all happened to me. Why in the heck did he do it?"

"No way of knowing now." He threw his hat onto the floor and sat on the bed.

"At least you got your job done," she said, going to him. "And saved my life."

He grunted. "Hell, Patrice, I didn't do it all. If you hadn't fought off those two men in the alley, well, I might not have had the opportunity."

She smiled and sat beside him, pressing her thighs to his. "Mother always said I knew how to take care of men. At least, most men."

He folded his hands in his lap and looked down. "So what happens now?"

Patrice lifted his chin. "I've got a few ideas."

He glanced up at her. Lust smouldered in the woman's eyes.

Spur laughed. "I mean *after* that. You planning on staying here and dancing for Mr. Weatherby, going back to Holmes, or returning to St. Louis?"

She shrugged. "Who knows? With Jack out of the way now I guess I could do anything. You know, I haven't even thought about it. All morning long I've just been lying here, worrying about you, wondering if I'd ever see your face—and the rest of you—again."

He nodded. "There may be more Jack Galdes out there."

She stroked his chin and sighed. "I know. But I refuse to think about such horrible possibilities. At least, not now." Patrice touched his chest and ran her fingers along the line of buttons that extended down it.

"I've got a hunch what you *are* thinking about right now," he said as her hand grasped his crotch.

"Mmmmmm."

Her fingers groped, rubbed, explored the bulge between his legs. Spur kissed her forehead and her eyes. "Look, Patrice, I'm just as willing as you—believe me. But maybe we better get a bath." He frowned. "Somehow."

She looked at him, delighted. "That sounds wonderful! And I know just where to go! The Crouching Lion has this incredible bath room. They showed it to me when I checked into my room. It only costs two dollars for two hours and it's all tiled and completely private. Shall we go?"

He removed her hand from his increasingly uncomfortable crotch. "As soon as I can walk."

She chuckled. "The way you talk, Spur!"

Steam hung in the air.

The room was completely covered with the finest gold inlaid tiles that had been imported from Italy. A pile of fluffy white towels sat heaped near an oil lamp which exuded thin golden light. In the center of the room sat the tub—a monstrous, claw-footed affair that could easily hold two or more people.

A sweating boy hauled up one last bucket of fire-warmed water and poured it into the tub. He wiped his forehead and smiled at Patrice.

"There you go, Miss Carlon," he said, grinning at her. "You and your *friend* can take your bath now," he said, surprisingly aware for his age.

"Thank you, Peter. Spur, give the young man a tip, would you?"

He handed the kid a silver dollar.

"Boy oh boy, thanks, mister!" Peter trailed off, bucket dragging along the floor, and banged the door shut.

McCoy locked it and turned to Patrice. She stood by the tub, staring into its steamy contents, looking for all the world like a seer at an ancient Greek oracle.

He moved to her. Tiny droplets of water hung to her blonde hair, flattening it around her face.

"What are you thinking of?" He rubbed her shoulders, feeling her soft skin beneath the thin material.

Patrice shook her head. "Just—just about—"

"Shhhh. The past is just that—the past. Only important thing is *now.*"

She glanced up at him and smiled. "Well, heck, I guess you're right. No sense in worrying about the hells we've been through."

They undressed, arms flying, hands gripping, unbuttoning, unstrapping, slipping off, removing. Her dress soon flew on top of Spur's shirt and hat. Boots thudded on the slick floor followed by petticoats and pants. Laughing, they raced to finish before the other.

Soon Spur went to her and gripped her slender

waist. Steam condensed on their bodies as they kissed passionately. When he lifted his head he knew that he was more than ready—throbbingly ready.

She looked down between his legs. "I thought we were going to take a bath, Spur," she chastised with mock despair. "Isn't that why you've dragged me here?"

He grunted. "Okay."

So they washed each other in the stingingly hot water, rubbing away trail dust, cares and worries from their naked bodies. He delighted in his exploration of her, rubbing every square inch of her marble-white flesh as she returned the favor to him. Muscles relaxed as the warm water soothed them.

"Stand up," Patrice said, grinning evilly as she held the huge cake of lye soap.

"Why?"

"You'll see later. Just stand up!"

He rose from the tub. As water sheeted down from his body, Patrice gripped his leg and urged him to turn around. Once he faced away from her the blonde jammed the soap between his buttocks and vigorously scrubbed.

"Hey!" he said.

"Never you mind," she said cheerily as she violated him. "I'm gonna make sure you're really clean."

"Oh . . . . ohhhh . . . kay."

She grabbed his penis and stroked it as she washed, stroked him to full erection.

"Damn it, woman, I don't know if I hate it or love it!" he thundered.

"That's the whole idca," she deliciously said.

Spur turned around and splashed down into the tub. "I think we've had enough of this damned bathing." He wriggled the suds from his body.

Her eyes were filled with innocence. "What've you got in mind?"

"Come on!" He grabbed her hands and pulled Patrice to her feet.

The naked, dripping couple walked to the pile of towels.

"Now that we're all clean let's get filthy." He pushed her down into the towels.

Patrice laughed as he turned to arrange them into a soft bed. She grabbed his hips and licked his left buttock.

"Hey!" he protested. "What the hell're you doing?"

"Mmmmmm. Kissing your ass." She moved her mouth to his right cheek. Then to the middle.

He shuddered from her unholy actions. "Where did you get all thcse crazy ideas, Patrice?" Spur asked as she licked up and down.

She moaned and removed her head. "I don't know. I guess it's just the devil in me."

"I'll put the devil in you—*my* devil. As soon as you—oh! Oh! Oh hell! You stop that, girl, you hear? You just stop that—ohhhh! Dammit, that feels goodd!"

"Mmmmmmm."

She moved between his legs, licking down to his hanging scrotum, sucking it into her moist mouth, humming and probing his fullness with her tonguc.

Spur shook as she squirmed and turned around, sliding her mouth up from his testicles to the root of his erection. She licked up it, pressing her lips around his shaft until she'd met its pulsing head. Patrice enmouthed him in liquid fire.

"Ahhh! Damn, that's fine, Patrice! Don't stop now!"

She slid her lips up and down along it, savoring it, staring into his steamy eyes as she pleasured him. Spur laid his hands on her shoulders as erotic sensations rocketed through him.

"Jeez!" He bent forward slightly and grasped her breasts, cupped them, squeezed them softly while thrusting into her mouth. Patrice groaned and quickened her pace, accepting his pumps, opening her throat.

Steam enveloped their bodies. All too soon Spur felt himself getting dangerously close. Patrice sensed it and released him.

"Now," she said, flopping down onto the towels. "Now I want you to do it." She pressed the backs of her hands against her thighs and stroked upward. "Do it to me, Spur. Put it in. Fill me up and make me feel like a woman!"

He got into position and rubbed his penis against her opening. "You've got me so worked up I don't know how long I'll be good for."

"I don't care!" The woman bumped her crotch against him, urging him to impale her. "Just stick it in!" Her gaze burned into his through the mist laden air.

He pushed into her, sliding, driving. Patrice came alive. She met his thrust, slamming him full-length into her. She groaned and squeezed her eyes in temporary pain before opening them wide and looking up at him.

"Oh yeah. Oh yes, Spur! Heck, you're gonna spoil me for any other man. But I don't care. I don't! Just fuck me. Fuck me! Fuck my pussy!"

He obliged, pulled out and pounded back into her. Their slick bodies joined, separated, joined as they worked out their mutual lusts. Spur felt strong and alive as he rocked in and out. They established a rhythm of slow thrusts and quick withdrawals that increased in speed with each push. Soon their bodies banged together and Patrice groaned and moaned beneath him.

"Faster. Open me up. Oh god oh god oh god!"

McCoy revelled in the pleasure that shot through him, surging through every part of his being, spinning his mind until all he was aware of was Patrice and their warm connection and her willingness to give her body to him.

He rode her harder until his testicles banged against her crotch. The blonde woman shook and shuddered, dug her fingernails into his back and thrashed her head from side to side as the pleasure built within her and mounted to an unbearable, undeniable peak.

"Yes! Yes! Yes Spur!" she said, rolling through her orgasm and clutching his body with unshamed lust as she shivered and bucked beneath him.

McCoy deepened his thrusts, puffing out his breath in short blasts, staring down at the climaxing woman, driving himself closer and closer until he couldn't hold back, couldn't stop the ultimate release that boiled up within him.

"Patrice!"

He yelled and pumped and exploded. A thousand stars wheeled before his eyes as he slammed into her, grunting and snorting and gripping her shoulders as every muscle in his body tensed and celebrated his orgasm. Lightning raced through him with each spurt, electrifying him, empowering him with the primal savagery of pure lust.

It finally ended. The incredible feelings washed through him to be replaced with sweet lethargy. He halted his thrusts and lay panting on top of her as their genitals clung to each other.

Spur closed his eyes and gasped. His breath shot against a curl of blonde hair, sending it flying into the air as he desperately tried to recover his senses.

Below him, Patrice sighed and grabbed him and held the spent man like she'd never let go.

It was some time later that Spur realized he was crushing the woman. He gripped her hip and rolled Patrice on top of him.

The woman kissed his nose. "Fun, wasn't it?" she asked with shining eyes.

He nodded.

"I thought so." She laid her cheek on his hairy chest. "But don't you think it's time we had a bath?"

Spur met her at the train station in Fagan. He'd ridden back to Holmes, paid her bill and rescued her belongings from her hotel room. He piled the leather bags at her feet.

Patrice was dazzling in the full sunlight, her blonde hair glowing beneath the white hat, her luscious body wrapped in a matching silk dress trimmed with white lace and real pearl buttons.

The woman was relieved to see him. "Just in

time. How'd you ever manage to bring everything back?" she said after kissing him.

He shrugged. "Just did."

Patrice smiled hesitantly as the train approached, whistling its impending arrival. "Look, Spur, maybe this was a mistake. Maybe I shouldn't go back to St. Louis."

"It's your decision." He wasn't too happy to see the woman go.

"I know." She closed her eyes. "If I could just be with you everything would be different." Patrice grabbed his hand.

He shrugged. "I told you I never hang my hat in any one place for long."

She blinked. "Yes. I guess it's for the best."

The train slowed as it clattered up, belching smoke. Air hissed from its brakes. Steel scraped against steel.

Noisy newcomers disembarked, flooding the platform around them with a confusion of activity. Flashy suits. Stained carpetbags. Crying children and drunken men.

"You'd better get on," he said. I'll help you with your luggage." Spur reached for the brown leather bags.

She looked at him, her beautiful blue eyes brimming, lower lip trembling. "Spur. Spur!"

"I know."

They embraced. Her tears dropped onto his clean gray shirt as men and women jostled around them. She finally stepped back, wiped her cheeks and sniffed.

He handed her luggage to the porter and walked

with her to the doors.

Patrice turned back to him as she placed her boot on the stairs. "Thanks!"

She was gone. Spur waited until the whistles blasted the morning air and the iron horse slowly surged forward, taking her back to her home.

When it was out of sight he turned and walked to the telegraph office, shaking off the memories.

It was time for a new job.

SPUR
PLAINS PARAMOUR

Thanks to Scott Cunningham for his contribution to this book.

CHAPTER ONE

I'm gonna kill him.

The thought pounded in his brain, blasted through every nerve in his body. He deserves to die. He *has* to die for what he did. It's justice. It's everything that's right.

He followed the man through the darkened streets of Quintoch, Kansas. The saloons were quiet and all decent citizens had long ago gone to bed. But not that one. He'd been out drinking, carousing, going over old times with his murdering friends.

It'd be the last time he did that!

Mark Inglewood couldn't quite keep his eyes open. He stumbled down the rutted, dusty street, knees bending, muscles sluggish. Okay, so maybe he shouldn't have had that last drink. But hell! He'd be home soon enough, safe in bed next to his woman who'd be snoring away.

He'd grab her, wake her up, want her. She'd turn over and refuse to touch him when she smelled the liquor on his breath. Inglewood sighed. Some things never changed.

But he couldn't help the drinking, he thought, staring at the shimmering crossroads ahead. He had to pack down all that whiskey. Things were so boring since the great war ended. There was nothing to do. No battles to be won. No goddamn fun!

Inglewood's stomach rebelled at the bitter liquid he'd poured into it. He felt it heaving, threatening to come up. He stooped over a hitching post, stared at the inky water of the trough and waited. Nothing. Feeling better, the tall, muscled man groaned and lurched toward Settler's Avenue. It wasn't far now.

Reeling forward, his feet refusing to work properly, Mark Inglewood heard something behind him. Normally he'd turn to see what it was but he just didn't feel like it. Besides, the town was safe. Never any problems here. No robberies, no killings, no shootouts—no fun!

He made it to Settler's Avenue. The cool night air had finally cleared his head. Mark straightened his back and moved toward his house. Just half a block down. Just half a block to his wife and the kid and sleep.

Half a block.

The dark figure twisted the rope. He worked quickly as he followed the drunken man, forming the knot as best he knew how. Hurry, he told himself. His shaking hands fumbled. He silently cursed himself and his pain-racked brain, pulled the rope apart and started over.

He'd practiced so long that night, waiting for that damn man to leave the saloon. It just figured he'd be the last one out.

Mark Inglewood had stopped moving.

That gave him just enough time to complete the long, wrapped knot with the loop at the end. He ran his fingers over the rough hemp, checking it. It should work.

The sleeping town was lit with thin moonlight, but the silver glow turned to red in his mind. He shook his head, trying to quench the internal fire that boiled within his skull. It didn't work. Whenever he thought about it, about what had happened, it seemed his head was about to explode. He couldn't stop the pain.

Don't worry about that now. Just do it!

His prey had turned off the main street. He was nearly home. Time to act.

The knotted rope slapped softly against his thigh as he hurried toward him. Fifty feet. Thirty. Twenty. He pulled the heavy iron hammer from the back pocket of his overalls.

Mark Inglewood stopped and turned to face him. "Hey, boy! What're you doin' up so late?" he asked, his words alcohol-slurred.

"Just this!"

The hammer went up and pounded down. Inglewood groaned and dropped to the street. His assailant returned the hammer to his pocket, threw the rope over his shoulder and lifted the unconscious man by his armpits. He dragged him to the tree behind the small house, working slowly, making no noise, ignoring the agony that surged through his head.

He knew the branch was high enough, he'd checked that while waiting. The man lugged Mark Inglewood to the base of the neatly-stacked firewood. He took a deep breath and surged into action.

Lengthen the loop. Push it around the head. Pull it tight until it cuts into the neck.

He threw the other end of the rope over the highest clear branch and hauled Mark Inglewood to the top of the five-foot high woodpile. It moved under his boots so he paused until he regained his footing. He quickly checked the length of the rope and the height. It should work.

He jumped down and secured the loose end of the rope around a thick, dead branch. It was taut.

The ache in his head lessened. His heart banged. Sweat squeezed from every pore in his body. He lifted the man to his feet and slapped his face.

Mark grunted and opened his eyes. "What's—what's going on here?"

"Goodbye!"

He pushed. The drowsy man swung out on the rope, legs kicking, arms flailing as the tension settled around his neck. Strangled cries blasted out from his throat. Inglewood swung back and forth in a slow arc, his boots a foot from the ground, gasping as he slowly died.

Watching from on top of the woodpile, the other man sighed. The headache was gone. He looked into the branches of the tree, smiled and slowly walked away. He turned back just once to see Mark grabbing the noose, frantically trying to dislodge it from his neck.

With any luck, Mark Inglewood would be dead in a half-hour.

Spur McCoy opened the telegram again as he sat in the barber's chair. The cheery clipper worked on Spur's reddish-brown hair, snipping and talking incessantly about his eldest daughter—ripe for marriage.

Strange job he'd been handed, the Secret Service agent thought. The telegram from General Halleck in Washington was cryptic, as usual, but he got the gist. The growing town of Quintoch, Kansas, was living in fear. Three men had been hung in the last two weeks, all in or near their own homes. The county sheriff was stumped. No one witnessed the hangings and he had no suspects.

But there was one lead. All three men had been members of the Kansas 14th Regiment during the Civil War. They'd been recruited rather late and had taken part in the deep push into Georgia that finally led to the fall of Atlanta as well as the South.

That was the only thing the sheriff had been able to come up with. Sheriff Andrews had requested state aid but Kansas had in turn contacted the Secret Service in Washington. They, in turn, assigned Spur the job of finding the murderer.

"Pretty as a peach!"

Spur folded the telegram. "What?"

"Pretty as a peach, she is. Cooks good, too!" The barber lopped off one last hunk of hair.

He looked at his reflection in the misty mirror across from the chair. "I'm sure she is, Sam. Sure she is."

"You better hurry up and meet her or she'll marry someone else!"

"I thought you said she was nineteen," Spur said as he pulled the hair-strewn cloth from his chest.

"She is!" The barber sliced some soap into a mug, poured some water into it and whipped up the shaving cream. "She's just picky."

"Hmmmmm."

The barber honed the straight-edged razor on the strop. "Best thing of all—I taught her how to shave!"

An hour later Spur tipped his wide-brimmed hat at a pretty woman on the train as he sat beside her.

"Morning, ma'am," he said cheerily as he fit his six-foot two-inch frame into the cushioned seat.

"Don't you morning ma'am me!" The woman straightened her lace collar and glared at him. She looked to be about 35.

"Only trying to be friendly," he said.

"Try somewhere else!" She arched her eyebrows, emphasizing her ice-blue eyes. "I'm a human being, after all, not just a woman!"

"What?" Spur shook his head. "I must have missed something."

She frowned. "All you men are just the same. You treat us like we're delicate flowers, like we'll wilt if we don't hear kindly words. I ain't no flower, mister!"

Spur sighed and looked at the woman. A white lace and pearl trimmed dress covered her from her neck to the toes of her red boots, but it didn't take much imagination to see what was under all that cloth. "Right."

"You treat us like queens and expect us to be happy with that."

"And why not?" Spur settled in on the bench. This was going to be a long trip.

She turned to him, eyes flaring. "We want more than that. The women of the United States are tired! Sick and tired of it! We want the right to vote! We want the same rights as men enjoy in this great country of ours!" She panted. "And we'll get them! Don't fool yourself about that! We'll get what we so richly deserve!"

Spur sighed. It had been a while since he'd met a suffragette.

CHAPTER TWO

Spur McCoy walked onto the train station in his city clothes. He collected his luggage and ambled into town. Quintoch was a growing city of 6,000, surrounded by rich farmlands and ranches, a once sleepy settlement that had blossomed since the Kansas-Pacific railroad had pushed through on its way west.

The streets were filled with buggies, wagons and riders. Fancy ladies lolled on the boardwalks in front of saloons, fanning their satin-draped bodies in an attempt to escape the heat. Cowboys and farmers bustled into the Quintoch County Bank. Hisses and metalic clanks issued from the two blacksmith shops that serviced the town. Horses of every color and description were lined up at the hitching posts.

Spur had assumed the role of a well-heeled businessman from back east and was wearing his best suit. He'd say he was looking for a place to start a business—any business, since he had so many and so much money. This story would work for him, allowing him to pierce the fabric of the town and discover the killer.

The Diamond Ridge Hotel (est. 1863) seemed an appropriate place for a man like him to stay. The three-story structure had just been whitewashed. Stain glass windows sparkled along its walls. It was indeed fine.

The lobby was roomy, filled with leather chairs, gleaming spittoons and transplanted easterners. He registered and went to his third floor room, dropped his luggage and headed for the sheriff's office.

A gaunt, kind-faced man looked up from his desk as Spur walked in.

"Sheriff Andrews?"

"That's right. Who might you be?" He rubbed the bald spot on the top of his head.

Spur looked around the office. They were alone, no deputies in sight. He might as well be up front with the man. "Spur McCoy. Washington sent me."

Andrews stood, smiled and extended his hand. "Sure am glad to see you, Mr. McCoy. I hadn't heard you were coming into town."

"Just got in on the train."

They shook hands.

"You know about my problem?"

"Yes. That's why I'm here."

"Have a seat." He gestured to the wooden chair in front of his desk. Jonathan Andrews frowned. "I can't figure out who's been doing it," he admitted. "Lots of folks are worried. Most of them are mad at me."

"But you figure it's the same man doing the

killing? That hung those three men?"

"Almost sure."

He opened a drawer and hauled out a hangman's noose. Frayed ends showed where it had been cut off a foot above the knot. "This here's the last one. Found it around Troy Benton's neck eight days ago. It was his wife who discovered him, hanging dead in his parlor."

Spur examined the knotted rope.

"If you'll notice—"

"It's different," Spur said, cutting off the sheriff's words. "Only twelve knots."

"Yep. The other two were just like it."

"So whoever killed Benton killed the others."

"'Pears so." Andrews sipped some tepid coffee. "I can't understand what kind of killer would hang a man in his own house. That's pretty risky."

"Maybe he wants to be caught. Stranger things have happened. Where was his wife?"

Andrews flushed. "She—ah—was out with the preacher's son that night. All night. Millie found him kicking the wind when she got back in the morning. She never has been the faithful kind. Known her since she was kneehigh to a cricket."

Spur nodded. He'd run into the type a few times himself. "So I'm looking for a man who's killed three men, using the same kind of noose. And all three were ex-soldiers from the Fourteenth Regiment."

"Yep. That's what started me to thinking. Since all those boys were down South during the war, maybe some Southerner's getting his revenge or something." Andrews shook his head.

"It isn't unheard of."

"Hell, I don't know. It's been rattling around my

brain for three weeks now. I been thinking about it for so long I'm going crazy. And last night I woke up and suddenly knew who it was!"

"Yeah? Who?"

The sheriff laughed. "I was convinced it was Stafford the undertaker tryin' to get more work."

Spur smiled. "Any other connection between the three men besides their army careers?"

"Well, they used to drink at the Prairie King Saloon. Them and four others. All of them were recruited right here for the Fourteenth Regiment. Have their own tables near the back. Get together most every day, talking about the old times. That's how I knew that the dead men were ex-soldiers—they were always there with their friends."

Spur nodded. "No Southerners in town stirring up trouble lately? No men with obvious bad feelings about Yankees?"

"None that I've seen. And I've been lookin'. Ever'where." He gazed at Spur. "I just don't get it. Hope you can. If any more men are hung the whole place'll go crazy. People'll start moving out. Hell, they might run me out of town!"

"I'll do my best, Andrews. And I'll be in touch."

"Thanks, Mr. McCoy." He rose with Spur. "You let me know if I can help you."

"I will."

Kay Fordham snuck into the hardware store, a smile playing on her delicious face. A young man in overalls was bent over, struggling with the locked lower door on a rifle cabinet. She padded up to him. Blue eyes sparkling with mischief, she swatted his big behind with her beaded purse.

Jack Hastings spun around, rage and confusion on his face. When he recognized Kay he grabbed her thin wrists. "Woman! You know I don't like that! Besides, what if my boss was around?"

Kay laughed throatily and wrestled away from him. "Old man Tompkins sleeps until noon. And anyway, I like it!"

"You—you—" Jack sighed. "What am I gonna do with a woman like you, Miss Fordham?"

"You know exactly what to do. And don't call me miss!" She lifted her left eyebrow and repositioned her white bonnet. "Come on, Jack. I haven't seen you for a week. Been out of town all that time—alone."

The youth turned his attention back to the case and chuckled. "Alone? I don't believe you. You're never alone. Unless you scared off all the men." He worked the lock. "Damn thing won't open! The key must be bent or something."

"Hey, Jack, I just got off the train and came here specially to see you!"

"So you saw me. I'm busy." He rattled the key, sending the wood and glass cabinet rocking back and forth. "Darn!"

"If that's how your gonna be, I'll leave!" she pouted.

"You believe in women's rights," Jack mumbled. "I believe in my rights. And right now I'm busy!"

"Fine! Just don't show up on my door some lonely night when you want some company—in bed!"

Kay swirled to the door, a vision in white silk and pearls.

Amos Tompkins held the door for her and tipped his hat. "Good afternoon, Kay!" he said cheerily.

She snarled. "I'm perfectly capable of opening it myself. And what's so good about it?"

The store owner sneered. "When you suffragettes gonna be satisfied?" he asked, watching her hips swaying back and forth.

Kay turned to him and yelled. "As soon as we figure out how to live without men!"

"Women!" Amos said as he made his way through the cluttered store to his clerk. "What's with that lady?" he asked. "How come she's more ornery than ever?"

Jack Hastings blew out his breath and stood. "Heck, boss, I don't know." He dusted his hands on the legs of his overalls. "She's just mad at me."

Amos crossed his arms. "Thought you two was getting on mighty fine. What'd ya do, take her arm while you was out strolling—or some other crime?"

Hastings grinned at the joke. "Course not! I'd never do nothing like that with her."

Truth was, Jack thought, he was starting to hate Kay—the Yankee with her high-falutin' ways, her double-talk about female *this*, female *that*. Why couldn't he find a nice Southern gal?

"I'll let you get to your work, son," Amos said, and reached toward a stack of tools. "These the new hammers?"

Jack glanced over at him. "No. They came in last month. Remember?"

"Oh, sure, sure."

The aged man set the hammer down. Hastings stared at it for five minutes after Amos left. He felt that old ache in his head again.

* * *

It could even be one of them, Spur thought as he watched four men splashing whiskey into glasses and playing cards. The informal 14th Regiment club was in session in the back of the Prairie King Saloon.

Maybe one of the ex-soldiers had a grudge against them. Maybe he was killing them one at a time. It could have something to do with the war, something that had eaten away at his mind until he'd gone crazy.

Spur settled back into his chair and surveyed the loud, smoke-filled, dusty saloon, thinking.

Say one of the Kansas regiment found out he didn't have the guts to do the job during the war. Maybe he'd disgraced his friends and had suffered through their disgust and anger. They'd forgotten all about it but he never had, and was working to kill off the old pain. It was a possibility.

The four men seated around the table near the stairs were cut from the same cloth. Unshaven, long-haired, tired-eyed souls who seemed to be drifting through life. They drank without stopping, argued at the end of card games, whistled at the plain-faced whores and spat on the floor.

Maybe they'd gone downhill faster since their friends started dying. Maybe they were running scared, thinking they were next. Maybe—

"Hello, East."

He looked up. An almost-attractive girl in a green dress that matched her eyes leaned over Spur's table, staring at him. Most of her chest spilled out from the low neckline.

"Hello yourself. Why call me East?"

The fancy lady smiled. "With a suit like that you gotta be from the East!" She fluttered her eyelashes. "Buy a girl a drink?"

"Sorry, no. I got some thinking to do."

"You can think with me!" She widened her smile, showing broken teeth.

"I have to be sitting down to use my brain."

She sighed. "Okay! But it's on your head! You're condemning me to a longer sentence in this hell-hole!" She wandered off and approached another man.

Spur turned back to the four men. Who was it?

CHAPTER THREE

"I loved my husband, don't misunderstand me," Millie Benton said as she looked out the lace-rimmed curtains. "He was good to me. Though he played cards and drank too much, he never hit me or nothing like that. But he—he was—"

Spur stood in the widow's parlor. "Look, Mrs. Benton, if you'd rather not talk about it, I'll understand."

The blonde woman touched her high cheekbones, smearing a spot of rouge. "I'll be frank with you, Mr. McCoy. Troy was boring." She poured a glass of sherry and sipped it. "All he ever talked about was the war. He'd go on and on about it, from the time he got up in the morning until he went to work at the telegraph office. When he came home it was the same thing all over again. That went on for years. Finally, he started hanging around the Prairie King so much he was practically living over there." She frowned. "So I found other friends—male friends, if you get my meaning."

Spur nodded. "Got it."

"When I walked in that morning I couldn't believe my eyes. I hadn't slept more than a few hours so I wasn't sure I was seeing straight. But there he was—my Troy hanging from that beam right there, dead as the frog I found in the garden yesterday morning." Millie's face went white. She drained the glass and set it down. "I'm sorry. I just can't help you. That's all I know."

"I appreciate the information, Mrs. Benton."

"You—you gonna catch the man who did it?"

"Yes."

Millie bit her lower lip. "I may not have been the best wife, or Troy the best husband, but we loved each other. We really did!" Tears brimmed in her eyes.

He patted her back and walked to the door. "I'm sure you did."

An hour later Spur was digging into a thick slab of roast beef. The juicy meat was expertly cooked, and the other guests at the hotel dining table raved over their meal.

As he was piling more boiled potatoes and carrots on his plate a woman sat next to him. He turned to greet her and nearly dropped his fork. It was the suffragette from the train.

"Why hello again!" she said sweetly, nodding to Spur as she spread the napkin on her lap.

Spur had to admit she was an attractive woman, despite what came out of her mouth. "Hello yourself!" He stuffed a hunk of carrot into his mouth and chewed.

"I'm sorry I was so rude on the train earlier today," Kay Fordham said. "I was just nervous, I guess. I hate those iron horses. Every time I'm on them I know the whole train's gonna fly off the tracks and kill me."

He swallowed and looked blankly at her.

"So do you accept my apology?"

"Sure." Another carrot.

"I'm Kay Fordham." She stuck out her hand.

Spur laughed and shook it. "Spur McCoy. You know, you're bound to get into trouble spreading around your ideas."

"Don't I know it! Half the men in this town think I'm plum crazy."

"More than half!" a bearded man said from the end of the table.

Kay ignored him. "Half the women, too!"

She stabbed two slices of beef and transferred them to her plate from the serving dish. "But some of them think I'm right. A few of us women get together every Saturday morning to talk, figure out what to do."

"Oh." A potato this time, drenched in melted butter. It was ambrosia, Spur thought.

Kay took off her bonnet and hung it on the back of the chair, revealing a mound of bright red hair. "I hate those things! So frilly and uncomfortable. They keep the sun off my face but there's no reason to wear them inside." She looked accusingly at the four other female diners who kept on eating, hats tied around their chins.

"What're you doing here tonight, Miss Fordham?" the bearded man asked. "Decided to eat some good cookin' rather than your slop?"

A white-haired woman cuffed the aged man's shoulder.

"It's true," Kay said, glancing at Spur. "I can do

lots of things better than cooking." Her blue eyes were warm and inviting.

"I'm sure you can, Miss Fordham. I'm sure you can."

After dinner the suffragette tagged along with Spur.

"Do you wanna?" she asked.

"Wanna do what?" Spur said it, though he knew darn well what she meant.

"You know—that!"

He laughed and considered it. She sure was a good-looking woman. "Sure. Of course!" he said. "But Kay, it's two hours till dark!"

"Well, we might be able to finish by then. Let's go!" She grabbed his hand and pulled him along the boardwalk.

Spur laughed. He wasn't about to say no to a woman like her.

Kay's house was austere and spotlessly clean, but Spur barely saw it as the wild woman whisked him to the bedroom. There was something so arousing about her, he thought as she stood panting before him, her chest heaving, eyes wild with desire as she yanked off her hated bonnet and unpinned her hair.

She might have been fighting for women's rights, but at the moment she was all woman. Spur kicked off his boots and removed his holster.

They stood before each other, staring, bodies tense, breath blasting from their lips. The man and woman almost dared each other to start.

Spur touched the neckline of her beautiful satin dress.

"Do it! Rip it! Tear my dress off, Spur!"

"Sure you're not having second thoughts—" he started.

"Damn you!"

He grabbed the material and tore it.

"Oh!"

Another rip.

"Yes!" she gasped.

He cleaved the bodice in half. Spur smiled in delight and surprise at her bare breasts. None of those fancy female underthings for this woman. Under the dress she was as naked as the day she was born.

Kay arched her back and sighed as Spur denuded her. Pearls and shiny threads rained down to the carpet. He unwrapped her like a package until she was completely naked.

The sharp-tongued woman's body glowed in the diffused sunlight. Spur felt the pressure build in his crotch. His eyes misted as he stared at the red patch between her legs.

"Are you here to do it or just to look?" Kay demanded. She grabbed his groin and squeezed it. "Get that thing out and use it!"

"Yes ma'am—I mean—ah!" He fumbled over the words as he took off his pants. "Yes, Kay!"

Stripped from the waist down, he grabbed the woman's shoulders and threw her onto the bed. She sighed as their bodies slapped together, as she took the full weight of the man.

"Oh heck, honey! Let me up there on top!"

Spur looked at her. "Huh?"

Kay squirmed. "Come on." She pushed him off her, rolled him onto his back and knelt over his crotch. "It feels just as good," she said.

"Okay."

Spur wasn't one to argue with a lady—even those who didn't think they were ladies. Her white breasts wiggled erotically as she lined up their bodies.

"This is gonna feel soooo good," Kay said, grunting. Finally in the proper position, the woman lowered her hips, impaling herself on Spur.

"Christ!" he hissed as he entered her.

"Leave him outa this!"

Lower, lower. Hot, wet sensations flooded through him. Kay shivered and threw her head from side to side. He watched his penis disappear into the woman's red pubic hair. The feelings grew more and more intense as she took him inch by inch.

"Spur, honey, I never thought it'd take this long!" Kay said. She panted as she slowly sank down.

"You complainin'?" he asked, gently pinching her nipples until they grew into hard, pink lumps.

"No. Never!"

Kay's round bottom finally pressed against his thighs. Spur grunted at the full penetration, at the erotic heat of her body. He lowered his hands to her hips and grabbed the soft cheeks. "This is kinda fun!" he said. "I mean, doing it this way."

"I know. Why'd you think I wanted it? Some of us women have good ideas, too." She pushed harder onto him for emphasis.

"Why Kay Fordham! How you do talk!" Spur said, reveling in their intimate connection.

She exploded into action, pulling up and slamming down onto him. Spur grunted as she hit home and bucked like a wild horse, hair flying, breasts bouncing, gasps blasting out of her lips as she pleasured herself.

He grasped her buttocks and guided her harder onto his erection. "Yeah, do it, woman!" he said. "Show me what you can do!"

"Oh, Spur!"

The bodies banged together at the hips, slick flesh slapping against wet skin. Spur stared at the woman who worked him over, at her lovely face radiating sexual bliss, her red lips and wide eyes, at the red mane of hair that flew around her head.

"Yes! Yes! Yes!" she chanted on each downward thrust.

Her cries intensified. Kay grabbed her breasts and squeezed them. She threw back her head and strangled out a scream, ramming harder onto him, shaking and shivering through an orgasm.

"Oh yes, Kay. Yes!"

His thighs tightened. Every nerve in his body strained for release. Spur bent his knees, lifted the sighing woman and jabbed up into her with powerful thrusts, pushing into her liquid opening.

"Give it to me. Give it to me!" she gasped.

He grunted and pistoned into her. The brass bed squeaked beneath them. The room blacked out. Spur drove home and ejaculated, gritting his teeth. He banged his head against the down pillow in time with each powerful spurt.

Spur drove into her ten times and fell back on the bed, exhausted, drained. Kay flopped onto him and kissed his neck. Their slick bodies melted together as they panted and held each other. McCoy closed his eyes and smelled the woman's hair, nuzzled it, kissed her ear and sighed as she continued to spasm around his shrinking penis.

Groggy, Spur pried apart his right eyelid. Diffused sunlight splattered the room. Kay smiled when he looked at her. They kissed, lightly touching lips.

"That was heaven."

"It certainly was." She moved off him but pressed her body against his.

"Who would have thought this would happen when we met on the train?"

Kay smiled. "I would. In fact, I did. I'm just sorry I opened my big mouth."

"No harm done." Spur luxuriated in the tremendous peace that oozed through him.

The bedroom door burst open. "Kay, dear, I know I'm late, but—"

They turned and looked at the horrified woman standing in the bedroom door.

"Oh, hi, Mrs. Germer." Kay's voice was sweet.

The middle-aged woman blushed and held her purse with both hands, mouth open, eyes wide, at the sight of their nude bodies.

"Oh, our meeting! I'm sorry," Kay said. "I guess I kind of forgot all about it." She smooched Spur's cheek. "I've been busy with Mr. McCoy here."

Spur laughed. They'd been caught so he might as well make the best of it. "Afternoon, Mrs. Germer." Spur smiled at her. Nothing could bother him now.

"Good afternoon!" Her gaze dipped below his waist. "A real pleasure meeting you!"

"I hope you're not shocked," Kay said. "After all, this is what we women have to fight for. The right to do anything we want, whenever we want. Right?"

"Why, of course. Of course, Kay! I'm not shocked. Maybe surprised, but not shocked. In fact, it's been a delight, Kay, Mr. McCoy." She nodded.

"If you wouldn't mind waiting in the parlor I'll be out soon."

"Fine, Kay. Take your time. And if I was ten years younger I'd take your place!" She cackled and walked off.

The door closed. Spur laughed with Kay as they jumped up and dressed.

"That's one of my most promising members," she said, selecting a new dress to replace the one that lay ribboned on the ground.

"Great. Just don't promise me to her." He pulled on his pants.

CHAPTER FOUR

Jack Hastings wiped his hands on his overalls. The air in the hardware store hung like a thick curtain. It smothered him. He couldn't breathe.

To make things worse, they hadn't had more than two customers that afternoon. Amos Tompkins had told him if business didn't pick up he might have to fire him.

Hastings closed his eyes and felt the flames of fire licking the back of his head. The pain grew more intense so he looked around the store, desperately searching for something to make him forget the awful throbbing in his skull.

The brass bell on the door, the one that Mr. Tompkins said had come all the way from India, clanged. Jack Hastings looked up from behind the counter and smiled.

"Hello," the vivacious, smiling woman said as she closed her parasol with white-gloved hands. "I hope you can help me. I need a pitcher and basin."

"We have a wide selection, miss," Jack said.

She waved the parasol. "Not just any pitcher and

basin—a proper one. White English ceramic with red roses and a hummingbird." The thin-waisted, pretty girl seemed firm on that point.

"Hmmmm." He stepped to the shelf behind him. "Why that particular design?"

She lowered her eyes. "It reminds me of home."

He heard it then—the slightest hint of an accent. A southern girl! Jack fought off his excitement and scanned the gleaming sets that he dusted off every morning.

"How about this one?" he turned to her and pointed at it.

She sighed. "No, that's not quite right. It has to be perfect."

"You from Georgia?" he asked, continuing to hunt.

"That's right. How'd you know?"

"So'm I. Just outside of Atlanta." He grasped a ewer and handed it to her. "This one should do it, ma'am."

She regarded it and held out her hands. Jack tenderly deposited the ceramic pitcher on her gloves, gazing eagerly at her.

"Well, it'll do. I know I'll never see the other one again. It's been gone these ten years."

"Yes, ma'am. Lots of us lost things in the—the—" Steely knives stabbed into his brain.

"Please, don't remind me." She shivered under her yellow bonnet. "How much you asking for this?"

"Ah, dollar-fifty."

She placed it on the counter and opened her purse. "Wrap it up, please, sir."

He grinned at her voice, the accent was coming

through. Visions washed through his mind—the scent of magnolias in the cool evening air, tree-lined drives, the young women in their hoop skirts, the smell of frying chicken, his father, his mother. . . .

Jack's hands were shaking by the time he'd fastened paper around the pair of utensils. He took the woman's money and deposited it in the cash drawer.

"Thank you kindly, sir." She nodded to him and reached for the package.

"Wait!" he said. "Uh, is there anything else I can interest you in?"

"I'm sorry. I must be leaving."

"But—but—" He grabbed the paper-wrapped ceramics and looked at the floor. "Sorry to bother you, miss, but it's been so long since I talked to a pretty girl from home," Jack grabbed his scalp and rubbed it.

"Well, ah, I really have to be going." The southern woman couldn't quite remove the package from his fingers.

Hastings glanced up at her. "Please!"

Her cheeks colored. "Sir, my husband is waitin'!"

"Alright, take it!"

The confused woman wrenched them from his hands and swirled away. "Good day!"

Jack slammed his fist onto the counter as the Indian bell tinkled and the woman left. Her husband. Probably some Yankee who'd robbed her parents blind, who'd gotten fat off the wealth of the South during the war.

Heck, he hadn't wanted to get into her bloomers.

All he wanted to do was talk to her. But she was just like all the rest—afraid to remember what had happened, afraid to relive the horrors of those last days before their world crumbled to dust, stomped under the boots of Northern soldiers.

Jack Hastings pounded his neck with his fists. He remembered all right. He was 11 on his parents' plantation. There was a squirrel in the pecan tree beside the cookhouse. He'd shinneyed up the trunk, innocently hunting when it happened.

It happened!

The memories seared his brain. He slumped over the counter. The muscled young man choked back a cry.

"I keep telling you, I'm not from the east," Spur McCoy said to the green-wrapped saloon girl.

"Oh, sure. Look, everyone out here's whatever they wanna be. I mean, look at me!" Gussie Granger guffawed and spilled some watered whiskey down her throat.

Spur was too busy looking at something else—at the demoralized men that constituted the local remnants of the 14th Regiment. They seemed darker than ever as they went through the motions of playing cards.

"You know, I didn't always do this," Gussie said, breaking his concentration. "I used to be a nice city girl in Philadelphia. Engaged and everything."

He glanced at her.

"Then that ape dumped me. I didn't know what to do! But this man said he'd pay my way out here if I'd be willing to work for him. Never said what I'd be doing, you unnerstand, though I had a hunch." She laughed. "So I've been here six months, still working for him, not earning a dime. He takes all the money and I do all the work!"

"I'm sorry, Gussie, but I really don't have—"

"Sure, you're sorry!" she said, cutting off his words. "Meanwhile I'm breaking my back trying to earn enough money so I can get outa this dump!" She crossed her legs and swung her leg up and down in front of him. "That real short guy over there at the bar's my boss. I still owe him a hundred bucks. Then I'll leave." She grasped his arm. "Hey, how about it?" Gussie's eyes were red with alcohol. "You know? Help a poor kid get back home?"

Spur sighed and shook his head. "I'm sorry, Gussie. I have this rule."

She retracted her hand and stood. "I know—you don't pay for it." The fancy lady straightened her bodice and forced a smile. "Wish me luck?"

"You have it."

Gussie slouched over to the back table near the stairs. "Come on, Sam," she said to one of the ex-soldiers, a beefy man with a thick brown moustache. "It's about time you saw me again. Ain't it?"

"Hell! I'm right in the middle of a game!" He hesitated and threw down his cards. "I guess so."

The angel of mercy winked at Spur as she took the man up to her room.

The remaining three men started talking. Spur moved to a closer table to pick up their voices.

"Least he's having a good time," a gaunt-faced

man said.

"He's trying, Les. I don't know about you boys, but I'm running scared."

"Hell, Hughes," Les said. "You wasn't never scared during the War!"

"Damn straight! But this ain't the war." Mike Hughes' left eyelid twitched as he stared at his hand. "We can't see the enemy. We don't even know who the hell it is!"

The men fidgeted in their chairs, laying down and picking up cards.

"Pure coincidence," Lester Fields finally said. "That's all it is."

"Bullshit!" a third ex-soldier said.

"Right!" Hughes patted his shoulder. "That's all it is. I—I hope."

Jack Hastings walked into the crowded Prairie King Saloon. He ordered a whiskey from the one-armed barback and gulped it down, staring at a group of men near the back of the big, smoky room. The fiery alcohol seemed to increase the pain in his head. Soon, he thought. Soon it'd be gone again.

He slapped a dollar on the bar and took the bottle. As he drank and watched the men, Jack drifted back in time, to the glorious days of his youth.

Jack remembered the plantation best—a huge, white collonaded structure. His boyhood had been as happy as it could be, growing up surrounded by money and power. His father had his hand in every aspect of Atlantan life. He called on the mayor whenever he had a problem. He owned five blocks of prime downtown property.

Life on Pecan Knoll was peaceful. Even after the Civil War had started it continued on much as it had been. His father fought for a few months before coming back home, wounded and readying to die. But he'd recovered and soon was back ordering the servants around.

At 11, Jack Hastings had been far too young to join up, and his father absolutely forbade him from pretending to be older to get into the army. He wanted him safe and sound at home. The Hastings had done their part to fight off the Yankees.

Jack closed his eyes and let his chin drop to his chest. That part was easy to remember. What came next was excruciating, but he remembered it. He had to.

The pecan tree seemed gigantic. Wearing a mended pair of pants, Jack had climbed up it, slingshot stuck into his back pocket, following a squirrel who was after the nuts. The scent of ten pecan pies cooling in the cookhouse window drifted through the air.

Sunlight blinded his eyes as he moved up the big old branch. The squirrel, alarmed at his intrusion, bolted up into a mass of emerald leaves.

"Come here, you ole critter," Jack had said. He stalked it as quietly as he could but soon lost it. "Darn you!"

He looked around. His parents weren't in sight. They'd warned him about climbing the tree but he just couldn't resist inching farther into its leafy heights. The branch slanted up, higher and higher from the ground.

He pushed into the tangled twigs and leaves.

Unripe pecans hung like jewels around his ears. He was fully meshed in the tree's fruitfulness.

He heard his father yelling somewhere far underneath but the squirrel was too tantalizing to back down now. He'd face his father later. Now—

Rifles cracked. Horses pounded the ground. The tree shook with the fury of their hooves. The squirrel popped into view, nibbling on a nut. More shooting, more shouts, more full-throated screams.

It was too much to ignore. Jack started down the branch, listening to the growing confusion. It was worse than anything he had ever heard. The smell of gunpowder drifted up into the tree, stinging his nose, giving him a headache.

Jack stopped and looked at the ground. Men. Lots of men in uniforms. He didn't recognize the blue suits at first. Then he knew.

Yankees! There, on his father's plantation.

His 11-year-old mind raced. Should he go down? Try to help? No. His father had told him what they do. They killed innocent children and women. They were ruthless, merciless monsters.

He hugged the branch, shut his eyes and tried to melt into the tree. Jack gasped as the squirrel hopped down his back on some kind of mission.

The sounds of the clash below him grew more intense. He heard his father yelling, then his mother.

No. Not his mother. God no!

Acrid smoke filtered through the leaves. Cannons blasted. Rifles discharged. Jack didn't know how long he laid there, hidden in the glorious pecan, immobilized with fear.

He heard loud popping sounds. Jack pried his

bark-imprinted cheek from the wood and looked out. The house was on fire, the huge white columns cracking and buckling, sending the upper porch crashing to the ground.

The bluebellies had left. They'd burned his house. But where was his mother, his father?

The little boy watched his home flare up into a spectacular blaze, unwilling to climb down the tree, afraid of what he might find there.

Finally, Jack couldn't wait any longer. He slipped down the branch, down the trunk. He huffed as his small feet slapped against the ground. Then he turned around.

He barely saw the 50-foot flames reaching for heaven, or the dead plantation workers and servants littering the ground, the broken rifles and bleeding, broken soldiers.

All his young eyes could take in were the two motionless figures sprawled near the front porch. His mother, her dress and underthings ripped off, her legs wide apart.

His father, a bayonet in his chest, blood soaked through his white shirt and white coat.

Dead. Both of them dead.

The scene telescoped. Jack Hastings started to shake as he stood there, staring at them, the air thick with the stench of death. His knees buckled and his eyes blurred.

The whole building trembled. He looked up as the second story fell, splintering into a black and white mosaic of destruction.

The innocent boy turned and ran into the pecan trees, stumbling over roots, crying as he realized what had happened. And his head pounded!

Jack Hastings opened his eyes. The saloon was emptying out, the fancy ladies were either busy or had gone to sleep now that their customers were leaving. He took one last drink from the glass and set it on the bar.

He stole a look toward the stairs. Just one man sat there—the one that looked thinner than a starved goat. Jack rubbed his neck, trying to massage away the agony, planning.

He needed rope. He needed the hammer.

He needed both things to clear his head.

CHAPTER FIVE

It's well past midnight, Spur thought as he sat hunched in his chair. Business in the Prairie King Saloon was slowly winding down. Spur got up and followed as the two ex-members of the Kansas 14th Regiment stumbled from the bar, out into the cool night air. They yelled goodbyes and wandered off in different directions.

He knew that all the hangings had occurred at night, so he'd decided to follow the men home, watching for any signs of trouble. He could follow one of them home at least. He chose Hughes, the one who'd admitted he was worried about the killings.

An owl circled overhead, flashing across the moon as Spur walked behind the man. Though Hughes might be drunk and afraid, his steps were sure, measured, as he automatically returned home, a task he must have done hundreds of times since the end of the war.

Hughes went down Mahoney Street and eventually disappeared into one of the small homes on the tree-lined avenue. Spur grunted. He should be safe enough.

McCoy returned to Main Street but the other man wasn't in sight. He checked the surrounding streets and, finding nothing, assumed he would also be safe in bed before too long. The Secret Service agent went to his hotel for a good night's sleep.

"Need some help?"

Lester Fields grunted. "Sure. My feet don't seem to work right," he said, slurring his words.

The stranger wrapped his arm around Fields' shoulders and gripped his ribs to prevent him from falling face-first into the dusty side street.

"Don't know what's wrong with 'em," Fields said.

"Seems like you had a few too many."

"Is that a fact? Maybe." Lester turned to look at his benefactor. "You sure seem familiar. Ain't I seen you somewhere around town?"

The man smiled. "Probably. I work in town. Jeez, you are drunk, sir!"

Fields laughed. "Yeah! And I don't care who knows it!" he yelled.

"Keep your voice down," he said gently. "You wouldn't want to wake up the ladies in town, would you?"

"Sure. But not with my voice."

Both men chuckled as they slowly progressed down the street.

"Now where'd my house go?" Lester Fields said, eyes rolling as he surveyed the darkened buildings. "I know it's around here somewhere." He stopped.

"Is it that one?"

"Nope."

"How about that one?"

"Uh-uh. Ah! There it is!"

"Good. Now let's get you home."

"Alright. And thanks." Fields pushed toward it, guided by the other man's strong hands. "You're a real pal, you know that?" he said, looking at him through bloodshot eyes.

"Yes," Jack Hastings said.

The light blinded him.

"Hughes!" the sheriff thundered. "You know what the hell time it is?"

"Yes, sir."

"It's a mite late to come courting my Annabelle!"

"Sorry, Sheriff Andrews," Mike Hughes said as he stood on the man's porch. "Fact is, I ain't here to do that."

He stared at the red-faced, sleepy-eyed man who held the kerosene lamp up to his face. "You see, I got this funny feeling."

Andrews snorted. "Hell! You should've taken care of that with Gussie or one of them other whores! Don't come here expecting Annabelle to take care of that. I still can't talk her into seeing you!"

"No, no, not *that* kinda feeling." Hughes wiped his sweating forehead. "Sheriff, I went home and took off my boots and—and I got—hell, I got scared like." He screwed up his face. "I don't know. I think somethin' bad's gonna happen."

The sheriff lowered the oil lamp. "Something

bad, huh? Something bad's gonna happen to you if you don't let me get my sleep!"

"But sheriff!"

Andrews sighed. "I know it's been hard on you lately, since your friends all started getting themselves killed!"

Hughes flinched.

"And it's only nat'rul that it'd start playing tricks in your head. But you gotta take it, boy! Hell, we were both in the war." He leaned closer. "We both know what it's like out there, facing the enemy. Never know when you might get it."

"That's just fine, Sheriff Andrews! There ain't no enemy to face!" He lowered his head in shame. "And it's eatin' away at me."

Andrews slapped his left arm. "Come on, Hughes. Don't worry about it. If something's gonna happen, it happens. Besides, I got me some help. Just came in today. He's gonna find the murderin' bastard!"

"Really?"

"Sure as shit. Now git back to sleep. Think about anything else—even Annabelle, that hot-blooded daughter of mine. Talk to me in the morning. Okay?"

Hughes nodded. "Okay, sheriff."

The door closed. He stood alone on the porch. Mike Hughes turned to face the street.

Now all he had to do was get home.

"Whew! I wouldn't have made it without you," Lester Fields said as he fell into a rail backed chair in his two room house. "Say, you wanna drink?"

"Sure."

"Bottle's over there."

Jack Hastings poured them both a healthy slug. His headache was getting so bad he could barely see the glasses well enough to splash the whiskey into them. The tattoo beating in his brain flooded red mists in his vision. He managed it and handed the drink to Fields.

"Thank ye kindly!"

They drank.

As the fiery whiskey poured down his throat, Jack saw his mother lying in front of the plantation house. He saw her lifeless eyes staring at the sky, her wide-spread legs, the wounds.

Hastings looked at the drunken ex-soldier. He'd done it. He was the one. He'd killed them! Now if he could kill him, his headache would go away. He reached into his back pocket and held the long, cold object behind him.

"Hey, Fields, I got something for you."

"Yeah? What?" the drunkard asked, smacking his lips after draining the glass. "Another drink?"

"Nope."

Hastings grunted and brought it down. Hard metal crashed against bone. Fields slumped in the chair. Jack replaced the hammer, ran outside and searched for the coiled rope he'd hidden in the azaleas earlier that evening. Suddenly he was back in Georgia in his mind, but it was different this time. Everything was different.

He didn't stay in that pecan tree, shivering like the little boy he was. No. He jumped down into the noise and confusion, at the bluebellies running around, killing and burning everything he'd ever known. He was too small to be noticed, too young to be of any interest to the rampaging northerners.

Hastings saw himself picking up his father's new hammer and knocking them out as they ran past, one after another after another. He conked them all on their heads.

Then he got the rope and hung them, one by one, using that strange knot the cook's husband had taught him. He hauled them up around that old pecan tree branch where he'd hid and killed them.

Jack Hastings panted as he made the noose. He stared down at the groaning man. Doubt clouded his brain but he quieted it. This wasn't killing. It's never killing during a war. It's doing a job that has to be done, and this was a war.

"You killed them," Hastings said as he knelt and slipped the noose around Field's neck. "You killed my parents! You raped my mother! You didn't think anybody was left but I saw it. I saw it all!"

He pulled the rope tight. Fields coughed and opened his eyes. "What—what—"

Hastings smiled. "You're getting what you deserve, Yankee!"

Lester Fields' voice was scratchy. "You're the one! You've been killing my friends!"

He laughed. "Yeah. And you're gonna join 'em in hell!" Jack yanked on the rope, causing Fields to cough and gag on the floor.

The drunken man clawed at the smooth wood below him, rose to his knees and then grabbed the noose. Hastings tightened it, staring down at him, nostrils flaring, forehead sweating as he watched the man struggle.

"You're already dead, Fields!" he whispered. "I hung you ten years ago. You've been a ghost a-haunting me all these years. That's gonna change!"

Smiling, he looked up at the open beam that crossed the man's parlor. It was solid oak, six inches thick. It should take the weight, should work to wring every ounce of life from the killer.

Fields stumbled to his feet. Hastings pulled harder, enjoying the sight of the coiled rope squeezing the man's neck. Lester crashed to the ground. Red skin bulged out around the rope. He yelled and passed out.

Hastings frowned as the man lay motionless. That wasn't the way it was supposed to be. He grabbed the bottle and poured whiskey on Lester's face. The man sputtered, wheezed and lay still again.

Furious at the change of events, Jack Hastings moved to him and stood on the burly man's chest. He grabbed the rope with both hands and pulled it upward.

Hard. Harder. He strained his shoulder muscles as the thick neck resisted his pressure, as his feet held down the man's torso with his weight. He let go; Field's head banged down. He pulled and released, pulled and released, working out ten years of guilt, a decade of agonized frustration and torture.

Fields' eyes bulged out. His tongue emerged from his mouth and gruesomely lolled over his lower lip. The tortured rise and fall beneath Jack's feet halted.

Hastings stepped off the man's chest and dropped the rope. Was he? He felt the man's wrist. Yes. He was dead. Probably died of fright. The noose hadn't done it.

At least he'd accomplished his mission. He'd set out to do what he had to do. Now it was over. His head cleared, the red veils lifted from before his eyes as if they'd been whipped away in a breeze.

Lester Fields was dead.

Jack found a knife on the table and sliced the noose from the end of the rope. Now, what to do with the body? He didn't want the other Yankees to find this one so fast. Let them wait, Hastings thought. Let them think they're safe.

Where could he put it? He mused for a minute and then smiled.

Yes, it would be perfect.

Mike Hughes sat on his hard bed. He was exhausted but he couldn't shake off the feeling. Something was wrong.

Twice he rose to his feet and started toward the door, but both times he fell back onto the pigeon-feather mattress. Sheriff Andrews was right, Hughes told himself. There wasn't anything he could do. He was just letting it get to his head.

Go to sleep! He stretched out and closed his eyes, too tired to even take off his boots. But sleep wouldn't come. He tossed from side to side, finally settled in and dozed.

Annabelle Andrews, the sheriff's blonde haired daughter, walked along a sunny trail. She turned, looked to him and laughed. In his dream Mike Hughes hurried after her but she disappeared behind a bend.

When he saw her again Annabelle was dancing joyously among wildflowers. All around her his friends from the army swung from ropes in a stiff wind.

A storm moved in. Hughes felt a hand on his shoulder. He turned around.

"Ain't no time to come courting Annabelle," Sheriff Andrews said. "She's busy killing all your friends. Don't she look pretty up there?" he asked, proud of his progeny.

Hughes woke up screaming.

CHAPTER SIX

Knock. Knock. Knock.

Spur raised his head from the pillow. Who the hell was waking him up this early in the morning?

He glanced out the window. It was barely dawn. Yawning and rubbing his eyes, he answered the insistent, nerve-shattering pounding.

"Yeah?"

"Mister, Sheriff Andrews says you have to come quick!" a red-cheeked young man blurted. "Found another dead man. He's been hung!"

"Great," Spur said.

"The sheriff wants you there right now!"

"Okay, okay. Where'd they find the body?"

"In the well, in the center of town. You can't miss it."

"I'm on my way."

The youth ran off. Spur dragged his wide brimmed brown hat onto his head and forced his legs to move. He was dead tired, unusual since he'd gotten so much sleep.

He woke up fast as soon as he left the hotel

lobby. The street was filled with men and women, shouting and running toward the stone-faced well. By the time he strode up to it Spur was sufficiently roused. He saw Sheriff Andrews standing beside the well, hands on his hips, staring down at something on the ground.

Spur McCoy pushed through the crowd. "You asked for me, Andrews?" he said, glancing down. A man lay sprawled at his feet.

"Yep." The sheriff snarled. "That's Lester Fields," Andrews said. "A friend of mine." His eyes were dark. "I played cards with him every once in a while."

The man's body was soaked, stripped to the waist, the noose plainly visible around his neck. Spur bent and counted the knots. Twelve.

"Who found him?" he asked, fingering the frayed end of the rope.

"You wouldn't know her. Kay Fordham. Seems she came out here this morning to draw some water for coffee, but the bucket wouldn't come up."

"Oh yes—Kay."

More Quintoch residents pushed and shoved against Spur and the sheriff in their early morning zeal to see the latest murder victim.

"She pulled and pulled. Something seemed to slip and it came up. Came up all right, with Lester's shirt wrapped around it." Andrews winced. "Some men who were passing by lowered Drake into the well and he brought up the body." Sheriff Andrews wiped his sweaty forehead. "I don't like this, McCoy. Not one damn bit!"

"You and me both, Sheriff." Spur stood.

"It's funny. Mike Hughes came around my place late last night. He said he had a feeling something like this was gonna happen."

"He was right. Looks like the same killer as before. Same knotwork. But he left the others where he'd hung them, in their houses. Why dump this one here?"

"Hell if I know, McCoy." He sighed. "I better get Stafford to take him away and put him in a box. Whoever's been doing this sure has been giving the undertaker more work."

A weary eyed, scrawny man burst through the crowd. He looked down at the dead man, pulled off his hat and stared. His lower lip trembled.

"Fields," he said. "It's Fields!" He lunged for the sheriff. "I tole you! I tole you last night but you didn't listen to me!" He grabbed Andrews' shoulders and roughly shook him.

"Hey, calm down," Spur said, wringing the man off the sheriff.

"Stay outa this, stranger!" Hughes said. "This ain't your business!"

"The hell it ain't!" Andrews said. "Go home, Mike. It's too late to do anything about him now."

"But you—you could have—" the man blubbered.

The sheriff shook his head. "Buy you a cup of coffee?" he said to Hughes.

The man looked at him, mumbled and walked off.

"I better get the undertaker. Stay here and see that things stay calm."

"Sure, sheriff." Spur nodded.

" 'Bye, father!"

Spur turned and saw a woman standing next to him. She was a gorgeous, well-rounded beauty in a light blue dress powdered over with yards of lace and ribbons. She wasn't wearing a bonnet, so blonde curls cascaded from her head past her shoulders.

The young woman looked at Spur and then at the body. Her smiled faded. "That's—that's—Lester Hughes!" she exclaimed.

Spur nodded.

"And he's—he's dead!"

She fainted. Spur caught her in his arms and easily lifted her. "Make room!" he said to the people surrounding the body. He carried her to the bench that fronted Tompkin's Hardware Store, sat on it, and propped her head in his lap.

McCoy fanned her lovely face, admiring the curve of her nose, her firm cheekbones, red lips and fluttering eyelashes. This morning was getting better, he thought, as he cradled her head on his legs.

The woman took a deep breath and opened her eyes.

"Are you all right?" Spur asked.

"I guess so. What happened?"

"You fainted."

"Did I?" She rolled her eyes. "I remember now. I saw Lester. How silly of me."

She started to rise. Spur gently pressed her back down.

"You better rest for a while. Looks like you had quite a shock."

"No, really, I'm fine. And that feels fine." She

rubbed her head against his crotch and happily hummed.

Spur laughed. "You sure look fine."

She bounced up and giggled. "I'm Annabelle Andrews. The sheriff's my father."

"I kind of gathered that. Does that mean Spur McCoy wasted his time rescuing you?"

Annabelle pressed her hand to his. "No. I—I really did faint. I just made sure I did it beside you."

"Why?"

"Why do you think, silly? I wanted to meet you. My father told me all about you last night."

He'd been trapped, but it was a kind of trap he enjoyed. "I see."

Her sea-green eyes sparkled. "Anyway, we must have dinner," she said, poking at her hair. "Wouldn't that be fun? Just the two of us. I can cook anything you want—almost anything." She moved nearer to him, pressing her thigh against his. "You like chocolate cake?"

He nodded.

"Apple pie?"

"Uh-huh."

Annabelle leaned closer and put her lips against his right ear. "Me?"

The word tickled him.

"Yes!" He gasped as she bit his earlobe. "Boy, I sure am hungry!"

Annabelle laughed. "Then we've settled the menu. But it's too early to have dinner yet. What will we do with all this time?"

Spur looked at the old man carrying away

Lester Fields' body. First things first. "I have some business to take care of, but I'll see you later."

"I hope you're a man who keeps his word," Annabelle said, pouting.

"Always!" He kissed her cheek. As he started to rise Kay Fordham approached the bench where he sat with the woman.

"Spur McCoy," Kay said, her face blanched. "The sheriff said I should talk to you about this morning. But I don't know what I can tell you."

He stood. "I was just going to look for you."

"Is this business or pleasure?" Annabelle asked him, her words clipped.

"Business."

She rose. "Well, I guess I have to be going. Morning, Miss Fordham."

Kay nodded to her. "Morning, Andrews—uh, Annabelle."

She walked off.

"Should we sit?" Spur asked Kay.

"I'd rather stroll." The woman wrapped the white shawl closer around her shoulders as she walked, though the air was warming.

Spur thought about taking her arm and quickly realized the suffragette wouldn't like it. "You found him. Isn't that right?"

She nodded. "I'd gone to the well just like every other morning. And he was in it." She stared at the distant spire of the Quintoch Community Church.

"You didn't see anyone walking away from the well, did you?"

"No. No one. Not many people were up and around. It was just after five."

They were nearing the end of the boardwalk.

Kay's gaze was still fixed on the gleaming white steeple. Spur grabbed her arm and halted her.

"Don't you take—"

He pointed down at the drop off to the dusty street.

She shook her chin. "I'm sorry. Thought you were pulling one of those manly tricks on me."

"No—just tryin' to save your pretty neck, Kay." He released her arm and they continued on walking. Spur asked her questions until he'd run out of them.

She didn't know a thing.

The bodies wrestled, the man grunting, the woman moaning as they grappled and bucked together. The headboard banged into the wall, matching the tempo of his powerful thrusts.

"Harder. Harder!" she said.

He blindly drove into her, pinioning her willing body to the mattress, lavishing kisses on her face, neck and breasts as his scrotum slapped against her groin.

It threatened to happen too soon, too fast, so he slowed down, easing into a relaxed movement. The man rode up high, raising himself off her onto his fingers and toes, changing the angle of his penetration to give her more pleasure.

The woman convulsed, eyes shut, mouth open in an erotic circle of red flesh. She arched her back, lifting her breasts as their slick bodies slid together at the waist.

Pound. Slap. Thrust. Both groaned and held back for as long as they could, but soon the pressure was so intense they couldn't resist. The world dissolved into a shimmering vacuum. He fell on top of her and they shook and rattled through their mind-bending orgasms.

Spur laid back on the mattress, panting. The sheets stuck to his body.

"Are you surprised?" Annabelle asked as she snuggled beside him.

"At what?" The ceiling still spun overhead, whirling in his mind.

"That the sheriff's daughter has been so friendly with you." She ran her fingers through his chest hairs.

"Yeah, a little. I figured you'd be a hard prize to catch, Annabelle Andrews!"

She softly laughed and pressed her ear to his chest. "You mean, you figured you should have climbed a greased pole to win me?"

"Something like that." He stroked her head. "Lots of sheriffs wouldn't cotton to their daughters doing what we just did."

"I can hear your heartbeat," she said. "So strong. So fast inside there." Annabelle tapped his ribcage. "My daddy isn't just any sheriff. Sure, he's trying to find me a good husband, but he knows I'm not about to wait around to have some fun. So he lets me do what I want."

"That's very considerate of him. Almost unbelievable." Spur was exhausted from their morning exercises.

"Of course, I was wondering if I'd get the chance to have any fun with you at all."

"What d'ya mean?"

"The way that Kay Fordham moved in on my territory this morning. Everyone in town knows that she's—well, she's worse'n me!" Annabelle looked up at him.

Spur laughed, feeling his breathing returning to normal. "That was business, just like I told you. She found Lester Fields' body this morning. I had to question her about it. It's my job."

The young woman settled back down. "Okay. I believe you." She sighed. "Poor Lester. Daddy never did see anything in him—no future. He wouldn't even let the man in the house. And I think he really liked me. I don't know."

"I don't know much of anything right now." He sighed. "I feel like I just ran ten miles. You sure can wear me out, Annabelle."

She thumped his chest. "Don't blame it all on me, Spur McCoy. It does take two."

"Right."

Later, after they'd dressed, Spur answered a knock at his door. The same young man who'd awakened him that morning thrust a folded piece of paper at him.

"Here," he said, glancing into the room. "Telegram just came in for you. Mister Drake down at the telegraph office said you'd told him to let you know if one came in. Well, it did so I brung it to you."

Spur dug into his pocket. "Here you go."

The youth flipped the silver dollar. "Gee, thanks, mister. And hi there, Annabelle!" he yelled.

"Git outa here, kid!" she yelled, and threw a pillow at him.

Spur closed the door and returned to the bed. He opened the telegram and read it.

"What is it?" Annabelle asked, looking over his shoulder.

He lowered his brows. "Trouble."

CHAPTER SEVEN

The Kansas Pacific Railroad locomotive slowly pulled away from the Quintoch train station, puffing its way on west toward the real frontiers.

A fiftyish man turned aside as steam blasted at him from the train. "Remember now, Maddie, we're respectable like," the mustachioed well-dressed gent said. He struggled with the four carpetbags.

A black haired woman 30 years his junior hurried across the platform, boots clicking on the worn wood. "Oh, I remember all right, Vincent!" she said, dodging other new arrivals. "I remember everything you tell me, *daddy*. But does that mean we can't have any fun?"

"Of course not, Maddie. But slow down, will ya? My arms are about to fall off. I don't have all that young spirit that you've got!"

She smirked and increased her speed. "Serves you right for leaving me in the lurch back there!"

"You shut your mouth, child," he said to the unruly young woman. "I didn't leave you anywhere. And besides, you don't even know where you're going."

"I don't care. All I wanna do is feel the solid earth under my feet for a change. Four days on that damn train's enough to make anyone crazy!"

"Crazier, you mean!"

She jumped down the last two steps and pressed her pearl-buttoned boots to the dirt. "Ah! Real dirt! At last!" She untied her bonnet, threw it into the air and caught it, then lifted her billowing gray skirt and revealed her ankles.

Vincent Vandermeer dumped the carpetbags on the ground and brushed away her hands. "Land sakes!" he said. "Be reasonable, girl! Last thing we wanna do is attract undue attention." Vincent smiled to a frowning elderly couple as they walked past them.

"Oh, I know, Vince. But this last week's been hell! Ever since we done it."

He pointed his finger at her. "And none of that foul language, girl!"

Maddie Pryor sighed. "Alright."

"Just think of how much fun we're gonna have. Hey, girl, you're rich! You can do anything you want. Go anywhere, be anybody. Start a business. Buy a house. Little lady, you've got it all!"

She turned to him, brown eyes flashing in the Kansas sun. "Yeah. As long as you don't double-cross me."

Vincent stepped back. "Me? Don't let that thought into your pretty little head, Maddie!"

"You know, Vincent, sometimes you treat me like I really was your daughter!"

He grabbed her waist. "Someone has to keep you

in line. Besides, you *are* my daughter. At least for the next week until the heat blows off and we can skedaddle to San Francisco."

"Okay! Let's just find us a hotel room so I can get out of this thing." She pulled at the thick cotton dress. "You know how much I hate these grown-up clothes!"

He sighed and picked up the back-breaking bags, wondering again if the 18-year-old girl was worth all this trouble.

Spur stared at the telegram.

SPUR McCOY, QUINTOCH, KANSAS
FRIENDS ARE COMING INTO TOWN STOP MAN AND WOMAN STOP MAY BE FATHER AND DAUGHTER STOP HE'S OLDER, TALL, DARK, GAMBLER STOP SHE'S SHORT, DARK, PRETTY STOP RECENTLY PICKED UP 25,000 SHIPMENT OF GREENS ON THE KANSAS PACIFIC FROM THE B.E.P. SHIPMENT STOP DEFINITELY COMING YOUR WAY STOP URGENT YOU SAY HELLO TO THEM FOR MOTHER STOP
JIM HALLECK, WASHINGTON, D.C.

He frowned. Though the general had couched the message in cryptic language it wasn't too hard to figure out what his boss was trying to tell him.

"What's that mean?" Annabelle asked as she read the telegram.

"You being the sheriff's daughter, I guess I can tell you. Seems this man and woman robbed a train. They're coming here and may already be in town. Must have crossed state lines after they did it or I wouldn't have been assigned to it." He rubbed his growling stomach. "They stole twenty-five thousand dollars from a Bureau of Engraving and Printing. The money was probably going to banks in the central U.S. My boss, General Halleck, wants that money back. They may or may not be father and daughter. Looks like I have something else to keep you occupied."

"A woman trainrobber?" Annabelle laughed. "Sounds like something that Kay Fordham would do. She's always saying women can do anything that men can."

"At least one woman's proving her right." Spur shook his head. "After the murder this morning I don't see how I can do both jobs."

She reached between his legs and massaged his over-stuffed crotch. "Oh, I think you're man enough."

He chuckled.

"But, Spur, I know my father's counting on you to find whoever's doing this. Four hangings." She grimaced. "Any more and I don't know what he'll do. Course, I'm not worried because no women have been hanged. But still . . . ."

"I'll just have to do both, won't I? I may not get much sleep for a while but it'll be worth it. Now, did I hear you mention something about food a while back?"

She jumped up and ran to the door.

After the noon meal, Spur started checking the saloons. There were so many men of every description and size gambling, that he couldn't begin to pick out a suspected train robber. Frustrated, he headed for the Quintoch County Bank.

"Yes?"

The man sat at a desk, dip pen poised over the inkwell.

"Hi. I'm helping Sheriff Andrews out with a little problem."

The banker's eyes narrowed. "What kind of a problem?"

"You'd have to ask him about that."

"Hmmmm."

"Has anyone deposited large amounts of cash recently? Say, in the last few days?"

The banker eyed him suspiciously. "I pride myself on being a good judge of character. I think I can trust you. No sir. In fact, just the reverse. Mrs. Tucker drew out her life's savings to buy the old Luria place on Franklin Avenue."

"You're sure?"

"Of course I'm sure!" He doused the pen with ink.

"Thanks for your time."

He started going into store after store. If the thieves had hit Quintoch they'd be spending money like it was water. The first place he hit after the bank was Tomkin's General Hardware. He walked into the dusty shop and blinked to accustom his eyes.

"Yes? Can I help you?"

"Hope so," Spur told the young man. "I'm looking to start a business in town here. I figured since everyone needs hardware I'd come here to ask how folks spend in this town. Is business good?"

Jack Hastings frowned and picked at his front

tooth. "Fact of the matter is, it's been pretty poorly lately. I don't know if Quintoch's the right town for you, sir."

Spur nodded. "So no one's been in lately spending lots of cash?"

Gaines laughed. "Hell, if that'd happen we'd be celebrating!"

"Maybe this isn't the town. Thanks."

Spur walked out into the building sunshine, frustrated. General Halleck definitely wanted the thieves caught before they could spend too much of the money. How was he going to do it?

At least he could check out the saloons again. There was four of them in town. The Bar S was the crudest of the places and would have fit right in a wild frontier town. It was a small, one-room saloon. Its bar consisted of a plank set up on two old barrels. A row of pegs behind it held the drinkers' weapons.

"Why do you make the men give up their hoglegs?" Spur asked the barkeep.

"Ain't no trouble in the Bar S," the greasy man said. "I aim to keep it that way. If you're here to drink hand it over!" He extended a fat paw over the plank.

"No, just looking for a friend."

The dirt floor was covered with wood shavings, broken here and there by a few nicked chairs that held snoring cowboys. The Bar S was strictly for serious drinking men and didn't seem a likely place for the thief to go.

Spur checked two more places, watching the men who sat hunched over their cards, faces taut, emotionless as they played. None of them were particularly well dressed; none were flashing around large sums of money and none were old enough to fit General Halleck's cryptic description.

He finally went to the Prairie King. It was the nicest of the gambling establishments. It had a dance floor, plenty of tables, pretty women, lots of liquor and a passable piano-player, an amiable guy whom everyone called Keno. Probably from his favorite game, Spur thought, as he sidled up to the bar. Though he wasn't there to drink, he had to fit in, so he nursed his whiskey and looked around.

Two fancy ladies, bored and hot, cooled themselves with ostrich feather fans.

Fancy ladies, Spur thought. Perhaps the thief had visited one of them. What was the name of the one who'd told him her sad story?

The two women saw Spur looking at them and misinterpreted his interest. They jumped to their feet and sashayed over to him. A sad-faced, bodice-busting woman grabbed their dresses and yanked them back. They squealed.

"Ain't nothin' doing," she said. "Just go back there and rest yer backs for a spell. This one's mine, girls!"

"Oh Gussie, we seen him first!" a pretty woman in a peach and white dress said.

"Yeah. You just wanna steal him from us! You don't need him!"

"Like hell! He's my steady. I've already had him two times." Her eyes flashed. "Now git!" Gussie strode over to him at the bar.

"Hello again," he said.

She was panting. "Howdy. A girl's sure gotta watch out for her own interests here. They was ready to eat you alive! Course, I wanted to have the chance to do that myself!"

Spur looked at her, all flushed, eyes sparkling, expectant. "Do you have a room?" he asked, and set down his drink.

Gussie laughed. "Do I have a room?" She grabbed his arm and pulled him to the stairs, tossing her head at her two competitors as she passed them.

Moments later they were inside. She turned up the kerosene lamp, since the window was covered with red damask drapes. "I sure am glad you changed your mind," Gussie said. "Should I take 'em off or you wanna do that?"

Spur sat on the bed. "Leave them on."

The whore squealed. "Oooh, you sure are a crazy one! You want me to pull up my dress?"

"No. Sit beside me, Gussie." Spur patted the quilt next to him.

She sighed and settled down on it. "So?"

"How's business been lately, Gussie?"

The woman rolled her eyes. "Oh lordy; you're not one of them talkers, is you? Why don't you just do what you came up here to do."

"I am. Fact is, I'm a businessman. I'm thinking of opening up a saloon right here in Quintoch."

"I—I see."

Spur spun his story as he told it. "Yes ma'am. That's why I'm here, seeing if this town could use another saloon."

She held up her hands as if to ward off a blow. "Don't go talking to me about it." She stood and walked to the cracked mirror that hung beside the wall lamp. "Soon as I can I'm getting out of his hell-hole. I got sweet talked into doing this once but it won't happen again." She poked at her reddish-brown hair.

"You misunderstand me, Gussie. I wanna know how much this place earns. How much you earn."

She turned to him and straightened her back. "One to two dollars a customer—depending on how he's dressed."

"I see. Ever make more than that?"

"Sure! Lots of times!" Gussie looked at the carpet. "Well, once in a while. Feller was in here not more than an hour ago. He gave me a twenty dollar bill for a quick one. Billy—he's the pipsqueak who hired me—lets us set our own prices. I saw this man, sized him up, figured he had money. I asked for five dollars. And he gave me twenty!"

"Not bad." There weren't many men willing to spend that kind of money for a woman, no matter how long it had been since they saw one. It was a possibility. "What'd this man look like?"

Gussie frowned. "Why you wanna know?"

"Sounds like a possible competitor. Maybe he's thinking the same thing I am. He might've been trying you out." Or maybe he was spending new money he'd just pulled off the Kansas Pacific Railroad.

"Oh, hell, I don't know. He was tall, skinny, maybe around fifty." She sighed. "Reminded me of my daddy."

"That's all you remember?"

She scrunched her eyebrows. "Clean shaven. None of those whiskers to chew up my face. And no moustache." She sat beside him again. "I also remember that you wanted to come up to my room. Whether we did nothing or not I gotta get paid." Gussie held out her hand. "If I don't come to him with money that pipsqueak boss of mine says he'll hit me."

Spur gave her a ten dollar bill.

"Land sakes!" the whore said. "You sure are a nice man!" She smooched his left cheek.

"You have many men like this rich one?"

"No. Lots of them are real strange. Like last night. This guy, who I recalled seein' around town once in t'while, took me up here. He didn't do nothing—didn't even talk. He just had me drop my dress and bloomers and looked at me. Finally he said something about 'momma,' gave me a dollar and ran out!" She blew out her breath. "Business really has been different!" Gussie stroked his thigh. "You sure you don't want nothing for your ten dollars?"

He smiled. "That's okay. I think I've gotten enough. Thanks, Miss Granger."

She rolled her eyes. "It's been a long time since anyone called me miss!"

Spur left her room and walked to the sheriff's office. Maybe Andrews could help him. Maybe the sheriff had some ideas about these train robbers.

Andrews was gruff. "Hell, I don't know nothing about that," he said. "So many people here in this town it'd be like tryin' to find a virgin over the age of fifteen!"

McCoy laughed and slid into the chair.

"So what're you doing about the hangings?" the sheriff asked.

"Not much right now. Investigating. Asking questions. I'm all tied up with these train thieves."

"You say you got a telegram? From Washington?"

"Yep."

Jonathan Andrews groaned. "And so now you can't look for the man who's been murdering my citizens. Is that the way it is?"

"Only for a while." Sheriff sure was acting strange, Spur thought. "No more than a few days."

"We could have ten more hangings in that time."

"My superiors decided that this takes priority."

"Well, I don't like that." Andrews rose to his feet. "I don't like that one bit. If I didn't know better I'd say there was something fishy going on here."

"Sheriff?" Spur said as the man walked behind him.

"Sure seems nice and tidy." He whistled.

Spur heard someone approaching from the jail behind him. He didn't bother turning around until his arms were pulled behind him. Steel jaws clamped around his wrists before he could begin to react.

"Hey!" he yelled.

"Spur McCoy, you're under arrest!"

CHAPTER EIGHT

Spur stood, struggling against the biting handcuffs. "What the hell do you think you're doing, Andrews? Have you gone out of your head?"

"I'm doing what I shoulda done first time I met you," Sheriff Andrews said. He glanced at his deputy, who stood smiling, arms crossed over his chest, staring at his handiwork. "Good job, Watson."

"Sheriff Andrews, you're not thinking straight." Spur let his bound hands fall to his back. "You've been blaming yourself for all the neck-tie parties going on in your town. You're not to blame and neither am I!"

He laughed. "Sure, McCoy." The sheriff's eyes were wild. "Why didn't I see it before? You must've come into town earlier and started killing the men. Then, for some reason you got scared so you came to me with that idiotic story about working for Washington. What bullshit! I believed you then—but not now." The sheriff rubbed his bald spot and turned to his deputy. "Watson, throw this killer in the left cell!"

"Yessir!"

"Yeah," Spur said to the young man as he hustled him into the jail. "And then go to room five at the Diamond Ridge Hotel. Look under my mattress. You'll find the telegram I just got today about the train thieves!"

"Good try, McCoy! You talk big, I'll give you that. Almost fooled me too."

Spur turned to the deputy. "Just do it!"

Watson shoved Spur into the cell and slammed it shut. His nimble fingers turned the key and yanked it out.

"Well, sheriff, what's the harm in it?" Watson asked.

"What's the harm in what?" he exploded.

"Might as well search his room. We would anyway—to see if there's anything in there worth taking—I mean, that might prove he's the killer."

"Oh hell! Alright." Andrews walked up to Spur, who pressed himself against the bars. "But I know we won't find anything that'll get you outa there. You ain't going nowhere, Spur McCoy!"

Spur banged his shoulders against the steel shafts.

The room opened and closed. "Did you do it? Did you go and do it like you said you were?"

Vincent Vandemere winced. "Hell, girl; keep your voice down! You want the whole hotel to know? These walls are as thin as your maidenhood!"

"I don't got my maidenhood anymore!" Maddie said in a shrill voice. "You took it from me!" She slammed the door.

"That's what I mean! Now pipe down!"

Maddie sighed and sat on the bed. "Well? Did you go and do it or not?"

"Yes. Rode out two hours ago. Hid it where no one'll ever find it."

"Not all of it!" Maddie said, eyes wide. "Vince, you didn't go and do something stupid like that! I gotta have some money to enjoy this town!"

"Of course not! I kept out a hundred apiece—just like we agreed." How could an 18-year-old girl be so loud, he wondered as he pulled the stack of crisp ten dollar bills from the pillow.

"Goody! Then I can buy some new dresses." She gazed at the money and frowned. "Doesn't seem like much when you think about what we have. Why couldn't you have kept out four hundred?"

"You know why. We can't go and spend up the town. Someone would notice us." He leaned closer to her. "They will be looking for us."

Maddie punched his gut. "No one would ever notice you Vince, darling. You're old and ugly."

"Well, they'd notice you. And stop calling me that! Might as well get in practice."

"Okay, daddy dear!" Maddie grabbed the money and squealed. "We're gonna leave tomorrow, right?"

"No! Three days from now we catch the west-bound train for Denver. Then we go all the way west."

She sighed. "If we make it." Maddie let the bills drop from her fingers.

"We will make it! If you can keep your mouth shut, child!" He looked at her harshly. "One slip of yer tongue and it's all over for us."

"I know, I know." Maddie played with the money, running a polished fingernail up and down the rectangles. "I just git all excited."

Vincent frowned. "Just stop getting excited around me."

Maddie whooped. "Why, daddy dear, I thought I'd never hear you say that!"

He sighed. "You know what I mean!"

"Yeah. I know." The girl glanced at the curtain-draped window. "Are we really safe here?"

Vincent Vandermere shrugged. "As safe as any place. Look, go out and buy yourself a new dress. I have some thinking to do."

"Okay." She kissed his forehead. "Goodbye, father."

Spur sat in the cell, cursing Annabelle's father. He knew the pressures the man had been suffering through, but that didn't make his current situation any easier to take. He had too much to do—find the thieves, stop the hangings—to spend the afternoon locked up.

McCoy watched a well-fed prairie mouse poke out from a hole in the wall, sniff the air and skitter across the floor until it had cleared the bars. If only he could get out that easily.

The front door banged shut.

"Well, what is it, Watson?" he heard Sheriff Andrews say. "I don't got all day!"

"You better look at this." The deputy's voice was

dark. "Found it right where he said I would—under his bed in the hotel."

Paper rustled. Silence. The sheriff exploded. "Damn!"

"Yessir."

"Well, I can't make heads nor tails outa this, but it sure ain't a normal telegram. Unless he's got a deal with Mr. Drake—which I can't believe—I guess he might be who he says he is. What's all this mean?"

Spur walked up to the bars. "You can't read it because it's in code," he yelled and waited. Soon enough the sheriff appeared.

"Talk!"

McCoy sighed. "My boss doesn't send telegrams describing train thieves. Any telegraph operator along the line could have picked up his message. Some of them are crooked and we don't want this information being spread around. So, while it's plain to me what it means, it wouldn't be to most other men."

Sheriff Andrews frowned and studied it. "I could see how it might be. Don't make any sense to me."

"Shouldn't we—ah—" Watson began.

"Hell, you trying to do my job?"

"No, sir. No sir!"

Andrews hesitated. "Well, hell. I guess I just lost myself a killer." He threw the keys to Watson.

"You never had one." Spur stepped back as the deputy unlocked the door. "Now the cuffs, if you don't mind."

"All right!"

A bit of maneuvering and two clicks later, Spur was rubbing his wrists. "No real harm done, sheriff."

Andrews reached for the bottle on his desk. "Hell, sorry, McCoy. I guess I went crazy there. It's this town. Kay Fordham's been by here three times today, worried she'll find another body. She's up in arms and it wouldn't surprise me a bit if she starts roaming the streets at night with that Spencer of hers."

Spur opened his mouth. "Kay has a rifle?"

Andrews nodded. "Damn right!" He slumped in his chair, the whiskey forgotten in one hand. "Hell, Spur; I'm afraid if I don't track down the killer soon the good people of this town'll turn nasty. They'll take the law into their own hands. We may yet have another lynching—" He frowned.

"What about this Mike Hughes? Know anything about him?"

The sheriff nodded. "His mother died bringing him into the world. Father got killed by a Southerner during the war. Mike inherited their ranch, but he sold it when he came back. Been living on the proceeds ever since, not doing much of anything besides drinking and cards."

"Have you considered that the killer might well be one of their own?"

Andrews stared at Spur and laughed. "Yeah. Hell; I've even wondered if I've been doing it. But I don't see the reasoning. And Mike Hughes looked scared to death that night he came to see me."

"Maybe he was scared he'd kill another one of his friends. Maybe he can't control himself."

"Maybe."

"Well, sheriff, I gotta find me some train thieves. You keep in touch. And get some rest!"

"I got my rest right here." He poured a glass of the amber colored liquid and drank it down.

Spur walked out into the sunshine. Time enough for the hangings later. Halleck gave the train thieves priority. He passed a shop filled with women's finery. He glanced in the window and grunted. It was worth a try.

The middleaged storeowner shook her head. "No, sir. We haven't had no fancy women in lately—except Gussie. She keeps on coming in to have her dresses mended." The double-chinned woman propped her glasses higher on her nose as she laughed. "I can't imagine how that poor dear keeps on tearing 'em! Course I don't mind the business. Her boss pays for it."

"Well, it wouldn't have to be a fancy lady. Just some young woman with lots of money."

"No. Don't rightly remember. Sorry, mister."

He tipped his hat. "Thank you." Spur hurried to the next store that catered to women—a milliner. It made sense. A young woman with plenty of cash would naturally get some new things, as long as she wasn't a woman like the rifle-toting Kay Fordham.

Sarah's Fine Hat Shop was closed. A sign on the door read: "Back in one hour. Picking up New Shipment imported Ostrich Feathers from train."

Spur pushed on and finally found a second dress shop: Tillie's Tailor Made Creations for Ladies. The dresses in the multi-paned window showed that Tillie was a better than average seamstress.

He went into the small store. A woman was dusting a mannekin. Spur walked directly to her.

"Sorry to bother you, ma'am."

Kay Fordham turned around. "Spur McCoy! I'll bet you're wondering what a woman like me's doing in a store like this."

He nodded. "Matter of fact, I was. Doesn't seem to be your kind of place. You don't wear this stuff."

Kay grimaced. "Tillie's a new friend. I'm trying to get her to join my society. Anyway, she had to go off and help birth a baby—she's the local midwife—and she asked me to watch her store for her. Normally she would've closed, but the train just came in and she wanted to catch the business." Kay looked squarely at him. "So what brings you in here? Something about them hangings?"

"Ah—well—something like that."

Kay laughed throatily. "Heck, old Jonathan told me everything. Don't worry, my lips are sealed."

"Just how much did he tell you about me?"

"Enough."

"Actually, I'm wondering if a young woman came in here today. Very young. With a lot of money."

The woman eyed him suspiciously. "Land sakes, man! Ain't me and Annabelle enough for you?"

He laughed. Was there anything the woman didn't know?

"She'd be spending brand new money. Not some old bills that've spent the last year folded up in some cowboy's pocket."

Kay touched the feather duster to his nose. "Aren't you gonna tell me why you're looking for this here woman?"

"Why should I bother?" He sneezed. "You'll just

find out anyway." McCoy brushed it aside. "Has a woman like that come in here? Come on, Kay. It's important!"

"Yes. I may have seen the woman you're talking about. She stormed in here, all wrapped up in the gaudiest.... Well, I showed her two dresses and she picked both of them. They're in the back waiting for Tillie to alter them to her size. She must've been about eighteen, I'd say. But an *old* eighteen. If I could just get her to dress plainly she might be the kind of woman who'd understand what I talk about," the suffragette said. "Anyway, she never asked the price of anything. Said she'll pay in cash."

"Did she leave her name? Where's she staying?"

"Let's see." Kay went to the table in the back of the shop and checked the ledger. "Yep! Here it is." She closed the leather-bound book and slammed her hand down on it. "What do I get if I tell you?"

"Come on, Kay; I don't have the time for that!"

"Mr. McCoy—" she began.

"Using feminine wiles on me, are you?" Spur moved close to her. "I didn't think you did things like that to men." His voice was flat.

Kay's cheeks colored. "Alright. You caught me. But you can't blame a woman for trying!" She looked at the ledger, studying it with her sea-green eyes. "Jennie Clowshare."

"Does it say where she's staying?"

"No, of course not. She's supposed to pick up the dresses tomorrow morning." Kay fixed her eyes on Spur. "Just what is this all about?"

"Sorry, Kay. I got business to do." He pecked her cheek and walked toward to the door, dodging yards of lace and feather-strewn hats.

"Spur McCoy!" she yelled, exasperated. "What am I gonna do with you?"

"Whatever you want—as long as it doesn't involve that rifle of yours." He stopped and looked back at her.

The woman gaped. "Who told you—"

"You're not the only one the sheriff tells everything to." He grinned and walked out.

Jenny Clowshare probably wasn't her real name, if she was the girl he was hunting for. He stood on the street, hands on his hips. There were three decent hotels in town, one rooming house and a few he wouldn't wish on his enemies. Spur bolted toward the closest one—the Livingston.

The front desk man was out, so Spur flipped through the registry. He searched the barely legible scrawls. No Clowshares.

He got lucky at the next establishment. Mr. Frederick Clowshare and Miss Jennifer Clowshare were registered in room 311. He glanced at the stairs and, seeing a dark-suited man coming toward the desk, McCoy casually walked to the landing.

He checked the tilt of his hat in the shiny spittoon that sat on the newelpost and made his way up the stairs. He nodded to an elegantly dressed couple on their way down, but the white haired woman didn't fit General Halleck's description of the train robbers.

He made the third floor and checked the closest room, 306, just in the middle of the corridor. Spur found the room he wanted and tapped lightly on the door. No answer. He knocked again, harder. Still nothing from inside.

The hall was empty so Spur checked the knob. It was locked. He removed his billfold, pulled back the lining and extracted a small set of skeleton keys. The first one did the trick. The latch clicked and the knob turned in his hand.

He went in quickly, stashing the keys and his wallet in his back pocket under his coat tails. The room was filled with carpet bags. The velvet and oak chairs were draped with women's undergarments and the closets were stuffed with dresses.

Spur sighed and searched the room, working quickly but neatly so that its occupants wouldn't know someone had been through their belongings.

After five minutes he hadn't come up with much. He'd found 100 dollars in new, crisp bills—that was all. They'd been printed in Washington D.C. and were uncirculated. Jenny and Frederick Clowshare—whatever their real names were—must be his thieves.

He pocketed the money and returned the room to its normal appearance. McCoy stepped out, closed the door and locked it with the skeleton key.

He slipped down the stairs and went outside. Somewhere in this booming town were two people who'd robbed the U.S. Government of $25,000.

Hundreds of men and women walked the streets and breezed by in buckboards and buggies. Young mothers comforted screaming babies. Merchants were shining their windows with fleeces. Couples walked arm in arm.

At least he knew where to start looking, McCoy thought, gazing at the confusion. He leaned against the hitching post that fronted the Livingston Hotel.

He'd be at Tillie's shop in the morning, waiting for a young woman to pick up her new dresses.

Hands slipped around his throat, squeezing, choking.

CHAPTER NINE

"I oughta kill you!"

His attacker's voice was soft and feminine. Spur pried the strangling hands from his neck and swung their owner in front of him.

"I should kill you, you know," Annabelle Andrews said. "Running off like that!"

Spur laughed and rubbed his throat. "Sorry, Annabelle."

"Where you been?"

"I had a little run-in with your father."

She rolled her eyes. "My father?"

He stood. "Yep. He had me under arrest for a while this afternoon. And I've been busy—"

Annabelle whooped. "Serves you right! You deserve to be locked up for what you did to me!"

"Annabelle!"

A portly man dressed in overalls and dirt walked up to their little scene. "Can I help you, ma'am?" He spat brown juice and warily eyed Spur. "This man bothering you?"

She hesitated and smiled. "Not really, but thanks."

The high-nosed man squinted at her. "You just say the word and I'll flatten him!" He raised a fist.

"No, really, it's nothing!" She grabbed Spur's arm. "See? We're just having a disagreement."

"Okay. It's your funeral." He shook his head and walked away.

"I guess that's just what I needed to liven up a boring day."

The sheriff's daughter frowned. "I'm sorry, Spur, but as soon as you left I got so hot I couldn't stand it." She shook her head. "Took three cold baths but that didn't help a whit! So when I saw you sitting there, doing nothing, torturing me, I just thought I'd get your attention."

"You got it alright. Annabelle, I have work to do. You know that." He touched her right cheek. "I'll get back to you as soon as I can."

"Work? You're just sitting around!"

"Annabelle, I've—I've—" His words trailed off. A man and a young woman were approaching the Livingston Hotel.

Maddie yanked on Frederick Vandermeer's arm. "Come on!" the girl yelled. "I just have to have something to eat! I'm starving!"

"Can't you ever just talk? The way you scream you'd think I was half a mile away." Vandermeer stopped walking and stared at her. "Maddie—I mean Jennie—you're driving me up the wall!"

"You're so tall it's a short trip." She stuck out her tongue at him.

He sighed. "Sometimes I wonder if this was the

right idea. Getting you involved in all this."

Maddie smiled. "Really? You didn't seem to mind two days ago when I distracted the guards on the train! Didn't I come in handy, daddy dear, by accidentally losing my dress in front of those four men and falling to the floor in a dead faint?" She laughed.

"I'll admit, you played your part." He dabbed sweat from his chin. "But it's high time you changed your tune. Remember, you're my daughter, a sweet, virginal girl from back east. Try to act like that!"

"How can I? You've ruined me for life!" She dramatically slapped the back of her hand to her bonnet. "Led me into a world of guns and money and sex! I'm a changed woman, Frederick; changed beyond belief. And I'll never forgive you."

"Maddie!" He said the word through gritted teeth.

"Until just before we split the money. Then I'll forgive you."

"Let's just get back to the hotel. I'm out of cash—for some reason." He eyed the sparkling amethyst pendant that hung around the girl's neck. "Then we'll get some dinner."

"You've what?" Annabelle demanded.

"Like I said, I've got work to do."

They sure looked like the right people, Spur thought, eyeing the tall man and young woman as they argued on the other side of the street. Her dress was expensive; his suit tailor-made. She still had the dewy cheeks of youth.

"Spur McCoy, you're impossible!"

"Impossible?" he asked, still looking at the pair.

They'd stopped fighting and were crossing the broad avenue, avoiding the steaming horse droppings that littered the dusty road.

"Impossible to make!" Annabelle blurted.

"I'll see you later, missy!"

"All right! I'll never cook for you if you keep this up!"

The well dressed couple passed by him and disappeared inside the Livingston Hotel lobby. Spur nodded to Annabelle, waited two seconds and walked in.

They were headed up the stairs. He followed at a discrete distance, taking his time, rounding each landing just as they moved up the next flight.

He watched them walk onto the third floor. So far so good. At the top of the stairs Spur glanced to the right down the hall. The door to room 311 closed.

That was them. He didn't need to wait until the morning to settle this. He could do it right now.

Spur dashed down the hall and pounded on the door.

"What the hell is it?" a gruff voice said. "My daughter and I are exhausted!"

"Fire!"

"What?"

Spur pushed his mouth to the thin door. "There's a fire in the hotel! Get out now to save your lives!"

"A fire? Vincent, no!"

It was the girl's voice. He heard some rustling from the room. The door finally opened.

"What's this about a fire?" the tall, dignified man said. "I don't smell smoke."

"It hasn't started yet." Spur pushed past him, entered the room and slammed the door behind him.

"What's the meaning of this?"

"Vincent—I mean daddy—!"

The 18-year-old girl grabbed the dress from the floor. She held it up to cover her bloomers and bodice.

"Settle down, folks," Spur said. "There's no fire, but there will be one if you don't cooperate."

"Cooperate? You can't barge in here and threaten us!"

"Sit down!" Spur drew his Colt .45. "Both of you! On the bed!"

"Vincent?"

"Damn!"

Spur followed the man's eyes to the holster draped around the doorknob behind him. "Not a smart move, mister."

"Tell me something I don't know."

"Shut up!" He spat the words. "Where'd you hide it?"

The man and woman looked at each other.

"Hide what?" she asked.

"You wanna play games?" He cocked the revolver. "I got all day."

"We don't know what you're talking about." The man straightened up on the bed. "My daughter and I are traveling to San Francisco. Her aunt died and we're to attend her funeral."

"Good story. Now where'd you hide the money? It's not in your room, I checked it."

The girl opened her mouth.

"Come on."

"Are you trying to rob us?"

Spur laughed. "I'm an agent of the Secret Service. They put me on your trail. Seems they're missing twenty-five thousand dollars. A couple who look an awful lot like you took it from the Kansas Pacific train a few days ago."

"You dare insult us with your accusations?" He rose.

"Git your butt down!" Spur waved the weapon in the air. "You can sit there until you drop dead, but I'd rather get this over with. Where is it?"

The girl was pale. She watched the man nervously, fidgeting with the scarlet dress that she'd lain in her lap. Maybe he could work on her.

"Sir, we can sit here until doomsday. We don't know what you're talking about."

"That's—that's right." The young woman's voice was hesitant.

"I went through your room a few minutes ago. Found five brand new twenty-dollar bills. Uncirculated. Fresh from the Bureau of Engraving and Printing. How do you suppose they got in your carpetbag?"

"You're lying!"

"Vincent," the girl began.

"Shut your mouth, Maddie!"

"No, Vincent, I can't stand it anymore." The girl stood. "I have to get out of these clothes!"

Spur watched the man as the girl lifted the bodice from her body. "Maddie? Maddie and Vincent?" he said, deliberately ignoring the girl. "I thought your names were Jennifer and Frederick."

The man sat tensely on the bed. Spur glanced at Maddie. She was lowering her bloomers, revealing her luscious, young body.

"Sorry, honey, that won't work." Spur kicked the dress to the woman. "Put it on. Now!"

"No!"

"Maddie!"

Spur lowered his aim on the man. "If you don't tell me where you hid the money I'll shoot your knees off. You'll be a cripple for the rest of your life, Vincent!"

He flinched and turned to the girl. "Maddie, get dressed." He sighed. "I guess it's over."

The naked girl gasped. "No, it isn't!" She threw herself at Spur.

He easily sidestepped, maintaining his aim. The girl flopped against the far wall and gasped at the impact.

"Talk!" he yelled.

Vincent sighed. "It's—it's not here."

"Obviously! Where is it?"

Dazed, Maddie made her way to the bed and dropped down on it, all curves and mounds and soft, pink flesh.

The man's face was stony. "Three miles out of town. I hid it near a clump of cottonwoods beside an old ranch." He sighed. "Take the east trail out of town and turn left at the first windmill."

Spur weakly smiled. "I thought you looked like a sensible man."

Maddie raised her head and grinned hopefully at Spur.

He turned back to the man. "Get your whore dressed, Vincent. I don't buy your story. We're all gonna go on a little ride—together!"

The girl's smile faded.

CHAPTER TEN

"Were you a good boy today?"

"Yes, mama."

"You know ah won't bake you no pecan pies if you weren't a good little boy!"

"I was mama. I was!"

Gussie Grainer sighed and pulled at her dress. Her room above the saloon seemed hotter than ever. Why couldn't he just do it to her like all the other men? Acting like this crazy guy's mother was tiring her out.

She'd been at it for 15 minutes while he crawled around on the floor in his longjohns, babbling away about his mother and the plantation. He'd even asked her to "talk Southern-like," so she drawled with the best of them.

She suddenly remembered her own mother. When Gussie had told her she wanted to become an actress the white-haired woman had threatened to jump off the roof. Now here she was, acting her heart out, making three dollars the hard way.

"Mama? Are you still there?" Jack Hastings asked, his voice cracking.

No, I'm not, Gussie thought. But money was money. Every dollar got her closer to home. "Yes, honey. Ah'm right heah." She struggled for something to say. "Don't the—the marigolds smell sweet-ah today!"

He looked up at her from the floor. "Magnolias!" he thundered. "They were goddamn magnolias!"

"Alright, alright, sugar. You can't expect me to remember everything!"

Jack twisted up his face in seeming confusion. "Yes, mama." He bent down and licked the pearl buttons on her boots.

Oh lordy, do I need a drink, Gussie thought. "Look, deah, do you want your mama to take off her dress right now? It sure is hot in heah."

"Okay!" He looked up at her like a puppy.

Gussie closed her eyes. Please, let him stick it in and get the hell out. She took off her clothes as her customer stared up at her from the floor. His face didn't change as she stepped out of the dress, shrugged off the lace chemise and her bloomers. He just kept his sad eyes locked on her, unseeing, almost as if he was blind.

"Ah do declar-ah," Gussie said. "That's much bettah." She stretched, showing off her breasts to their best advantage. That usually did it.

"Mama?" Jack Hastings shot his head from side to side as if he was looking for her.

"Honey, I'm right here! I mean heah!"

"Mama, where are you? Where are you?"

Jeez, this guy's weird. "Look, Jack, what in Hades is going on?"

"Mama?"

"Shut up!"

"The squirrel, mama! The squirrel!"

"Now look, mister, I don't mind doing some strange things, like taking it up the ass, but this is too bizarre for me! Either shove it up me or pay and get out!" Gussie folded her arms on her naked chest.

"But the plantation!" he said desperately. Jack Hastings grabbed her boots. "Please, mama! I'm not ready to leave you yet!"

"No!" She kicked him away and picked up his pants. Three dollar bills were folded together in the front right pocket of the man's worn Levi's. Gussie tucked the money under her pillow and sat on it. "You just used up all your time, honey. See you later."

"Come on, mama!" Jack rose to his knees. He held out his hands to her.

Gussie shook her head. "No way! I can't do it! No more mama, no more pecan pie, no more plantation and no more marigolds!"

Jack Hastings winced. "Magnolias!"

"Whatever!"

"Go ahead and put on your dress, Maddie," Vincent Vandermeer said.

She sighed. "I knew this would happen!" She started for the closet.

"No, the red one!" He pointed to the dress she'd worn earlier that day, mounds of stiff taffeta.

She looked at him.

"No sense in dirtying up another one of those expensive do-dads!"

"Okay. What about my others?" She pointed to

her underthings.

"No time for that," Spur said. "Just hurry!"

He leaned against the door, feeling the man's holster pressing against his hips. "Pretty good idea, using her," he said to Vincent, who sat on the bed, hands folded on his knees. "Your biggest mistake was coming into this town."

"I know that now. Have to rub it in?"

Maddie had made herself as decent as she could. She turned around, showing Spur a slice of bare skin between the unbuttoned flaps. "Would you help a girl out?" she asked sweetly.

"No. Why don't you have your *father* help you?"

"Oh, alright. Come on, Vincent."

The man rose and walked to her.

"Turn sideways and don't try anything, girl!" Spur said.

The man dutifully fastened the buttons into their cloth slots. Spur didn't believe the man had given up. He'd try something, sometime. And so would the girl.

"How old is she anyway, Vincent?"

"Eighteen."

"Uh-huh. And how old was she the first time you—"

"Eighteen!" The 50-year-old man fumbled with the buttons. "I've only known this paragon of virtue for six months. Six months of heaven and hell!" He finished the last one.

"Let's go."

Spur made Vincent lead the way, keeping the girl on a short leash. "You try anything and I'll shoot you," he whispered.

The girl nodded and walked down the stairs.

They didn't give him any trouble as they went to Henry's Livery stable. There Spur rented a serviceable buckboard and two rested horses to pull it. When it came time to talk money, Vincent Vandermeer—Spur had finally learned his last name—pulled a new 20-dollar bill from his pocket. McCoy quickly snatched it from the man's hands and paid Henry with good circulated currency.

Soon they were bouncing out of town. The sun was two hours down from noon in the sky. He made Vincent handle the reins with Maddie sitting beside him. Spur rode in the back seat, keeping his Colt trained on the man's back.

Two cowboys on horseback approached them on the trail. "Keep your mouth shut, sweetheart," he said to Maddie. She dutifully did so as they waved and passed on by.

They ate dust for a while, moving through the brown cloud that the horses had kicked up. It must not have rained in Quintoch for quite a while, judging from the haze that filled the air.

Maddie started sneezing. "Achoo. Achoo. Excuse me."

"Stop that, Maddie."

She did. "Vincent, there must be some way we can get out of this."

"Hey, lawman, what're your plans for us after we give you the money?"

"Have the county sheriff lock you up. I'm sure you'll get a fair trial." Spur ignored the rumbling in his stomach. He sure could have used the lunch Annabelle promised him hours ago.

"Trial? All we did was take a few lousy bucks!"

Maddie said.

"Twenty-five thousand, to be exact."

"So? What's the big deal?" Maddie asked. "We're giving it back."

Spur glanced at the back of her head. "That's right. It'll look good. Maybe the judge'll take that into account, as well as your, uh, tender years, Maddie."

"But what about Vincent?"

"I couldn't say."

"Will you two shut your mouths?" Vincent said. "Just drive."

They rode in silence. A half hour later Spur saw a ranch to the south. A windmill, half its vanes torn off, flapped from side to side in the light breeze. The buckboard continued on down the trail.

Vincent looked over his shoulder at Spur and shrugged. "So I lied."

"I figured."

Ten minutes later eight horseshoes bit into the sandy soil. Vincent drove them out onto the prairie, past clumps of yellow and white flowers. Spur saw the clean tracks that showed someone else had recently been here.

"You better be taking me to the money," Spur warned him.

"I am. Believe me! And it'll be a relief to get Maddie off my hands! Even jail's better than her!"

"That's so rude! Vincent, you oaf!" She slapped him.

"Cut it out!"

The horseshoe prints tracked back near a clump of straggly trees. Vincent reined in the beasts and sighed. "This is it. This is where I hid the money."

Keeping his Colt trained on the man's back, Spur surveyed the ground. Darker soil was spilled onto the lighter top layer of dirt. Someone had moved it. Maybe Vincent was telling him the truth.

McCoy jumped out and stood beside the buckboard. "Okay. Out. Both of you!" he barked.

Vincent tried to hand the reins to him. Spur waved him off with his weapon so the man dropped them and stepped onto the ground. Maddie huffed her way out at the same time.

"Dig, Vincent! Use your hands, since we didn't bring a shovel!"

The man laughed. "Don't need one. It's right there in those trees, between their trunks. I found a mighty fine place to hide it. You'd never think there was anything in there if you didn't know."

Spur looked. The slender trunks formed a dense jungle. Inside, it was dark and there seemed to be plenty of room. But he didn't like it.

"Okay. Take it out and let's get going."

Vincent hesitated. "I'd rather not do that."

"Why not?"

The man looked at Maddie and shrugged.

"Then we'll have her do it!" He motioned her over to the clump of cottonwoods with his revolver. "Go on, Maddie, get the money."

"No, Maddie! I—ah—" He bent down and handed her a dead tree trunk. "Shove this in there first!"

"Why, Vincent?"

"Girl, just do it!"

Spur watched her. Maddie clutched the thick

branch. "Lord, this thing's heavy!" She swallowed hard and poked it into the dark opening. "You put a snake in there or something?"

"Or something."

Two metallic clanks sounded from the trees. Maddie yelled and dropped the stick.

Vincent sighed. "It's okay. Pull it out now."

The girl tugged on the branch, revealing two bear-traps. Their shiny jaws had nearly bitten through the four-inch-thick wood.

"Nice, Vincent. Not very original, but effective." Spur said. "Get the bags!"

Maddie bent down.

"Not you, him! Come on, Vandermeer!"

The girl stepped back. Vincent knelt beside the trunks, pushed away the deadly traps and reached into the pocket formed by the trees.

"Well?" Spur asked.

"I'm looking." He scrunched up his face, moving his arm back and forth.

"I'm warning you, Vincent!"

"Ah. There they are!" He hauled out one bag and sat it on the dirt.

Spur relaxed as the next three emerged from their hiding place. The large canvas bags were stuffed so full the man had barely gotten them tied shut. Vincent looked up at him. "Well? What now?"

McCoy blew out his breath. It was almost over. "Put them in the buckboard. You and Maddie have an appointment with Sheriff Andrews." Spur glanced toward her. The 18-year-old girl was fumbling with her skirt.

"What's wrong, Maddie?" Spur asked.

She smiled up at him. "Nothing's wrong—with me."

"Maddie!" her partner called.

"Vincent! Use your gun!"

Spur turned toward the man. In that instant an explosion rocked the air. Hot lead tore into his left shoulder. The searing metal burned a hole in his flesh, ripped through veins and grazed muscles before it blasted out the other side.

Stunned, Spur looked at the girl. She smiled and showed him her derringer as Vincent tackled him, grabbing for his Colt .45.

CHAPTER ELEVEN

Vincent Vandermeer knocked the Colt from Spur's hand. The Secret Service agent ignored the fire burning in his torn shoulder and elbowed Vincent's midsection. The man backed up, doubled over in pain. Spur scrambled for the gun.

"Hurry up and kill him!" Maddie said.

Vandermeer launched his body from the sand and slammed down on top of Spur's revolver. McCoy lunged for him. Vincent rolled onto his back and threw the Colt to Maddie.

His shoulder wouldn't work properly. The burn turned to a cold numbness as shock set into his bullet pierced flesh. Spur shook his head and turned toward the girl. Maddie aimed at his heart, gripping the Colt .45 with both hands.

"Kill him!" Vincent said.

She laughed. "No, he's too cute. Just beat him up and let's get the hell outa here!"

"Damn you!"

The man slugged Spur's wounded left shoulder. It exploded in pain. He groaned in renewed agony and twisted around to face his attacker. Spur got off one solid punch to the jaw but Vincent easily recovered and slammed his fist into McCoy's oozing wound.

Pain blinded him. He couldn't block it out. It slammed into his brain, disorienting him. McCoy stumbled around, struggling to regain his senses.

"Do it!" Vincent yelled.

Something hard crashed down on his skull. Spur groaned and dropped to his knees, groggy, aching, every nerve in his body screaming.

"Again!"

Another solid whack. He slumped to the hot dirt. His vision blurred.

Then he saw nothing at all.

Sand coated his lips. The sun burned down on him. Spur coughed, wiped his lips and sat up. He felt the big lump on his head and realized he wasn't wearing his hat.

They'd gone, left him there to die. The memories of those few tense moments jolted Spur back to reality. He grabbed his hat and looked around. Vincent and Maddie had taken the money, his revolver and the buckboard. He'd have to walk.

He didn't know how far it was. They'd probably driven for about a half hour. Maybe a few miles. He trudged along the trail. It was covered with so much loose dirt that his feet sank to the ankles as he pushed ahead. Thirsty, well aware of the dull ache in his shoulder, Spur walked back to town.

He had to get his wound patched up. Rent a horse. Buy a rifle. Get those damn thieves!

The sun was much lower in the horizon by the time he straggled into Quintoch. No one noticed him as they bustled about their business. Spur McCoy headed for the white house he'd noticed earlier. He hoped the doctor/barber was still there.

The door was open. A pudgy man dressed in striped pants and an open-collared shirt looked at him.

"Gunshot wound? Don't see many of those around here," he said cheerily.

"Just plug the leak. I got work to do." Spur slumped on the chair the doctor motioned him toward.

"Okay, okay. You should rest until at least tomorrow, but I got a feeling you won't."

The doctor removed Spur's shirt and inspected the wound. "Pretty clean," he said, leaning over him. "Went through high up. No major damage." He grabbed a small bottle.

Spur grunted as the whiskey seared his exposed flesh.

"Where'd you get this hole? How'd it happen? No shootings in town today, was there?"

He winced. "No. Just do it!"

"Okay, okay!"

The plump man wrapped a bandage around Spur's shoulder and tied the ends tightly together. "That should keep you in good shape. But don't do any wrestlin'. You hear?"

"Yeah." Spur gave the man a dollar and headed for the livery stable.

Ten minutes later he'd bought an old Navy revolver, ammo and two hanks of rope. He rode out of town, heading back for the place where Vincent had burried the money.

He felt pretty good, all things considered. The

buckboard's tracks leading east were clear but he didn't see a second set that indicated Vincent and Maddie had gone back to town. They were out there—somewhere.

He rode west on his rented horse for another ten minutes. "Whoa!"

The horse stopped and looked around, bored.

The flat impression of the buckboard's wheels headed toward him and veered off to the north.

North, Spur thought. The train?

He kicked the mare's flanks, jolting her into a gallop. The bare ground flew by as he followed the fresh ruts. They were probably going to try to stop the train somehow, he thought, and remembered the sight of the smiling young girl seconds after she'd shot him in the shoulder.

What a pair they were.

A line of trees up ahead showed the path of a small stream. He splashed across it. The horse was eager to drink but Spur couldn't take the time. "Soon, girl," he said.

The long, monotonous railroad tracks stretched out before him, fading into the distance on the flat prairie. Vincent and Maddie weren't in sight.

Cursing, he urged his horse to a fast walk. Not many features broke up the terrain. Clumps of trees and waist-high bushes grew sparsely. But he saw the remains of an abandoned house about a mile away.

It sat near the tracks—on his side. The perfect place for the two of them to wait for the train. Spur galloped up to it for a half mile and slowed his horse to a walk.

The sod house had long ago lost its roof to the

blinding sun, wind and rain, but its walls were seven feet high. He pulled out his rifle and held it ready with his right hand, keeping the reins in his left.

The horse's subtle movements made his shoulder complain but he blocked out those feelings. He had too many other things to think about.

Spur warily approached the old house.

"It'll never come."

It was Maddie's voice.

"Yes, it will. I'm pretty sure I remember what the conductor said. Should pass by here before dark."

They were on the other side of the house. He quietly rode up to it and dismounted. Spur tied the reins to a crumbled brick and checked his revolver one last time. Fully loaded.

"Land sakes, Vincent, can't you keep your hands to yourself?"

Spur padded along the far wall.

"Not with you lookin' so pretty, my dear."

"Vincent, not now!"

"Come on, you little cutie! Didn't I make you a rich woman? Look at all the money!"

He heard the sounds of boots shuffling in the dirt. Spur waited.

"Oh, all right." Maddie's voice was resigned.

"That's the spirit! Now you just let me eat this for a while."

Spur turned the corner. The side wall was shorter. He inched along it, rifle ready, slowly working his way toward them.

"Ouch! You bit me!"

"Grrrrr!"

He cleared the wall and stepped past it. Vincent Vandermeer's face was inside the girl's dress. She leaned against the sod bricks, enjoying his ministrations.

Spur fired over their heads. Vincent stumbled back, spit drooling from his lips.

"Damnit!" Maddie screamed.

Vincent grabbed the Colt stuck down his pants. Spur peeled off a shot with his Navy revolver. The slug slammed into Vandermeer's arm, ripping, tearing into his flesh. The man screamed and dropped his weapon.

"Goddamn!"

Maddie bent toward the Colt.

"Don't, girl," he spat. "Unless you wanna be next!"

The girl shook her head and straightened up. "Whatever you say."

"You shot my firing arm!" Vincent said, rubbing the bloody wound.

"Be glad I didn't kill you!"

They'd set the buckboard across the tracks, probably hoping to stop the train, give them some story and hop on. The four large money bags sat on the ground near its rear wheels.

"Planning on going somewhere?" Spur asked.

Maddie clenched her fists. "I knew this wouldn't work! I knew it the minute I—"

"Shut your mouth, girl!" Vincent yelled. He rubbed his wound, his face twisted with pain.

Spur stared at Maddie. "Got any more surprises in your dress? Where's your derringer?"

She sighed and reached into her voluminous skirt.

"Gently—gently pull it out and throw it to me. If you try anything you'll wish you hadn't."

Maddie extracted the tiny gun and tossed it to him.

"Kick my revolver over here. Now!"

She frowned and stabbed her boot at the downed weapon. It skittered two feet on the sand.

"Farther!"

Maddie's next attempt sent it behind him. "Good girl," he said sarcastically.

"Damnit! It hurts!"

"Yeah." Spur grabbed the Colt and stuck it into his empty holster. "Walk to the other side of the house. Both of you!"

The despondent pair did as they were told. Spur followed them closely, switching his aim from one to the other. The horse stood patiently in the shade.

"Alright, Maddie. You should enjoy this. Tie him up!" He threw a coil of rope at her.

"Gladly!" She caught it and set to work. "I never done anything like this before."

Spur guided her. The girl worked with gusto. Her skirt flew around her as she wrapped the rope around Vincent Vandermeer's wrists.

"I told you all along!" Maddie said to him.

He closed his eyes. The dark stain on his right arm slowly spread out. "Hurry up, Maddie!" he yelled. "I'm bleeding to death!"

"Come on, Vincent, you've cut yourself worse'n that shaving in the morning!"

Finished, she stepped back, almost proud of her work. Spur examined the knots. They seemed fine.

"Now it's your turn."

Spur bound the girl's wrists. He helped both of

them into the back seat of the buckboard. Then he hauled the money sacks into it as well, tied his rented horse to its rear and set off for Quintoch.

"I'm never going to take another train ride with you!" Maddie said.

"Shut up!"

"And you're a lousy father!"

An hour later Spur spotted Deputy Watson walking into the sheriff's office just as he was driving up to it. "Watson! Get Andrews out here! Now!"

"Okay!"

The man disappeared. Sheriff Andrews came out and stared at him. "What's this all about?"

"I got two for you," he said, pointing to the man and woman on the front seat. "They robbed the Kansas Pacific." He lowered his voice. "I have the money too. Lock 'em up!"

"Okay, okay."

Andrews and his deputy hauled the thieves into the jail. "You come by later and tell me all the details."

"Will do."

Spur drove the Quintoch County Bank. He hauled the four bags inside and watched as the president placed them in the vault. Once they were safely stashed there he dropped off the horse and the buckboard and went to the telegraph office. He wired a short message to General Halleck saying they'd been caught and the money recovered. Exhausted, he trudged over to Annabelle's house.

It was just getting dark as he knocked on the

door. He was looking forward to some home cooking.

The young woman opened the door and peered out at him. He felt better just seeing her. Annabelle was the prettiest woman for miles around.

"Sorry, drummer; I don't wanna buy anything." She started to close it.

Spur grabbed her wrist. Annabelle giggled and pulled him inside. She looked at the blood stain that plainly showed on his shirt.

"You're hurt! What have you been doing?" she asked with genuine concern.

"Business. It's fine; got it patched up. But I'd kill for supper."

Annabelle smiled. "Only if you promise you won't run out on me again."

He grinned. "I promise."

"Okay. I was just going to start cooking. Why don't I heat some water so you can take a bath?" She wrinkled up her nose. "Think you could use one."

"Okay. Won't you join me?"

Annabelle laughed. "It's too small. Besides, I have some cooking to do."

Soon Spur was luxuriating in an iron-clawed tub of sudsy water. He kept his shoulder high and dry but scrubbed the rest of his hide, freshening it for the lovely lady who hummed as she chopped, sliced and cooked in the kitchen two doors away.

Scrubbing trail dirt and sweat off his body, Spur remembered the Quintoch killings. He'd taken care of the train thieves but his job wasn't done yet.

The washroom door opened. Spur turned toward it.

"Sheriff, Sheriff Andrews!" he blurted.

CHAPTER TWELVE

Jonathan Andrews laughed as Spur sloshed around in the tub. "Relax, McCoy." He grinned.

"Well, okay." He sat upright in the sudsy water.

"I know all about you and Annabelle. Just wanted to stop by and say that the two you brought me are safe and sound. The man looks like he's ready to kill the girl and vicey-versa."

"I see." Spur relaxed. "That's good to know."

He shrugged. "What can I say about what I did to you? It was stupid. Sorry I locked you up."

"No problem." Spur stared at him. "You really don't mind my being here? Taking a bath, getting ready for your daughter?"

"Hell no!"

"You sure are one hell of a father, Sheriff Andrews."

He laughed. "And she's one hell of a girl. That's why I don't care if you fool with her. I don't want her seeing the idiots that come around here all the time." He winked. "Better be getting back to work. Old Missy Forster found her buggy missing. She swears it's been stolen, but she always forgets where she's left it. Enjoy yourself!"

Spur shook his head as the sheriff closed the door.

Soon he was digging into Annabelle's cooking. She sat watching him, amused. Spur didn't waste time talking. He just ate.

The fried chicken was scrumptious. He wolfed down four pieces, had two helpings of the peas and carrots and four cups of coffee. When she showed him the chocolate cake Spur nearly fell off his chair.

"You're a fine woman, Annabelle!" he said, watching the thick slice fall onto his plate. Nearly an inch of fudgy frosting covered the dessert. He ate it slowly, savoring every rich morsel of her handiwork.

"You like it?" she asked.

He tried to answer her with his mouth full. Annabelle watched him in amusement.

When he'd finished, Spur pushed back from the table and slapped his belly. "Best meal I've had in years!" he said. "Now, come on over here!"

Annabelle went to him and wiped a chocolate smudge from his lower lip. "Still have room for me?"

"You can bet on it."

They went to her bedroom—a confection of lacy pink curtains, antique dolls and even a few books. Annabelle's bed was a huge canopied contraption.

"Looks like a man could get lost in there," Spur said.

"Not when I'm around."

They undressed each other, throwing off various

pieces of clothing, eager to see each other's naked body. Stripped to the skin, Spur rubbed his bandaged shoulder and watched as Annabelle lowered her bloomers. She was as beautiful as he remembered—smooth skin, firm breasts, curved hips, a flat stomach and the erotic patch of hair between her thighs. And, for the moment, she was his.

"Jesus, you're incredible!"

"Come on, Spur!" She banged into him, sending Spur sprawling onto the mattresses. He groaned as his shoulder hit the quilts.

"Hey! Take it easy on me. I'm a wounded man. Remember?"

"Oh, I'm sorry." Annabelle kissed the bandage. "Is that better?"

"Yeah. Feels better all over." He took her hand and moved it between his legs. Spur smiled as she gripped him, wrapping her soft fingers around his awakening penis.

"That's nice," Annabelle said. She stuck her tongue in his ear.

"Oh, girl!"

Her hand moved up and down, hardening him. Spur gritted his teeth and gently pushed the woman onto her back. He fit his knees between her legs and gazed down at her.

"Annabelle, you really are—"

She touched his lips. "Don't talk, Spur. Not now. We have better things to do!"

"Right!"

McCoy nodded and bent down. She squealed at the hot contact of his tongue on her left breast. He licked around her nipple, rousing it until it stood up. Groaning, he pushed her breast into his mouth and sucked.

It was delicious, Spur thought as he feasted on the globe of soft flesh. He slipped it out and attacked the other one, chewing lightly on her nipple until Annabelle was squirming beneath him.

"Do it, Spur!" She said. "You make 'em feel so good!" Annabelle grabbed his head and moved it back and forth between her breasts, urging him to satisfy her desires.

He looked up at her. "Just tell me if you don't like it, Annabelle."

A laugh spilled out of her throat. "And you tell me if this isn't your cup of tea!"

The woman scrambled out from under him and turned around so that her head was at his crotch. Surprised, Spur looked at her lovely bush. He knew what was coming. He knew that any second she was going to—

"Ohhh. Oh! God, Annabelle!"

Her mouth was warm and fluid. She worked him over, bobbing up and down, taking him, taking all of him in her lust-crazed heat.

"Jesus!" Spur looked down to watch her happily sucking away, then moaned and burried his head between her legs. He spread her lips and tongued her delicate opening. The musky taste exploded on his tongue. Spur lapped at her clitoris, stabbing his tongue against it, banging it back and forth and enjoying her grunts. His moustache meshed with her pubic hair as he ate.

They happily licked and sucked each other, forgetting everything else, sinking into a world of sex. Annabelle used her throat incessantly, taking him to the hilt again and again. The pleasure increased within him. Soon Spur felt the tightness in his testicles, the danger signs of too much excitement too fast. He started to lose control.

She moved faster.

"Maybe you better stop that!" He gently pulled her head away.

"Okay!" She wiped her lips and gasped for breath. "Do it to me, Spur McCoy. Do it!"

He crossed his arms, grabbed her waist and flipped her around on the bed. Annabelle sighed as she sank into the quilts. She spread her legs and reached up to him.

"Gimme gimme gimme!" she said.

He got into position and thrust forward, sinking into her liquid fire. Spur grunted at the tight penetration. He pushed deeper and deeper until she'd taken every thick inch.

Annabelle flopped around on the bed as he transferred his weight to her. Their bodies were connected. Spur felt her breasts crush against his chest. Kissing her sucking lips, he withdrew and pushed.

He wanted to go slow. He wanted to stretch out their pleasure. He wanted to give her orgasm after orgasm before his last, final drives into her body. But it didn't work out that way.

Spur was too excited by the woman. He pumped between her smooth thighs. Their hip bones banged together as he pleasured Annabelle. She broke the kiss, turned her head to the side and gasped at his masculine thrusts.

"Oh hell, Spur; ram me!" Her voice was soft.

"What was that, Annabelle?" He slowed down. "What did you say?" All he could see was the fire in her eyes.

"Ram me."

"Louder!"

"Damnit, Spur; ram me!"

He pulled out to the limit and slammed into her. Annabelle groaned as their hips slapped together. She bit his neck.

He grimaced and rode higher into her, rubbing his erection against her clitoris. Annabelle shivered at the intensified sensations coursing through her body. Her hands locked around his waist. She met his thrusts, pushing her hips toward him, impaling herself on his penis.

"Oh. Oh. Oh!"

Harder. Faster.

Annabelle exploded. She shook through a tremendous release, lips wide, huffing and moaning. Her fingernails drove into his back, urging him as her world melted.

Spur stared down at the orgasming woman. The lust on her face, the intensity of her passion aroused him even further. He drove blindly into her. He was too close but he didn't care. He bucked and arched his back.

McCoy shut his eyes and roared as his seed rushed into her. His body spasmed, jerked backward with each spurting thrust. His release went on and on. Annabelle's groans mixed with his own as Spur drained himself deep inside her body.

He ejaculated one last time, grunting at the incredible feeling, then collapsed into a sweating heap on top of the woman.

His brain fried from the sex, McCoy was dimly aware of Annabelle panting beneath him. He grabbed her shoulders and pressed his lips to hers, thrusting his wet tongue into her mouth until they both had to stop for breath.

"Spur McCoy," Annabelle said dreamily between gasps. "I'll—I'll cook for you every day."

He kissed her again and drifted off into a wonderland of soft feminine skin.

A half hour later, rested, refreshed from their exertions, Spur and Annabelle slowly dressed. She looked at him as he hauled up his pants.

"Let me guess—I'm not the first woman you've ever bedded." Her eyes twinkled.

"You're right about that. But you're the best."

Annabelle smiled. "Really?"

"Really."

She looked at the rug. "Can't—can't you stay the night? We could have lots of fun together. We could do it again and again and again!"

"Sorry, Belle. I have work to do."

"Belle. No one's called me that since I was a little girl." She reached behind her and buttoned up her dress. "I like hearing it from you."

"I sure like saying it—Belle." Spur stuffed his feet into his boots and grabbed his hat. "I'll be seeing you again." He tenderly looked at the woman.

Her face was dark. "You mean before you leave?"

"Yeah."

Annabelle finished the buttons and turned fully to him, hands pressed against the smooth material that covered her stomach. "And when's that?"

Spur smiled. "Not until I find the man who's been doing all the hanging in this town."

She shivered. "I don't know if I want to wish you good luck or not."

He kissed her, a lingering, tongue-lashing kiss. With difficulty, Spur pulled his head from hers. "I know. Thanks for dinner—and everything."

Annabelle nodded as he walked to the bedroom door.

Don't turn around, Spur told himself as he went through the big house toward the entrance. He heard her feet pattering along the floorboards.

"Spur!" Annabelle called, her voice breathy.

"Yes?"

She hesitated, so he looked at her.

The woman's lower lip trembled. "Hell." She forced a smile. "Good luck."

"Thanks."

It was dark outside. Light showed through thousands of panes of glass. Figures moved inside the buildings that lined Oak Street. So many people. And he wasn't any closer to finding his man.

Spur shook off the lethargy that had invaded him ever since he'd finished with the young woman. He looked down the long avenue that led to Main Street. Where was that murdering bastard?

There was one place to start looking again. The Prairie King Saloon. Maybe he'd talk to the remnants of the 14th Regiment.

The crisp night air awakened him as he strolled along the dust. Spur stretched his arms, lifting them high above his head and locked his hands around his wrists.

He entered Main Street and turned toward the saloon, passing drunken cowboys, rich ranchers, a few fancy ladies scurrying to work, women with screaming babies, and fresh-faced young couples enjoying the evening together.

Spur surveyed every face, looking for the visage of a killer as he made his way through all the humanity. He didn't know how he'd recognize it or even if he could. But he'd try.

Something hard and cold pressed against his back.

"Don't think about going nowhere!" a low voice said.

CHAPTER THIRTEEN

Spur froze. The revolver's muzzle dug into his lower back. Alcoholic breath blasted around his head.

"I thought things like this didn't happen in Quintoch," he said wryly.

"Shut up! How much money you got?" his attacker said. The voice was grave.

"Why? You interested in a loan?"

"Don't mess around!" The barrel nudged against him. "I gotta get another drink and I'm flat broke. How much you got on you?"

"Check for yourself. My moneyfold's in my front pocket. The right pocket."

"No. You pull it out and hand it over!"

Spur was silent.

"Damn you! Do it!"

"You want it so much—you go for it." Spur was playing with him. This wasn't an experienced, cool thief. And he wasn't about to get his money.

"Well, well...." The man thought about it. "Awright."

The pressure eased on his spine. Spur elbowed his unseen attacker's ribs and wrestled the revolver from his right hand. He spun and smashed his boot into the man's groin. The chunky man howled and doubled over in pain.

"Thanks for the weapon." Spur pushed it into his pants.

"Damnit!" The would-be thief lifted his head. "Damn you!"

McCoy plowed his fist into the man's jaw, sending him reeling back.

"Come on; you've got an appointment."

Spur grabbed the man's belt and hauled him a half block down to the sheriff's office. Jonathan Andrews nearly spit up his coffee as he looked at him.

"Thought you were with my daughter!" he said.

"Was. This joker tried to rob me." Spur pushed the groaning man to the ground. He landed on his butt and shook his head.

"Sam? Sam Feingold?"

"Take care of him, would you? I've got something that needs my fullest attention."

"Sure, sure McCoy." The sheriff stared down at Feingold, shaking his head. "Mighty big crime wave we're having."

"Right."

"Well, come on, Sam. Sleep it off."

Spur grunted and walked outside. Just what he needed—more distractions. But nothing could distract him from his mission.

He got a whiskey in the Prairie King Saloon and glanced at the back tables. Just two men sat there. He recognized one of them—Mike Hughes, the one who'd been talking about being scared the night of Lester Field's murder. The one who'd knocked on the sheriff's door that night. The one with the nervous tic below his bushy eyebrows.

McCoy frowned. Could be. It just could be. Maybe the man couldn't stop himself. Maybe he had to kill to root out some old, ugly problem that had been brewing in his gut since the war.

He walked over to the table.

"Damnit, where's Feingold?" Hughes said. He flipped off his hat and mopped his sweating forehead.

"Easy, Hughes. You know sometimes he's late getting away from his wife."

Hughes fidgeted with his bottle. "Never been this late before."

"You lookin' for Sam Feingold?" Spur said.

Hughes turned to him. "Who wants to know?"

McCoy smiled. "He's at Sheriff Andrews' little hotel. Your friend got drunk and tried to take my money."

Hughes rose to unsteady feet. "You accusin' my friend—"

"Calm down, Hughes!" the other man said.

"Don't worry," Spur said. "No one got hurt. He's sleeping it off, nice and safe in the jail."

Mike Hughes slumped into the chair. "Well—well" he stammered.

"So he's okay. Nothing's happened to him."

"Obliged for that. I'm 'Ketch' Ketcham," the smaller man said. "Ol' Hughes here's been pissin' in his pants."

"I just don't wanna bury Feingold too!"

"Heard there's been some trouble in this town."

Spur slid easily into a chair at the table with the men. "Hangings, wasn't it?"

Hughes sucked down a swallow. "Yeah." He wiped his chin. "Four of 'em. All my friends. All dead. There's only three of us left."

Spur turned to Ketch as if he needed an explanation. "We wuz all together during the War."

"I see. You think someone's still fighting that war against you boys?"

"Hell, I don't know." Ketch drummed his fingers on the table.

"Ketcham here thinks it's co—co-" He scratched his head. "What'd you say?"

Ketch weakly smiled. "Coincidence."

"Right. But it ain't. They're all our friends. Andrews ain't done a damn thing about it!"

Spur could see the anger and fear inside the man. He was convinced that neither Hughes nor Ketcham had anything to do with the hangings. It was truly and outside party. "Guess there's not much to go on. A town this size—"

"Blast this town!" Hughes downed the last of his whiskey and hurled the bottle onto the floor. He didn't wince as it smashed into a fine layer of sparkling crystals. "I'm gonna leave. Just pick up and go somewhere else."

"Might be a good idea," Spur said.

Ketcham frowned. "He's been saying that for a week now. I'm starting to believe him. But that won't do nothing, Hughes! If someone is after us—all of us—he'll track us down. No matter where we go."

Hughes put his head on the table and banged the boards with both fists. "I know! I know!"

"Nice talking with you," Spur said as the man went into near-hysterics. He tipped his hat and took his drink to the bar for a refill.

"Hey, got something to tell you!"

It was Gussie Granger, wearing an even tighter, smaller lime green dress that covered less of her than ever.

"Yeah? What is it?"

She shook her head. "Not here! Come on!"

He was surprised when the whore dragged him outside onto the front porch. At least she didn't expect him to screw her, Spur thought.

"Okay." He leaned against the pillar five feet from the front door.

"How much'll you pay?" she eagerly asked, her face glowing in the diffused light seeping from the saloon.

"What's this all about, Gussie?"

"Sheriff Andrews tole me all about what you're really doing here. You're not looking to start a saloon!"

He sighed. "I see. So you know something about the hangings?"

She nodded, then shook her head. "Hell, I don't know. It could be." Gussie lifted her eyebrows.

It was worth a gamble. "Five dollars."

"Jack Hastings. Know him?"

Spur shook his head.

"He works at the hardware store. A young 'un. He's the one who came to see me the other day and didn't do nothing to me. Remember I tole you about him?"

Spur nodded.

"Well, he saw me today—middle of the

afternoon! Woke me up and everything. Said he was supposed to be eating lunch." Gussie fanned her ample bosom. "That boy's weird, I tell you! He made me do all kinds of things—but not like you might think." She paused for effect.

"Go on," Spur said.

"Made me pretend I was his mother, living on the plantation. Made me rattle on about the magnolias, pecan pies and the squirrels." Gussie shook her head. "He never tole me what it was all about, but I got a sneaking suspicion it's something about his mother. I think she's dead."

Spur frowned. He vaguely recalled the man in the hardware store. "How old would you say he was?"

Gussie shrugged. "I don't know. Twenty. Twenty-one. A babe in arms, 'cept that's the last place I had him. It's something to do with the War. He must've been a little tyke back then."

His mind churned, digesting the bits of information. Jack Hastings. He's from the South. "Did he say where you were supposed to be during all this?"

She rolled her eyes. "Georgia. Somewhere near Atlanta."

He gave her a five dollar bill. "Thanks, Gussie. You've made me a happy man."

"I have?"

"You have. Now get on back in there and earn some more money so you can go on home!"

"Yes sir!"

He slapped her behind as she scooted inside.

Jack Hastings sat alone in his house. Though the

place was small it was crammed with silver candlesticks, broken furniture, charred paintings and every other piece of his home he'd been able to recover after the Northerners had ransacked it.

When the bluebellies had left, Jack had wandered around the burned mansion for two days. No one came near; no one came to help. He slept in trees and ate whatever food he could find in the cookhouse. Once in a while he forgot and ended up near the porch. The boy had tried to avoid seeing his dead parents but he couldn't push them out of his mind. He couldn't pretend nothing had happened.

Everything had happened. All at once the life he'd known had been shattered. His father and mother lay cooking in the sunlight. Even his pet pony, the one his father had sent all the way to England for, had disappeared. He waited and cried and waited.

Finally an aunt of his from Augusta rattled up in a rickety wagon. Four other men were with her, distant cousins of his, Jack remembered. She'd heard about what had happened and had come to see what was left—if anything. She was surprised to see that Jack was alive and well.

"God was good to you," Aunt Esther had told him. "Now it's time you were good to God."

She'd packed every salvageable item onto the wagon and took the boy to her home—an austere, lonely horror. For six years, until he turned 18, his aunt forced him to be her servant. He washed, painted, scrubbed, waited on her hand and foot. The old biddy had hated her sister, Jack's mother, and she took it all out on him.

One thought kept Jack going during his youth—he would avenge his parents' death. He'd kill the murdering bastards who'd destroyed his whole life.

When he was 17, his aunt suddenly died. Jack had loaded up the memories of his youth into the same old wagon and rode it across the country until he landed in Kansas. He moved from small town to small town, looking for men who fit in with his childhood nightmares.

Hastings finally settled in Quintoch and planned his revenge. He knew about the group of seven ex-14th Regiment soldiers. And a few weeks ago he'd finally started exorcising the pain.

Jack sighed and looked at the cast-iron kettle that his mother used to use for soap-making. He remembered her outside in the back, throwing fat and lye into the monster. He recalled the nose-numbing smell and the harsh results that she used to scrub the rich Georgia soil from his little body.

A knot formed in the back of his head. He squeezed his eyes shut. No, he shouldn't have. He shouldn't have thought about old times. He shouldn't have thought about his mother.

Now it was too late. There were still three more men to go, three men between the pain and the pleasure of revenge.

His head aching, Hastings checked the carton near the door. Out of rope again? Jack sighed. He'd have to get some from the store.

Spur found the gray, blank-windowed store huddled next to the Quintoch County Bank. He didn't figure Jack Hastings would be there at that time of night—it must be around nine—but he might as well check it out.

The street was relatively quiet. This was wild frontier town, most of the locals seemed to take to their beds early. So Spur was surprised when a figure approached the store with a determined gait.

The man walked directly to the door.

"Excuse me. You Jack Hastings?" Spur yelled.

He turned around and regarded McCoy. "Ah—ah yeah, that's me."

"You're not opening the store, are you? I sure could use some ammunition. Someone told me you were the man to see."

"Ah—sure. Just a minute." He pushed his hands into his pockets. "Dang! Hell, I gave the keys back to the owner. Guess not."

Spur shrugged. "Okay, I'll come by in the morning. When you open?"

"Eight."

"Thanks."

Spur turned and moved down the boardwalk. He settled back on a hitching post and casually looked down the street. Jack Hastings walked into the darkness, slamming his fists against his thighs.

He disappeared.

CHAPTER FOURTEEN

Spur hurried down the darkened street after Jack Hastings. He found him again, wandering past a brick house. Hastings was taking his time getting home, McCoy thought, as he faded from shadow to shadow.

Soon the big, opulent houses were in the distance. Hastings kept on walking, rubbing the back of his head. Spur heard the man groaning softly into the night air.

He finally turned a corner and moved down a half-block past small, single-story dwellings. Jack Hastings walked to a squat house and went inside.

Seconds later the glow of kerosene light yellowed the solitary expanse of curtains.

He must be home, Spur thought. He found a comfortable tree to lean against a half-block from Hastings' place and pressed his back against the thick trunk. Might as well watch him for a while.

Jack Hastings seemed harmless enough, not exactly the shooting, killing kind. But then again, the killer had hung the four men.

Rope. Working in a hardware store Hastings certainly had access to plenty of rope. So did most of the other citizens of Quintoch, for that matter. But Gussie's vivid account of Jack Hastings' peculiarities made him wonder. The Civil War. Georgia. A plantation. A possibly dead mother. And the murders of the Kansas 14th Regiment, all of whom had helped bring down the South. Did they all fit together?

Possibly.

Spur yawned and hunched over. The tree was dark; anyone glancing outside wouldn't see him. He settled in for a long night, peering at the small house in the distance. The house that may hold a killer.

Three hours later the light went out. Jack Hastings must have gone to sleep. His knees and back were cramped from the awkward position, so Spur stood and rubbed his eyes.

Hastings might have been planning something that night when he'd met him at the hardware store. Maybe he'd scared the man off.

Spur watched for another hour until well after midnight. Still nothing. No sign of movement, no lamps being lit. Hastings was apparently fast asleep.

You should be too, Spur told himself. Nothing's going to happen here tonight. He just had that feeling. Spur shook his head and walked toward Jack's home, moving slowly. McCoy peered at the tiny structure. It looked grey in the thin moonlight. Weeds had grown up around it save for a patch that led straight from the street to the covered porch. Nothing seemed unusual.

Sighing, Spur walked back to his hotel room. He had a bad feeling about Jack Hastings.

Spur opened his eyes with the dawn. He heard horses and buggies moving in the street below his window. The sounds of Quintoch coming to life roused him. McCoy went to the pitcher and basin and splashed his face. The water stung him with its coolness, washing away the last traces of sleep. Alert and ready for anything, Spur strapped on his holster, put on his boots and hat. He'd just wear his fine shirt, vest and pants. No coat today, he'd decided—too hot for that.

McCoy opened his hotel door and was greeted by Kay Fordham—pointing a rifle at him.

"Kay!" he said. "Watch what you do with that thing!" Spur eased the barrel to the side.

She laughed. "I'm sorry, Spur. I was just gonna knock."

"Uh-huh." He eyed her curiously. "What brings you to my room—with that?"

If she'd been any other woman she would have blushed. As it was, Spur saw a faint tinge of color on her cheeks. "I wanted you to show me—"

"How to use it?" Spur said, blocking the entrance to his room. "You own a rifle and don't know how to shoot?"

"No, no, no. I shot lots of rabbits and things when I was a little girl. My father always wanted a boy. But I don't know how to clean a rifle."

Spur nodded. "Fair enough. But why come to me? You must know lots of other men in town."

Kay bit her lip. "Most of 'em won't talk to me. They won't come near me—afraid I'll turn their wives against them." Kay delicately pushed her left hand against Spur's chest. "Hey, can I come in?"

"Okay." He made room for her.

"Thanks." She barrelled in like she owned the place. "I do want you to tell me what to do with the rifle, but I was also hoping you'd clean me out." Kay Fordham said the words without the slightest hint of coquettry.

"Sorry, woman. I gotta eat some breakfast and go to work. Unless you'd like to cook for me."

She smiled. "Sorry, Spur. I—uh—wouldn't want to hurt my chances later on. My cookery's that bad." She handed him the rifle. "So what do I do?"

He carefully explained the simple procedure to her, telling her how to break it down, what to oil, how to wipe it off and reassemble the rifle. Kay eagerly absorbed every word, nodding every once in a while.

"Got it. Thanks. You're a real pal!"

Spur flinched. "You look like one, but you sure don't talk like a woman."

"I know. There's only one time I act like one." Kay touched his thigh. "You sure?"

"I'm sure." He gave her back her rifle. "I've got to be going. Nice seeing you again, Kay."

"You too."

He walked her down the stairs. Two men hooted as they entered the lobby.

"Lookit that!" a grizzled man said, slapping his knee. "Old Kate-the-freight-train done nagged herself a live one!"

"Hell, Marcus, he won't be breathing long after a

few hours with her." His friend was an earlier version—same beady eyes, same double chin, same jug-handled ears.

Spur looked at Kate.

She straightened her back. "That's just Jim Fletcher and his son. I'm used to it—from them."

"Whoo-whee!" the codger exploded into laughter.

McCoy walked up to the father and son, who sat on a couch near the front desk. "You got a problem, mister?"

Fletcher controlled himself. "Hell no. Looks like you do, though." He poked his son in the ribs.

"That's no way to talk about a la—" Spur bit off the word, sending the two men bouncing up and down on the leather couch with guffaws.

"Spur, it's okay!"

"Now look, Fletcher," McCoy said. "I want you to apologize to Miss Fordham."

"Heh heh. Whew! Apologize to her? I'd as soon kiss Sheriff Andrews!"

"Yeah, or his daughter!" Marcus Fletcher threw in.

Kay Fordham stomped up to them, shaking the rifle in her hand.

"Don't!" Spur said.

She transferred the weapon to her left hand, made a tiny fist and blasted it into Jim Fletcher's jaw. The connection was surprisingly solid. "Shut up!" she screamed.

The man's head jerked back from the blow. He stopped laughing and rubbed his chin.

Kay glared at him, face flushed, panting.

"This means we're married?" he joked as his jaw slowly turned bright red.

"You want more?" She shook her fist at him.

"Alright, alright! Jeez, Kay!" Fletcher said. "Just kidding around! Nothing serious like!"

"Come on, Spur; let's get out of here."

She grabbed his arm and led him out of the hotel. Spur went with her, admiring the woman's spunk. Not many females would have done what she'd just done.

"You probably think I'm some kind of monster," Kay said as they stood on the front porch. She leaned her rifle against her right shoulder.

"No, Kay. I think it's admirable that you showed that man the, ah, error of his ways."

"It was so womanish of me!" Kay shook her head.

"Womanish? You—I—I can't think of many women who would have hit that man. Even if he was saying things like that!"

"Not what I mean," she said. "I lost control. I let myself go like a foolish girl." She moved the rifle to her right hand. "I hope I didn't embarrass you, Spur."

He laughed. "No, not at all, Kay."

"Good." She pecked his cheek. "Guess I'll go home and try to figure out this rifle. Nice seeing you again, Spur."

"Likewise, Miss Fordham." He nodded and turned toward Sheriff Andrews' office.

The suffragette was some kind of woman, though Spur didn't know what kind. If there were just a few more like her they'd carve the west into hospitable land that much faster. But how could the men handle them?

Spur sighed and went into the jail. The sheriff was busy wolfing down a plateful of scrambled eggs, bacon and biscuits. He waved as McCoy sat in the chair opposite his desk.

"Your daughter's cooking?" McCoy asked.

Andrews nodded, chewing. He grabbed a tin cup of coffee and splashed some into his mouth.

"She sure knows her way around a stove." The smells rising from the steaming food made his stomach grumble. He realized he hadn't stopped for breakfast in his hotel's dining room. A whirlwind in feminine form had distracted him.

"What's on your mind, McCoy? Any more train thieves?"

He glanced back at the door to the jail proper. "Nope. You know a Jack Hastings?"

"Hastings. Hastings." Andrews scratched his scalp and chewed half a biscuit. Melted butter dripped down his chin. "I've heard of him," he said, his mouth full.

"Know anything about him?"

Andrews shook his head. "Can't say I do. Never been in any trouble far as I can remember. "Why?"

Spur reached toward the plate. "Do you mind?"

The sheriff smiled and wiped his lips.

"Thanks." The bacon was still warm, and Spur enjoyed its crisp saltiness. "I have a feeling he's up to something. One of the girls at the Prairie King told me a little story about this Jack Hastings. I'll check up on it."

"And you let me know." Another forkful of eggs slid into the sheriff's mouth.

"I will."

Spur went to the hardware store. It wasn't open yet, so he grabbed breakfast at the communal dining table in his hotel. He was alone save for a gun-packing youth who almost looked old enough to shave.

He barely noticed the brown-haired kid as he devoured the food.

"You ever shoot anybody?" the boy asked him.

Startled, Spur looked at him. "Why?"

The boy shrugged. "Just wondering." He fingered the thin hair on his upper lip. "But did you?"

McCoy shrugged. "Yeah. And it isn't fun."

"My daddy's dead. He got hung. Last week." The youth's face was expressionless.

"Sorry to hear that, boy. What's your name?"

"Clemons MacArthur, sir."

"Well, Clemons, I'm gonna find the man who hung your daddy. Don't you worry about that!"

The boy looked down at his plate. "I hope so. Momma took sick and I have to look after the place, coming in here to eat."

Spur finished his meal and glanced at the grandfather clock in the corner. Seven o'clock. An hour to go before the hardware store opened.

The ache in his knees matched that in his head, but Jack Hastings continued kneeling on the floorboards, praying his heart out.

"Yes, mother, I'm doing your will. I've done it to four of them so far."

His face squeezed up. "But mother! I couldn't do it last night! I didn't have any rope! And that man scared me. I coulda been caught. Might've been taken prisoner by the bluebellies or killed."

Jack lifted his head. "What's that? What're you saying, mother?" He sighed. "Well, it's too soon. I can't do it yet!"

He listened to the shrill voice in his head, accusing him, berating him for his lack of faith.

Hastings looked into space, his eyes glazed. "Alright, mother. Tonight. I'll hang another one tonight." He banged his hands against his skull. "Can't you make this headache go away?"

Spur watched the hardware store all morning long. He even went in to buy some ammunition he didn't need, just to see Jack Hastings in the light. The man seemed pleasant enough. Spur confirmed he didn't have a trace of a Southern accent, but a man could do that if he tried hard enough. Lots of former Georgians and Alabamans had lost their former accents since the end of the War.

He checked the stolen money he'd recovered. It was still safe and sound in the Quintoch County Bank. Then he took up his post again, waiting for night, waiting for Jack Hastings to make his move—if any.

It was just getting dark when Spur heard feet shuffling up behind him.

"Mister?"

It was Clemons MacArthur, the youngster he'd eaten breakfast with.

"Yeah?"

The boy looked at his feet, then at Spur's holster.

"My momma says I'm the man of the family now. I have to protect her. So I was wondering if you could teach me how to shoot."

Spur smiled down at him. "Maybe you should learn how."

"I know guns ain't toys and all that," Clemons said. "And I'm a fast learner. My father taught me how to do practically everything else. Now he'll never teach me."

The poor kid, McCoy thought. "I'm real busy right now," he said.

Clemons turned down his mouth. "Okay. I figgered you'd say that."

"But try Sheriff Andrews. He might help you out. In fact, I'll ask him to. How's that?"

"Sure. Thanks, mister!" His eyes shined up at him.

Spur started to feel like a hero. "I'll talk to him today. See you, kid."

"Great!" Clemons ran off.

Two hours later, Jack Hastings walked out of the store and locked it. He had two coils of rope in his right hand. Nothing suspicious about that, McCoy thought, but he followed the man as he walked down the street.

Hastings kept clutching the back of his head, rubbing it. The rope swung back and forth in his arm as he moved. To Spur's surprise Hastings didn't head for home, but turned down a side street. He walked up to the front door of a large house and knocked.

Spur shrank back in the darkened street and watched.

A woman answered it and, reluctantly, it seemed, invited Hastings in. McCoy was too far away to be able to hear what they were saying. The front door closed.

He darted across the street and walked up to the window. Mike Hughes came into view.

"Who the hell's that, Angela?" Hughes asked, arms crossed on his chest. "You invitin' your boyfriends over to the house now? You gonna take him into the bedroom?"

Angela Hughes was calm. "Now, dear, don't get all riled up. This poor man needs help with something or t'other."

Hughes scratched his chin. "Go find someone else!" He turned and walked out of the room.

Mrs. Hughes smiled at Hastings. "I'll try to talk some sense into him."

"Would you let me?" Jack smiled at her and went in through the doorway.

Spur watched the woman circle around on the floor. A dull thud issued from inside the house.

"Mike?" Mrs. Hughes asked. "Are you all right?"

Jack Hastings lunged for her, hammer in hand, the rope coiled around his neck. "He's just fine, Angela."

"What'd you do to him?" She backed away from the man. "What have you done with my husband?"

"Nothing."

"You stay away from me!" she shrieked. Mrs. Hughes grabbed a cobalt blue vase from the mantel. "I'm warning you!"

"Now, now. None of that!" He advanced on her. "That isn't ladylike behavior!"

Angela hurled the vase. It sailed three feet and smashed onto the floor. "Don't hurt me! Please, don't hurt me!" She stared at the hammer.

"Maybe I won't if you keep your mouth shut!" Jack walked up to the terrified woman.

She nodded, eyes wide.

Hastings tied her hands behind her back. He worked quickly, methodically knotting the rope. Jack pushed her into a chair and secured her ankles to the thick oak legs. "You just sit there and have a good rest, hear me?"

"Don't do this!" Angela Hughes said. She broke into sobs. "Leave us alone!"

"I don't wanna do nothing to you. It's your husband, Angela. Your murdering, bastard husband! He's the one I'm gonna kill!"

"No!"

He grabbed a lace doily off the table and stuffed it in her mouth. Hastings pushed it so deep that the woman couldn't spit it out.

"If you scream again I'll kill you too! Maybe if you were from the South I might forgive you. But you're just a goddamn Yankee. So shut up!"

Spur watched the scene with growing unease. He fought off the impulse to rush in and free the woman. He had to catch the man in the act of hanging. That was the only way to connect him with the earlier killings.

"I'll be right back," Jack Hastings said. "And when you see me your husband'll be dead."

Angela struggled against her bonds as Hastings walked into the other room.

Spur moved to the next window. Mike Hughes lay unconscious on the kitchen floor. Hastings whistled as he tied the noose. He hurried through it but soon got a serviceable knot.

"Who said the War was over?" He slipped it over Hughes' head and pulled it tight.

CHAPTER FIFTEEN

His head ached.

Nearly blinded with pain, Jack Hastings opened the door and started hauling the unconscious man out to the woodshed. He'd checked out the small building a few days ago and it seemed perfect. It had an open beam just the right height for his purposes. Sure, it wouldn't be a fast death, but soon Mike Hughes would be dead just the same. Then only two of his parents' murderers would still be alive.

Blood pounded in his brain. He gasped at the intensity of the internal torture and halted. "Soon, mother," he whispered. "Soon you can rest in peace."

He got the man fully out of the kitchen.

Crouched outside the window, Spur watched Jack Hastings prepare for his latest hanging. There was no immediate danger. He'd have to move the still unconscious man.

Sure enough, Hastings dragged Mike Hughes to

the kitchen door and opened it. Spur slid up beside it and waited. Hastings backed out, dragging the man.

He'd seen enough. Spur stepped from the shadows. "Going somewhere, Hastings?"

Jack stumbled and dropped the man's torso. "Who—what're you—"

Mike Hughes groaned. His right arm moved aimlessly in the dirt.

"The War's over, Hastings. It's been over for a long time. Stop fighting it!"

Hastings held his hands toward Spur in earnest. "No! He—he murdered my mother and father! He torched my home! He killed my whole life!"

"Him? This man?" Spur shook his head. "No. You can't be sure of that."

"He did! I'm just finishin' up the job!" He grabbed his head. "Damn, it hurts!"

"Come on, Hastings." Spur gripped him and pushed the man into the house. Once in the parlor he patted the man down. He wasn't armed, just crazy. "Untie the woman!" he said, shoving him toward her.

Angela Hughes, still bound to the chair, looked up at the two men in fear.

"It's okay, Mrs. Hughes," Spur said. "I'm not with him. I'm on your side."

She struggled against her bonds, shaking her head, trying to spit out the doily that gagged her. Spur pulled it out and stroked her hair. "Okay now?"

The redhead gazed at him, then nodded.

"Good. Get to work, Hastings!"

"Damn! Oh, sorry about that, ma'am." He

moved around her and loosened the knots, his face expressionless, distant.

For safety's sake, Spur drew his Colt .45. He glanced toward the kitchen. Just outside Mike Hughes stirred, sat on the bare earth and rubbed his scalp. He looked into the house and saw Spur.

"What—what happened?" he asked.

"What's that around your neck?" Spur asked.

His hands went to it and felt the rope. "God-damn!" Hughes grabbed at it, struggling, finally loosening the knot. Then he threw the noose behind him. "You mean it was Jack Hastings? From the hardware store? He's the killer?" Hughes pushed himself to his feet and stormed into the house.

"Take it easy." Spur turned back to watch the woman's untying.

"Like hell!" Hughes thundered. "That asshole just tried to kill me!"

"You're still alive."

He pushed past McCoy, looked at the man who was busy untying his wife, cursed and ran into the bedroom.

"You about finished?" Spur asked.

"Yes, sir." Hastings pulled the end free. The last knot dissolved and the rope slapped onto the floor.

Angela Hughes stood and moved to the wall, staring in fear at the young man. Her face was pale and tight, her throat bobbed up and down as she nervously swallowed.

"Hughes, get in here!" Spur shouted.

The man appeared, holding his old Army rifle. "It's time you got a taste of your own medicine, Hastings!"

"Michael!" Angela shouted.

"I'm gonna plug that bastard," Hughes said, gripping the weapon with both hands. "If you try'n stop me, mister, I'll shoot your head off, too!"

"Kill him!" Angela viciously shouted. "Kill the son of a bitch!"

"Calm down! Both of you! I'm a federal law enforcement officer," Spur said. "I'm taking this man into custody. If you stop me I'll have you arrested for—"

"Piss on you!" Hughes swung up the rifle and blasted a hole through the wall, ten feet from Hastings.

Angela covered her ears as the explosion reverberated in the parlor. "Kill him!" she screamed.

"That's enough!" Spur tackled Mike Hughes. The two men banged onto the couch, knocked it over and spilled onto the floor. The rifle skittered away from them as Spur grabbed the man's hands.

"Grab the rifle, honey!" Mike yelled.

"Too late for that!" she said. "He's getting away!"

Spur tried to break free but Hughes clutched him with his left hand and vainly tried to punch with his right. Spur rolled on top of him and smashed his fist into Mike's face. He broke from the groaning man and sprang to his feet.

"He's gone and it's all your fault!" Angela screamed. She attacked him, slapping at his face and shoulders.

Spur ignored her, grabbed the rifle and started for the door. The ex-soldier crashed into him.

"I warned you, didn't I?" Hughes said.

McCoy swung around and planted his fist on the

man's chin. The woman screamed as her husband reeled back, lost consciousness and flopped onto the couch.

"You killed him!" she said, rushing to him.

Spur snatched the rifle from his hands. "He'll wake up. Keep him here!"

"I—I—"

He was out the door.

"Mister! That man grabbed the horse out back and rode off that way!"

Spur squinted. The young boy he'd spoken with during breakfast stood beside his own mount.

Clemons patted the horse's rump. "You can borrow her if you want!"

"Thanks, MacArthur. I owe you one!" The kid must have been watching him. Smart boy.

Spur slid onto the saddle and kicked the horse into a gallop. It easily responded and soon he was racing toward the south into the night.

Jack Hastings couldn't have gotten far.

The horse was lazy, he thought. "Come on, girl, faster!" Hastings' stomach was queasy from the pain. His brain felt like someone had driven a hair pin clear through his skull. It pounded in rhythm with the unwilling horse's hooves.

Fast. Faster. Come on!

He didn't know what went wrong. Nothing should have gone wrong! He had him. He'd almost done it when that man showed up. The same one who was there when he tried to get the rope from the store last night. The same one who bought a box of ammo from him that morning. Damn him! He'd been watching him.

Hastings enjoyed the cool air blasting against his face. It seemed to make the pain in his head subside somewhat. It didn't matter anymore. It didn't matter what happened to him. He'd done most of what he'd set out to do.

He looked around him. The moonlight showed a stark, barren landscape. Not much place to hide anyway. He might as well stop and wait for the man who was surely following him.

The image of his dead parents flooded through him. The anguish surged anew through his veins. The years of toil at his aunt's feet sprang into life.

No. Damnit, no!

He jabbed his heels into the horse's flanks. "Move!" he yelled.

Hastings sighed as the horse reluctantly obeyed his command. He never had had much call for the beasts, but this one sure was coming in handy.

He'd get away, somehow. He'd get away and hang the three murdering bluebellies. Then, and only then, would he be free. Even if they killed him for doing his duty he wouldn't mind. He'd die in peace and happily join his mother and father in heaven.

"Faster, girl!" he screamed, fearing he'd hear the sound of a rider behind him.

Spur slowed his horse. No sense in racing in the wrong direction. He couldn't tell if the man had continued on in a straight line, and the night was so dim he couldn't see any details on the earth below him.

He reined in the boy's mount, jumped to the ground and lit a lucifer match. The tracks were there, plain and crisp on the dew-covered earth. Hastings was still heading south. But to where?

Spur continued on, occasionally glimpsing a freshly trampled plant that showed the man's trail.

Jack Hastings was a strange character. Why would he set out to kill another man without bringing along a weapon? Some sort of protection? It didn't make sense, unless it was part of some elaborate revenge plan.

Or unless he was out of his head.

McCoy continued following the invisible trail, stopping at frequent intervals to check the tracks with a match or a torch twisted from dried prairie grass.

On the sixth such stop Spur cursed. The ground was hard-packed, as if it had been flooded recently and dried to an impenetrable crust. There were no hoof prints in sight.

He walked in circles around his horse, fanning out farther and farther away. He came across nothing but an owl resting on a scrubby bush.

Jack Hastings had vanished.

He sighed. He had two choices. Keep on going and trust his instincts, or wait until sunrise to start tracking the man again. Spur walked back to his horse, who stood shifting its weight as if eager to be on. The mount whinnied at the flame before he crushed it out with his heel.

He'd lost time trying to pinpoint Hastings' tracks. The man could be miles ahead by now. Or he could have stopped and was now snoring away on the ground. Somewhere out there.

He slid back into the saddle. No time like the present, he thought, and kept going in the same direction.

The moon began to set in the west. The enlarged orb off his right shoulder seemed to temporarily give off more light. Soon Spur saw a dark track stretching into the distance.

A trail.

Hastings must have been heading for it. He was a local man and knew the surrounding area. Though Spur didn't have any idea where it led, he urged the horse along the well-worn track for five minutes, lit a match and searched the dirt.

Fresh horse prints. Hastings must have come this way.

He rode south until dark blue light tinted the eastern horizon. It was dawn.

Tired from the saddle, weary from lack of sleep, Spur surveyed the territory as the day began. It was flat, featureless prairie land. A few ranches—big, fenced-in spreads—broke up the monotony. But the clean tracks led straight down the trail. Hastings—if it was indeed his horse—hadn't stopped.

A half hour after the sun broke over the horizon, Spur reined in his horse. The hoof prints veered to the right, down a lane between white picket fences.

He followed them, peering at the golden-tinted ranchhouse in the distance. Maybe Hastings had spent the night there.

The ranchers seemed to be asleep. Spur halted his horse at a hitching post outside the farmhouse and was pleased to see an ungroomed mount standing there. He tied up his mare, watching a plump woman in a bonnet and a calico dress heading toward the henhouse with a basket.

"Ma'am?"

She kept padding by.

Spur ran up to her. "Excuse me, ma'am," Spur said.

The ranchwife turned to him and pleasantly smiled. A pair of spectacles was perched on her nose. "What can I do for you, stranger?"

"Did a man ride up here last night? Someone you don't know? Maybe he asked for food and lodging?"

She smiled. "Yes. Came in—land sakes, it was late. James put him up in the spare bedroom."

"Can I see him?"

"You a friend of his?"

"Sort of."

"Of course. Go in through the front door, down the hall and up the stairs. It's the first room on thc right. Now I have to be getting those eggs. Good morning!" She trotted off toward the coop.

Spur sprinted to the two-story house, quietly opened the door and went in. He walked over the rag rugs that covered the wooden floors and eased up the wide stairs. There was the door. McCoy turned the knob and pushed it open.

It was a plain room, with a huge oak bed covered with smooth quilts. It hadn't been slept in. Nearby was a small stand with the indispensible ewer and basin. But Jack Hastings wasn't in sight.

Spur's guard went up. He drew his Colt and stepped into the room.

"Don't!"

Jack Hastings sat in the corner, knees folded, an antique flintlock rifle in his hands. He stared at McCoy's weapon.

"I'll shoot you!"

"I thought you only hung men, Hastings."

"I shoot 'em, too. Did lots of shooting in the War fighting against the North!"

Spur shook his head. "You weren't in the War, Hastings. Remember? You were too young."

"Yes I was!" Hastings said. He stood, supporting his back with the wall. "I killed lots of them Yankees. Shot and hung 'em!" Sweat squeezed from his forehead; dark half-circles showed below his eyes.

"And you're still hanging men. Aren't you? You hung Lester Fields."

Hastings shook his head and showed his teeth in anguish. "Never heard the name."

"You know him. And you tried to kill Mike Hughes last night. I stopped you."

He choked out a laugh. "I see. You're trying to fool me." Hastings' eyes grew dark. "Hell, you're one of them Yankees too!" He pushed off from the wall.

"Put that rifle down," Spur said. "You're gonna hurt yourself."

"No I won't! But I'll hurt you. I'll shoot you! It's loaded and everything!" Hastings smiled. "I don't have a rope but this'll have to do! Just hold still and let me kill you." He pointed the rifle in Spur's direction, but his aim wavered back and forth.

"Give it to me." McCoy tentatively took a step forward. "You can't win."

"No, Yankee!" Hastings fired the primitive

weapon. The lead ball slammed into the wall. Blue smoke filled the air, mixing with the explosion. The recoil sent him stumbling backwards.

"What in hell's going on here?" an old man in a nightshirt yelled as he appeared at the door.

"Nothing I can't handle," Spur said. "We'll be out of your hair soon."

"You can't go and shoot up my house!" the farmer said. "Hey, that's my rifle!"

"I'd take cover if I were you, sir!"

"Okay, okay, sonny." The man mumbled and ducked out of sight.

Still dazed by the explosion and lack of sleep, Hastings pulled the trigger again. Nothing.

"A flintlock only fires one round. It's over, Jack. Come on."

"No!" He rushed for the door.

Spur smashed the butt of his Colt into Jack Hastings' neck and banged the top of his head. The muscular youth screamed and dropped to his knees. He moved his face between his legs and started crying.

McCoy shook his head and retrieved the rifle. He laid it on the bed, helped Jack to rise and escorted him down the stairs.

"My rifle alright?" the rancher asked.

"Yeah!"

It was over.

CHAPTER SIXTEEN

Hastings was silent during the long trip back to Quintoch. Spur looked at him occasionally, taking in the man's sad eyes and slumped shoulders. He moved gently up and down on the saddle, his hands bound before him, emotionless.

"You know it wasn't right, don't you, Hastings?"

No answer.

"Even if you did lose your parents and the plantation during the War, that doesn't give you the right to kill innocent men! How can you be so sure they were the ones who did it?"

No response.

"I figured as much." The man was out of his head. It was that simple. Spur sighed and hurried toward town.

Almost two hours later they trotted past the houses on the outskirts of Quintoch. Jack Hastings looked up at the Hughes house and shook his head.

"No more," he said, his voice soft and raspy. "I won't get any more of 'em."

"Haven't you done enough?"

"There's still three more!"

"Look, Hastings, terrible things happen during wars. The Civil War wasn't any different. I'm sure you suffered as much as anyone. But you didn't have to hang those men."

"No more." Hastings raised his face to the sky.

They moved out to busy Main Street.

Not far to the sheriff's office, maybe a half mile.

"That him?" a man shouted.

"Yeah! It's Hastings! The one who tried to hang me last night!"

Spur recognized Mike Hughes' voice behind him.

"We don't want any trouble," McCoy yelled.

"We do!"

A bullet whizzed past Spur. He turned around. Three men stood with their weapons drawn, staring at Jack Hastings. Women and children scattered.

"Put your guns away, boys. I'm taking this man to jail. He'll get a fair trial."

"No way!" Hughes bounded up to him and grabbed his horse's reins. "I've got some unfinished business with that man!" He hefted a huge coil of rope.

"Lynching's murder. You wanna get what's coming to Hastings?"

Hughes laughed. "No judge'd blame me! Now ride outa here, McCoy! I could shoot him but I wanna do it up right! Just like he did to my friends!"

"Yeah! Let's take him to the walnut tree!"

Three other men joined the group of ex-soldiers. Spur sighed. At six-to-one he didn't like the odds.

He wrested the reins from Hughes' hands and

pulled Hastings' mount beside his. "You're talking crazy, Mike!"

"Enough! Let's get him!"

The six men rushed Hastings' horse, screaming, hands outstretched. The mare bolted at the surge of humanity, whinnying and rearing up on her front legs. Jack Hastings fell off the saddle and rolled on his shoulder, his hands still tied.

Spur fired over their heads but the men didn't flinch. They grabbed Hastings' arms and legs and started hauling away the dazed man.

Cursing, McCoy dismounted and attacked the mob. He grasped Hughes' waist and hurled him away, then punched a few chins and took a fist to his left shoulder.

The old wound surged back into memory, the bullet hole magnifying the pain. He winced and drove into them again, succeeding in knocking two of them on their butts. Hastings broke free from the men and aimlessly ran right into Sheriff Andrews' arms.

"Now you boys stop it!" Andrews said, holding Jack. "This man's in my custody now."

"Like hell!"

The bloodthirsty mob surrounded him.

"We ain't gonna stop until we've finished what we came here to do!"

"Hastings hung four men! He's gonna kick from a rope before the day's done!"

"Stand back, Andrews, unless you want it too!" Hughes threatened him.

The sheriff sighed, released Hastings and walked toward Spur. "They're not too friendly this morning," he observed, folding his arms on his chest.

"That's one way to put it."

"He's the one that hung all those men?"

Spur nodded.

"Well, at least that's over."

"Not yet," McCoy said, watching the fracas. "We should try to stop them."

Andrews chuckled. "Don't see how we can. Don't think anything would. They're out for blood." The sheriff drew his revolver and fired into the ground a yard from Mike Hughes' feet. The man didn't even notice. "See what I mean?"

"Yeah."

A group of citizens flooded into the street, watching the fight.

"Hey, this is better'n Dr. Marvel's Traveling Patent Remedy Show!" one young man yelled.

Annabelle appeared among them, saw Spur and ran over to him. "Are you still in one piece?" she asked, looking at him with concern.

"Oh, Annabelle, he's all right," her father said.

She looked at him. "I just wanted to—"

The violence intensified. The men kicked and punched Hastings, screaming their lungs out.

"What?"

"I'm just glad that you're—"

"How's that?" Spur shook his head.

"Glad you're not hurt!"

He smiled. "Me, too."

Annabelle turned to the sheriff. "Father, aren't you going to stop them?"

"We already discussed that, me and your beau."

"I see."

They all turned to watch. "You won't charge

them with anything, will you, Andrews?" Spur said, taking the hand that Annabelle thrust into his.

"Don't rightly know. I completely understand why they're doing it, though I don't approve." He paused. "Maybe there won't be any witnesses willing to testify against Hughes and the rest of them."

Spur frowned. "That's not exactly by the book."

"True. But in this case . . . ."

Clemons MacArthur waved to McCoy from the crowd.

"Andrews, see that boy over there?"

"Yep. That's Clem's son."

"He helped me out. Loaned me his horse. Think you could give him a few shooting lessons? Teach him how to safely handle a revolver?"

The sheriff laughed. "Of course! Hell, you saved my butt from these folks. That could be me out there."

"Thanks. I'll be right back." Spur retrieved the boy's horse, who'd wandered over to the nearest trough, and took her to him. "Thanks for the loan, kid." He handed him the reins.

"Sure. Anytime! I'm glad you caught the man who murdered my father." The boy's face shined with admiration.

"With your help. The sheriff said he'd be glad to show you how to shoot. Oh, and one other thing." Spur dug into his pocket and took out two silver dollars. "For the use of your horse, son." He flipped them to him.

Clemons MacArthur watched the shimmering metal discs arc up and then hurl downward. He caught the coins and squeezed his fingers around them. "Thanks, mister."

Spur tousled his hair.

Sheriff Andrews grabbed the rope from Hughes' hand. "Ain't no more hanging gonna go on in this town!" he said.

Mike Hughes started to argue, then nodded. He wiped a trail of blood from his lower lip. "Whatever you say, sheriff!" He took a breath and rejoined the others who were still whacking away at Hastings.

"What d'ya say we go over there in the shade? It's powerfully hot this morning," Sheriff Andrews said to McCoy.

They walked under the porch of Millison's Grain and Feed, purposely avoiding watching the altercation in the street.

"Thanks, McCoy. I couldn't have done it without you."

"That's my job, Andrews. That's my job."

Annabelle laid her head against his good shoulder and sighed. "How about some of my cooking?" she asked.

Spur's eyes lit up. "Annabelle, I'd love it!"

CHAPTER SEVENTEEN

"You've done what you came here to do. Now git on home before I lock you all up!" Sheriff Andrews shouted.

The exhausted, bloody men walked off without comment, revealing a battered Jack Hastings lying in the middle of the street.

Annabelle gasped and turned her head.

"Is he still alive?" Spur asked.

The sheriff felt his neck. "Barely. Come on, McCoy. Let's get this man to Doc Lemmon."

"I'll wait for you at home," Annabelle said. She kissed Spur's neck and hurried off.

The two men carried the bleeding killer to the doctor's office.

Stu Lemmon was grim. "I was expecting you," he said. "Lay him down there."

"Not a pretty sight, eh?" Andrews asked.

Hastings gasped on the table. His breath was hollow, tortured. He lay motionless, his eyes closed, life oozing out of the dozens of wounds that fists and boots had made all over his body.

The doctor opened his shirt and lowered his pants, examining him.

"What do you think?" Spur asked him.

"It's bad." Lemmon wiped his forehead. "He won't last much longer. In fact, I'm surprised he's still with us."

Hastings gurgled sickeningly. A long, drawn-out hiss of air escaped between his lips. He was dead.

"That's it." Doc Lemmon said. "Nothing I could do. Sorry, Jonathan."

Andrews shook his head and looked at Spur. "We should have stopped them."

"No, sheriff."

"Why in hell not?"

"They would have killed us. You saw them! They were blinded with hatred. And if we did manage to stop them they would have stormed the jail. Mowed you down to get at Hastings." Spur shook his head. "It was a no-win situation. Two men alone can't stand against a dozen with murder on their minds."

"I guess you're right. At least there won't be any more hangings in my town."

"Yeah." He glanced at the lifeless body. "Your daughter's waiting for me."

"Yeah." Sheriff Andrews touched Spur's arm. "Make her forget what she saw this morning. Okay?"

"Sure."

"I'm pretty tired, Annabelle," Spur said as he sat down at the dining table in her house. "Didn't get any sleep last night. Too busy watching Jack Hastings."

"You poor man!" she clucked. "Bet you're hungry, too. Right?" She held a platter full of steaks under his nose.

Spur smiled. "That's a fact."

"Then I guess you'll just have to eat these." Annabelle set the plate down in front of him.

"You're a good woman."

He dug into his food. The meat was hot, liberally seasoned with pepper and salt. He ate without talking, thinking about the morning's events.

When he'd arrived, Annabelle was depressed, anxious and upset. After she saw him, the young woman came back to life. Soon she had acted as if nothing had happened that morning. Spur made certain he didn't bring it up.

Spur shook off the memories so he could fully enjoy the meal she'd prepared for him. Annabelle ran from the kitchen to the dining room, bringing coffee, hot buttermilk biscuits, corn on the cob and other delights.

She finally sat down beside him and ate.

"Thanks for cooking me this fine dinner so early in the morning," Spur said before sinking his teeth into the buttery corn.

"I was hungry, too. Besides, I never heard of a law that says you have to eat bacon and eggs for breakfast." She delicately wiped her chin. "Spur, you aren't too tired to—well, you know. Are you?"

He laughed and swallowed. "No, Annabelle. I'm not."

"Good!"

They eagerly finished their meal. As the young woman took the dishes to the kitchen, Spur went to her bedroom. Might as well have a surprise for her, he thought, and kicked off his boots.

Annabelle walked in a minute later and gasped. "Why're you all naked like that?" she asked in mock indignation. Her green eyes locked onto the thick organ hanging between his legs. "And in my bedroom! I'll call my daddy, the sheriff. He's gonna throw you in jail!"

"Take off your dress, Belle." Spur stood before her and smiled.

She threw up her hands. "Well, alright. I never could say no to a man. Especially a naked man."

Annabelle laughed. Staring at his aroused organ, she sat on the bed and unbuttoned her tiny black boots. Then she rose and opened the front of her dress, unfastening the mother-of-pearl buttons that ran down to her groin.

Spur enjoyed the spectacle of the girl denuding herself. Annabelle threw off the dress, dropped her petticoats, yanked the bodice from her torso and slid down the snowy bloomers.

"I hope you're happy!"

"I am, Belle. I am. Come on over here."

She walked to him, completely comfortable in her nudity, and pressed full-length against him.

Her skin was soft and warm. Spur groaned as his erection smashed between their bodies. He passionately kissed her, their lips searing, his tongue darting into her mouth, pushing toward the back of Annabelle's throat.

She grabbed his shoulders and writhed as their tongues fought. Spur felt her breasts pushing against his chest. He reached down and cupped her round hips, pulling her closer to him, increasing the pressure of his trapped penis.

Annabelle threw back her head. McCoy kissed her ear and trailed his mouth down her neck, across her shoulder and to her left breast.

"Oh, stranger, I don't know who you are but you sure know how to make a woman happy."

She wanted to play games? Okay, he'd play a game with her. He bit the nipple, hardening it, teasing it with his teeth. Annabelle sighed and grabbed his head, forcing her whole breast into his mouth.

They both groaned. Spur sucked it, pushing it deeper into him, savoring its womanly flavor. Sweat sprang out of his body as he worked her over.

He pulled back and gasped. "You sure have some fine ones, Belle!"

"Don't stop!" She directed his head to her left breast and sighed at his mouth-work.

Sexual heat flooded through him but he controlled himself, nipping her tenderly, taking care not to hurt her as he feasted on the delicious mound.

He finally stepped back. Annabelle looked down at his firm organ and sank to her knees.

"You—ah—you don't have to do that!"

"I know." She moaned and took him.

"Oh. Oh Annabelle, darling!"

The woman filled her throat with him.

Spur gasped and ran his fingers through her blonde curls. The woman was incredible, he thought, as she pulled up and stuffed it into herself again.

The feeling was unique and incredibly erotic. Spur felt his knees start to buckle as she grabbed his buttocks and pulled him full-length into her. She didn't choke or gag as every inch of his penis disappeared down her throat.

Spur couldn't take much of that. He grabbed her head. Annabelle willingly rose, a devilish look in her eyes, and allowed him to lay her on the bed.

"Come on, Spur!" she said.

He raised his left eyebrow. "What happened to the 'stranger'?"

"You're no stranger to me."

Spur moved on top of her. Annabelle squealed as his fingers ran between her legs, probing, parting her lips. Her opening was soft, wet and ready.

He removed his hand and rubbed the head of his penis back and forth. "Do you want it, Annabelle?"

"Yes."

"Really?"

"Yes, Spur!"

He pushed into her. She arched her back and sighed as their bodies joined. Spur jabbed and thrusted, sinking into Annabelle, staring down at her lovely face as he penetrated.

"Oh!"

"Yeah, Belle!"

He went slowly, taking his time, trying to cool the fires that burned inside him. Spur finally drove his erection into her length.

She came alive. Her eyes widened; her hands slapped onto his back. "Yes! God, it's so—so—"

"So big?" he guessed, withdrawing and plunging back into her.

"Yes! You know it is!"

In. Out. In and out. Spur held her shoulders and

pumped between her legs, moving as slowly as possible to maximize their pleasure. He kissed her again, his tongue mimicking the movement, opening her up at both ends.

Sex musk rose up and filled the air as they made love. Annabelle's canopy bed squeaked in rhythm with his thrusts. He pushed faster into her and bit her ear.

Annabelle's nails raked his back. "Ram that thing into me! Come on, Spur!"

He lifted himself onto his hands and grinned down at her. The new angle of his thrusts drove Annabelle crazy.

"Harder. Harder, Spur! Please!" Her face glowed with sexual heat.

"Anything you say!"

Their bodies slammed together. Nothing like making love to a woman, Spur thought as he moved faster inside her. Nothing at all.

Soon he was beyond all thought. His hips pumped with supernatural speed. Annabelle's groans rose to breathy cries as he drove into her again and again.

"Yes. Yes. Yes!" she chanted. Her body undulated below him; her head hit the bed frame.

Spur moved her down, slowed his penetrations, giving them both time to rest. He pulled out to the head and held it there, poised.

"Take it!" he yelled, and rammed full-length into Annabelle.

"Oh!"

He was relentless, out of control. "Jesus, Annabelle!" he yelled.

A low moan issued from her throat. "Oh no. Oh

God! Here it comes. Here it comes, Spur!"

He sped up his pumps, deliberately pushing her over the edge. The naked woman rattled and shook beneath him. She tore at her hair and clamped her thighs around his legs, squeezing his erection with her genitals.

Annabelle cried the timeless roar of a climaxing woman. Her breasts bounced crazily and flushed a bright red as she shuddered through the intense experience.

"Yeah, Belle!" Spur shouted above her.

The sight of her pleasure, the contractions around his thrusting penis and her open lust intoxicated him.

"Join me, Spur!" she gasped.

He pushed into her like a wild animal, holding back his orgasm, forcing her body to its peak again and again until she was panting from the effects of his work.

Her screams rose higher. "Goddamn it, Spur! Come! Join me, you son of a bitch!"

His scrotum tightened as it slapped against her body. Spur gasped and pounded into her, oblivious of everything but her warm opening and the shining eyes below him. He yelled and slammed into her, driving deeper than he'd ever been. His crotch exploded, his nerves shattered in a warm breeze. Every muscle in his body tightened and relaxed as he drained himself deep inside the sheriff's daughter.

"Oh Belle! Oh God!"

"Shoot it!" she said, and sunk her teeth into his sweaty neck.

It went on and on. Spur's mind dissolved. The

woman clutched him. The spurts grew shorter until he'd coated her vagina with his warm seed.

Spur slumped onto her, spent, useless. His breath blasted against her shoulder. Annabelle sighed and moaned. She ran her fingers through his wet hair.

He knew he should say something to her, about how wonderful it had been, but the words were still locked in his lust-fogged brain.

"You know something?" Annabelle muttered, her voice breathy.

"Hmmm?"

"I'll miss you."

"Mmmm."

"I guess you'll be leaving Quintoch soon, now that you've done your job."

"Uh-huh."

She grabbed his ears and lifted his head. "I don't want you to leave, Mr. McCoy!"

What could he say, Spur wondered.

Annabelle released him. He settled down on her breasts. "I'll never see you again."

"No."

"Damnit! It's not fair! I finally find the perfect man for me and he's slipping away from me!"

"I'm sorry, Belle. There's nothing either of us can do about that."

"At least I'll have my memories. They can't leave me." She stirred beneath him.

He looked at her. "I'll always remember you, Annabelle. I'll always remember the sheriff's daughter in that little town in Quintoch."

"Really?" Tears brimmed in her eyes.

"Really."

She sighed. "Well, I guess that's all I can ask for. Isn't it?"

"Yep."

They held each other until they'd cooled off in the light breezes.

The next morning, Spur boarded the Kansas Pacific train just as it left Quintoch. Riding in a specially equipped security car, he'd brought along a special cargo—four sacks of freshly printed money.

Yesterday, he'd wired General Halleck in Washington, telling him of the death of the mad hangman. Six hours later he received a reply.

His superior's response was short and terse. Spur had a new assignment, beginning immediately. He was to escort the currency shipment, stopping to deliver the money to various banks scattered throughout the mid-west. He'd be riding shotgun on the currency until he'd dispersed the last dollar bill, protecting it from any further misadventures.

The job would take two weeks, and General Halleck told him he'd already lined up another job for him when he was finished with that.

He glanced out the window as the train pulled away from the station. He saw the blonde-haired girl waving goodbye, a brave smile on her face. Sunlight glinted in her hair; the steam from the train ruffled her pink dress.

Spur lifted his hand and returned her farewell. The train picked up speed as it drove westward. He bent nearer the tiny window and strained his eyes, watching as the woman on the platform gradually diminished in size and dissolved into the moving landscape.

Don't think about her, he told himself. That's dangerous territory. Think about your new assignment, about Washington, about anything else. Don't let that pretty little woman get to you!

McCoy shook his head. It had been just another job. He'd been given an assignment and he carried it out like any Secret Service agent would do.

He should be satisfied with himself. He'd corraled two train thieves. He'd found a man who'd been terrorizing the whole town.

But he'd left something undone, Spur told himself. A job that he should have assigned himself.

A green-eyed creature named Annabelle.

Spur looked at the canvas money sacks and sighed. Some day he'd have to go back to Quintoch, Kansas.

Some day.